Andrea Boeshaar has a heart for God that shows up on the pages of every book she writes. I've been honored to work with and know Andrea for many years and have very much enjoyed her tender stories of hope and love.

—Tracie Peterson
Best-selling author of *The Song of Alaska* series

Andrea Boeshaar's novels always thrill and inspire, and *Undaunted Faith* is no exception! She writes with great insight and consistently writes stories that are rich with excitement and romance. Add these elements to Andrea's talent for delivering non-preachy messages of God's love, and you have a true "keeper" to add to your bookshelf.

—Loree Lough
Best-selling author of *From Ashes to Honor*,
#1 in the First Responders series

I have thoroughly enjoyed this series by Andrea Boeshaar. She has taken us through multiple settings scattered over a large area of the United States, and she's nailed the setting every time. With *Undaunted Faith*, I could see it, feel the sun beating down, smell the dust storm, taste the native food. And in front of that tapestry of setting, she played out an amazing story of self-discovery and spiritual growth along with the not one but two romances. I could hardly put the book down.

—Lena Nelson Dooley
Author of *Love Finds You in Golden, New Mexico,*
and the McKenna's Daughters series

Once again Andrea Boeshaar has given us a heartwarming adventure filled with colorful characters and true-to-life faith.

—Louise M. Gouge
Author of *The Wedding Season*

UNDAUNTED
FAITH

Seasons of Redemption

BOOK FOUR

UNDAUNTED
FAITH

Seasons of Redemption

BOOK FOUR

ANDREA KUHN
BOESHAAR

REALMS

Most CHARISMA HOUSE BOOK GROUP products are available at special quantity discounts for bulk purchase for sales promotions, premiums, fund-raising, and educational needs. For details, write Charisma House Book Group, 600 Rinehart Road, Lake Mary, Florida 32746, or telephone (407) 333-0600.

UNDAUNTED FAITH by Andrea Kuhn Boeshaar
Published by Realms
Charisma Media/Charisma House Book Group
600 Rinehart Road
Lake Mary, Florida 32746
www.charismahouse.com

All Scripture quotations are from the King James Version of the Bible.

The characters portrayed in this book are fictitious unless they are historical figures explicitly named. Otherwise, any resemblance to actual people, whether living or dead, is coincidental.

Cover design by Bill Johnson

Visit the author's website at www.andreaboeshaar.com.

Library of Congress Cataloging-in-Publication Data:

Boeshaar, Andrea.
    Undaunted faith / Andrea Boeshaar.
        p. cm.
    ISBN 978-1-61638-205-6
    I. Title.
    PS3552.O4257U536 2011
    813'.54--dc22
                                        2011001033

E-book ISBN: 978-1-61638-433-3

11 12 13 14 15 — 9 8 7 6 5 4 3 2 1
Printed in the United States of America

To Daniel—my hero.

And a heartfelt *thank you* to Anne McDonald
& Anne McDonald Editorial Services.
No one but a true and faithful friend
would stay up with me all night
so I could meet a deadline!

Also special thanks to Carol Brooks,
curator of the Yuma Historical Society
for answering my many questions—
and, again, to Annie who asked them!

PROLOGUE

Journal entry: Monday, April 1, 1867

I, Bethany Leanne Stafford, am writing in a leather-bound journal, which my dear friend Mrs. Valerie McCabe gave me for a going-away gift. She suggested I write my memoirs of my impending journey West and about my new life as a schoolteacher in the wild Arizona Territory. Valerie said she wished she'd have kept a diary of her escape from New Orleans and a loveless marriage from which her husband Ben had rescued her.

For continuity's sake, I shall back up from the day I left Milwaukee, Wisconsin. In September of last year, upon leaving the city, I took the train to Jericho Junction, Missouri. My traveling companions were Pastors Luke and Jacob McCabe and Gretchen Schlyterhaus, a German widow.

Mrs. Schlyterhaus had worked as a housekeeper for Captain Brian Sinclair, who, at the time of our departure, was declared dead—drowned in a boating accident on Lake Michigan. Mrs. Schlyterhaus felt her livelihood had ended too, until Pastor Luke convinced her to go West with us. Weeks later, the captain was discovered alive in a Chicago hospital. Mrs. Schlyterhaus had been certain that he would insist upon her returning to her duties in his household; after all, she'd signed a binding contract with him. But to her surprise, the captain allowed her to resign and even sent her a *bonus (a tidy sum, I heard). Richard and Sarah brought it with them when they came for the Christmas holiday. Uncharacteristic for the captain, but Sarah said he's a changed man. He found the Lord—and a good woman, whom he married—and he's living happily in Milwaukee where he owns a shipping business and a store. Richard is now his business partner and an equally important man in Milwaukee.*

But I digress. After a full day's train ride, we arrived in Jericho Junction, where I've lived for the past seven and a half months and earned my teaching certificate. In that time I've gotten to know Sarah's relatives. How I wish I were part of this family! Pastor Daniel McCabe is a thoughtful, gentle man, unlike my own father who is a hard, insensitive soul. Mrs. McCabe has been more of a mother to me than I've ever known. My own mother died when I was eight. My father remarried, and my stepmother is as lazy as she is lovely (and she's beautiful!). My half brother Tommy was born when I was nine, and nearly every year since my stepmother bore another child for me to look after in addition to my chores on the farm.

Forever, it seemed, I dreamed of escaping the drudgery of my life by marrying Richard, except God had other plans. Richard married Sarah. At first I felt jealous, but seeing how much Richard loved her, I couldn't begrudge them their happiness. I did fear, however, that I'd be forever trapped on my father's farm caring for my brothers and sisters and working my body to the bone. I couldn't bear the thought of dying as a spinster who'd never accomplished anything meaningful.

So when Luke McCabe offered me this chance to teach in the Arizona Territory, I jumped at it. In spite of my father's protests, I packed my meager belongings and stayed next door with the Navises until the day of my departure. Needless to say, I left my family on a sour note. My father said he never wanted to see me again. I can't say as I give a whit. I'm glad to be gone!

And as for the trip itself, we will depart in just a few short hours. We will follow the Santa Fe Trail along with other migrants—most of them families whom we met last night in the hotel's dining room.

I am ever so excited about my adventure. Still, I'm quite aware that traveling by oxen-drawn, covered wagons may, indeed, prove to be a hardship, but both Mrs. Schlyterhaus and I are ready and eager to face each new challenge. As required by the United States, more than one hundred wagons are signed up to leave this morning. Due to the threat of Indian attack no less than a hundred can travel the trail.

But I must cease my writing now. Luke is knocking at the door. It's time for breakfast…and then we'll be on our way!

Journal entry: Wednesday, June 12

There has been no time for me to write. It's been a long and exhausting journey thus far. During the daytime I walk beside the wagon while Luke and Jake take turns driving and scouting the trail ahead by horseback. After we make camp I prepare dinner, and then we clean up and get some sleep. But this evening by lamplight I simply had to pen what occurred today. I saw, for the first time in my life—a rattlesnake!

On the farm in Wisconsin, I never saw anything larger than a pine snake, and even though they can bite, pine snakes are not poisonous. But I happened upon this deadly reptile quite accidentally as I unloaded our wagon this evening. I nearly stepped on the horrid thing and it poised, ready to strike me. In those seconds that passed I was sure I'd be bitten and die. But Luke saw the snake the same time I did. He pulled out his rifle and shot it dead before it attacked me.

Afterward I just stood there, gazing at the creature's lifeless, beady black eyes. I burst into tears, realizing how frightened I had really been. Luke put his hand on my shoulder and said, "There, now, Beth, that buzz-worm's dead as a doornail. He can't hurt you anymore."

Luke saved my very life that day, and I thank God for him.

Journal entry: Friday, June 14

Yesterday a horrible thing happened involving another rattlesnake, but this time it resulted in a trag-edy. A five-year-old boy named Justin McMurray got bit. His passing was the saddest thing I ever witnessed.

The strike happened during the day, but the McMur-rays didn't want to make the entire wagon train stop because of Justin. By the time several men and one doctor went by the McMurray wagon to see if they could be of help, it was too late. The poison had gotten into the boy's system, and he had a raging fever.

Then Luke and I went over and talked to Justin. Despite the fever and chills, he was coherent and in a tremendous amount of pain. My heart immediately went out to him, but also to Mrs. McMurray. She looked so sad and helpless as she held her child whose life was slipping away with each passing second.

Instinctively, I put my arm around the woman's shoulders in an effort to comfort her while Luke talked

to the boy about heaven. Justin listened intently. I
choked back a sob and glanced at Mrs. McMurray, who
had tears rolling down her cheeks. Luke's eyes looked
misty too, but instead of weeping, he started singing.
He knew so many songs about rejoicing in heaven
that Mrs. McMurray actually smiled, and Justin even
laughed a couple of times.

Finally the Lord took the boy home, and while I was
happy that Justin is in the Savior's arms, I felt a bit sick
inside. I still do.

Journal entry: Sunday, June 30

For the past two weeks since little Justin McMurray's
death, I've been having nightmares. Each time I doze, I
envision rattlesnakes everywhere—in the wagon, even
in my hair! I awaken with a start, and Mrs. Schlyterhaus hushes me, since we both sleep inside the wagon
while Luke and Jake make their beds on the ground
below us.

My fear of rattlesnakes grew along with the exhausting desert temperatures to the point where I refused to
get down from the wagon and stretch my legs during
the day. At night I begged Mrs. Schlyterhaus to start
the fire and make supper. I did not have any appetite
and would lie down inside the wagon and pray for
some peaceful sleep...which never seemed to come.

Finally last night Luke said, "Bethany Stafford, you
climb down off that wagon this minute!" I told him I
would do no such thing. He asked me why, but I could
not admit how afraid I was to leave the wagon and
have a rattlesnake kill me. However, Luke guessed the
trouble. He said, "There's no snakes around, so come
down now or I'll climb up and get you myself."

Still, I refused, but I tried to be polite about it. Next thing I knew Luke had his arm around my waist, lifting me out of the wagon. Then he announced we were taking a stroll around the wagon train encampment.

I begged to stay back, but he would not be dissuaded. I went so far as to threaten him, saying if I died of snakebite, it would be all his fault. He said, "I'll take my chances."

So I pleaded with him to at least carry along his rifle. Luke replied, "No, ma'am, we're only taking the Lord with us tonight."

The fear inside of me increased. My heart pounded and my legs shook with every anxious step. At last Luke said folks were going to get the wrong impression about us if I did not begin to walk in a ladylike fashion. To my shame, I realized I was stepping all over him in order to keep away from the rattlesnakes that I knew lurked beneath the sands of the Cimarron.

Luke's voice became very soft and gentle. He said, "Beth, God does not give us the spirit of fear, so don't be afraid. Our heavenly Father was not surprised when Justin McMurray got bit by that snake. That homegoing had been planned since the beginning of time."

I knew he was right, and somehow his straightforwardness caused me to relax. Then he mentioned what a nice evening it was for a stroll, and for the first time I realized the sky looked clear and the air felt cool and clean against my face. Amazingly I even felt hungry then. I loosened the death grip I had around Luke's elbow. He chuckled as though he was amused. I felt horribly embarrassed, and he laughed again. I like the sound of his laugh, so slow and easy. And it's a funny thing, but with God and Luke right there with me, I didn't fret about rattlesnakes the rest of the night.

Journal entry: Sunday, July 21

After walking in oven-hot temperatures for ten to fourteen miles every day, except Sundays, we finally arrived in Santa Fe. I'm not sure what I expected, but I'm ever so disappointed with what has met my weary eyes thus far. Santa Fe is not at all lush and green like Wisconsin during the summer months. Everything is a dismal brown. Most houses are single-story adobe structures with dirt floors. There is a telegraph office, and we learned that Sarah gave birth to a healthy baby boy. His name is Samuel Richard. I must say that Luke and Jake seem quite proud of their youngest sister and newest nephew. I'm genuinely happy for Richard and Sarah.

As for myself, I am bone-thin, and the traveling dresses I made for the journey hang from my shoulders like old potato sacks. Luke is worried about me, and so we will remain here for a couple of weeks while I regain my strength.

On the last leg of our journey we escaped both Indian attack and bad weather. But we did encounter a buffalo stampede, the likes I hope to never witness again! The ground shook so hard my teeth rattled. That same day we saw abandoned wagons and fresh graves, which proved an almost eerie forewarning. Days later, a strange fever made its way around our wagon train, and several people died, including four small children. Although both Luke and Jake gave encouraging graveside messages, having to leave the little bodies of their children behind, coupled with the fear of animals discovering them, proved more than the three young mothers in our camp could bear. They wept for days, and my heart broke right along with them.

Luke soon enlisted my services, and I prayed with the mourning women and helped with their daily chores. Luke said I was a blessing to them. Oddly, in assisting them, my own heart began to heal. When Mrs. Schlyterhaus took ill with the fever, I nursed her back to health as well. Both Luke and Jake said they didn't know what they'd have done without me.

As for Mrs. Schlyterhaus, Jake has decided that, although her health is improving, she will remain here in Santa Fe permanently. He has arranged for her to stay with a missionary family and work as their house-keeper. Mrs. Schlyterhaus is very accepting of this arrangement, although I will miss her. She has softened considerably since leaving Milwaukee and has come to realize how unhappy she has been since her husband's death. But she said the thought of another four weeks traveling through Indian territory frightens her sense-less.

In truth, it frightens me also. But, as Luke is fond of saying, God does not give us the spirit of fear, and from the human standpoint, he and Jake have taken precautions to ensure our safety. He hired a guide—a physician named Frank Bandy, one of the few white men who have made peace with the Apaches. The Indi-ans allow him passage through their territory because he has been able to minister medically to their people.

But, alas, I must stop writing for now as there are numerous tasks I would like to accomplish—although if Luke discovers I am not resting, I may have some explaining to do.

Journal entry: Monday, October 7

I have discovered I keep a poor journal. Truth is, I forgot about my diary these past months as it has been tucked away in my trunk of belongings. However, this morning I shall do my best to bring the events up to date.

I fully recovered from my journey and now spend much of my time becoming familiar with my surroundings and the people here. We arrived in Silverstone on August 27, and I had only a few days to prepare the classroom as school began on Monday, the second of September. I have thirteen children in my class, ranging from first to eighth grades. Three of my students are from one family. They lost their mother just a few short months ago in childbirth. I hope to be able to help them deal with their loss as they might prove to be the brightest children under my tutelage this year.

Meanwhile, the Arizona heat has been ghastly. Rain compounded the misery by turning everything to mud. I doubt I shall ever get used to this place. I find myself looking forward to my cool baths every morning at the break of dawn when several of us women go down to the riverbank, as is the custom of the Mexican women here. The muddy water looks red and the river's current is swift; however, after wilting in the previous day's heat, it is a welcomed respite.

Silverstone itself is located twenty miles north of Arizona City and the Yuma Crossing on the Colorado River. Beyond the town the scenery is breathtakingly beautiful. The majestic mountaintops seem to touch an ever-azure sky, and the swirling red river water flows beneath them. But the town is an eyesore by comparison. It's a hot, dusty, unpainted freight town. The people here are an odd mix of prospectors, ranchers, freighters, Mexicans, and Indians, and they keep Main Street (if it may be called such a thing) lively with regular brawls, which I abhor.

On one side of the rutted, unpaved road there is an adobe government building, which houses the sheriff and a jail. Ironically, right next door, there is a rickety wooden saloon called Chicago Joe's and, above it, a house of ill repute. On the other side of Main Street is the Winters' Boardinghouse, in which I am presently residing. The Winters also operate a dining room and the post office. Beside their place is a dry-goods store and next to it a freight office and a bank. Luke maintains the church at the end of the thoroughfare and delivers the Sunday morning message each week. Jake does carpentry work when he is not riding the circuit and preaching. Beside the church there stands a small one-room schoolhouse, where I teach.

As one might guess, the two sides of Main Street are largely at odds with each other. Mrs. Winters says we are the "good" side, and those across the way (particularly the women in the brothel) are the "bad" side—all save for Sheriff Paden Montaño, of course. Silverstone's sheriff has been commissioned by the United States Army and oversees the shipping and receiving of government freight landed in Silverstone by river steamers. Then it is transported across the Territory by wagon. Sheriff Montaño's father was a rugged vaquero (cowboy), and his mother was a genteel woman from back East.

I think the sheriff seems to have inherited traits from both parents; however, he is a sight to behold. He is a darkly handsome man with hair so long it hangs nearly to his waist. One would never see such a man in Milwaukee, Wisconsin!

At first glance, he resembles a fierce Indian, but his actions are polite and refined. Like his vaquero father, he is a capable horseman and masterful with a gun. Like his mother, with whom he was raised, he is well educated. Some say Sheriff Montaño is a Mexican and Indian sympathizer, out to use his status as a United States lawman for his own purposes, but Luke says he's a fair man. I must admit I have found the sheriff to be charming.

And then there is Ralph Jonas, who is quite the opposite. He claims to be a Christian man, but he can be quite disagreeable. His wife died during childbirth just before we arrived in town, and Mr. Jonas is desperately trying to replace her—just as he might replace a mule. I was insulted when he proposed to me, and I find his philosophy on marriage highly distasteful. Thankfully, Luke had a talk with him. I don't know what he said, but now Mr. Jonas keeps his distance for the most part.

I must admit that I hate it here in Silverstone. I want to return to Jericho Junction. I'm praying the McCabes will find something for me to do there, but first an opportunity will present itself. But worse is the next wagon train won't depart for Missouri again until next spring.

Six months. Six long months.

Will I be able to survive that long, here in this God-forsaken land?

ONE

A KNOCK SOUNDED ONCE. THEN AGAIN, MORE INSISTENT this time.

"Coming." Bethany set down the quill and capped the inkwell. Closing her journal, she stood from where she'd been sitting at the desk Jake had crafted for her use. Then, before she could open the door, Trudy poked her round, cherubic face into Bethany's bedroom.

"Mama says breakfast is ready."

"Thank you, Trudy. I'll be down shortly."

A grin curved the flaxen-haired girl's pink mouth. "Reverend Luke and Reverend Jake are already here. Sheriff Montaño is too."

Bethany wasn't at all taken aback by the familiar way in which Trudy referred to both Luke and Jake. Because the men shared the same surname, the townspeople called them by their first names.

"I'll be down shortly." Walking to the looking glass, Bethany brushed out her long brown hair. It had dried from her earlier bath in the river.

Thirteen-year-old Trudy stepped farther into the room and closed the door behind her. "I'll bet we'll hear some lively conversation. Something about cattle stealing. Papa said the Indians have been causing trouble again."

"Oh, dear." Bethany tried not to show either her discontent with this town or her unease with the natives of this land. She gathered her hair then twisted it into a coil and pinned it at her nape. "Was anyone killed?"

"I don't know, but I expect we'll find out at breakfast."

With her hair in place, Bethany turned to Trudy. "I'm ready."

"Good." The girl strode to the door and paused. "Miss Stafford, who do you think is more handsome, Reverend Luke, Reverend Jacob, or the sheriff?" A conspiratorial expression spread across her face. "I fancy Sheriff Paden Montaño is a handsome curiosity, is he not?"

"I don't notice such things," Bethany fibbed. She folded her arms in front of her. If truth be told, only a woman deaf and blind wouldn't notice Paden Montaño; however, she wasn't about to encourage Trudy. The young lady was one of her pupils, and Bethany wanted to set a good example. "And what would your parents have to say if they heard you talking like this?"

Trudy gasped. "You're not going to tell them, are you?"

Bethany raised a contemplative brow. "Well, maybe not this time." She strode earnestly toward the young girl. "But you must stop allowing your thoughts to be consumed by romance. You're going to get hurt."

"Pshaw!"

Bethany gasped. "Trudy, really!"

The girl continued unabashed. "Miss Stafford, if you haven't already noticed, you and I are the only *eligible* women in Silverstone—well, except for Dr. Cavanaugh. But she's too busy to notice men. Even so, you and I can have our pick of any bachelor we want."

"You are not *eligible*." Bethany knew both Mr. and Mrs. Winters wanted their only child to receive an education before she married. "And I am not...interested."

"Are you certain about that?" A taunting glimmer entered her eyes. "You and Reverend Luke seem to spend a lot of time together."

Bethany felt her cheeks flame in a mixture of embarrassment and aggravation. "Trudy, I'm a teacher, and Reverend Luke—and Reverend Jake, I might add—are starting a school. It's only natural that we'd spend time together... to plan and organize."

"Well, fine. But *I* am interested—in getting me a husband!"

"You're much too young."

"Am not! My friend Emma got married last year, and she's only two years older than me!"

"Than I," Bethany corrected. "And every circumstance is different." She knew girls in remote places were married off as young as age fifteen or sixteen. "But we're talking about you, and you're not ready for marriage. You have a lot of schooling left."

"So I can end up like Dr. Cavanaugh?"

Bethany's jaw tightened. "And what's wrong with Dr. Cavanaugh? She seems like a remarkable woman. She's come all the way from Parkersburg, West Virginia." Bethany felt a kinship between them, both being women from east of the Mississippi River who had survived the journey along the Santa Fe Trail. But it seemed the physician wasn't interested in making friends, although she was pleasant enough.

"She's a spinster."

Bethany shrank. That shoe could fit her foot as well.

"Besides, no one wants her here. They put an ad in newspapers out East for a male doctor. They thought they were getting one too, until Dr. Cavanaugh arrived in town a month ago."

"Yes, I know about the mix-up." Although Bethany couldn't be sure it was an oversight on Dr. Cavanaugh's part. According to Jake, she'd signed her letter of application *A. L. Cavanaugh.* Everyone just assumed the rest. Since the day she arrived, Dr. Cavanaugh didn't appear to be offering up any explanations for her behavior, even though plenty of men besides the sheriff and Jake weren't pleased.

"Folks say she's running from something back East, and I just wonder if it's true."

"That's gossip, Trudy. Christians ought not indulge in it." Bethany had heard Jake say the sheriff checked Annetta Cavanaugh's background thoroughly—at least as far as the law was concerned. "As for you, young lady, you need to pay attention to your schoolbooks instead of romance and gossip."

Trudy gave her foot a stomp. "I'm not a child. Why do you and my parents treat me like one?"

Could be the tantrums. Bethany quelled an impatient sigh. Trudy Winters posed a challenge to be sure.

But in spite of the vexation the girl caused her now and again, Bethany felt determined to befriend her and become her trusted teacher. Perhaps she'd somehow make a difference in Trudy's young life. However, she certainly wouldn't accomplish such a feat by arguing with her.

Turning to the looking glass again, Bethany gave her reflection a final inspection. She smoothed down the skirt of her cotton printed dress. The leanness she'd acquired from walking those seemingly endless days on the trail had gone. In the past few weeks she'd put on some weight, so now her clothes fit nicely again. She tugged at her bodice. Perhaps too nicely. In fact, her dresses were almost snug, thanks to Mrs. Winters's good cook, Rosalinda.

Bethany made a mental note to purchase some material and make a few new clothing items.

She whirled back to Trudy. "I'm famished. What's for breakfast?"

Trudy's countenance brightened. "Omelets with Spanish tomatoes, peppers, and onions...and biscuits, of course. Papa loves biscuits." She paused, looking thoughtful. "Ever wonder why men insist upon biscuits at nearly every meal?"

Bethany laughed lightly. "I suppose the biscuits help to satisfy their voracious appetites." She took Trudy's arm. "Come along. Let's go downstairs."

Trudy complied, and they strolled into the hallway and to the stairs. "Aren't you the least bit interested in getting married, Miss Stafford?"

She paused on the landing as a vision of Luke McCabe flitted through her mind. "I guess I'd be a liar if I said I never wanted to get married. Doesn't every woman?" She'd marry Luke in a heartbeat. But he treated her like he would another younger sister. Jake did too.

"Then why don't you?"

"Trudy, I've learned there are other things in life of greater importance. Serving others, showing them the love of Christ—"

"Yes. I think so too."

"Then steer your thoughts toward reading and arithmetic."

Trudy groaned.

They finished descending the stairs, and Bethany felt hopeful. So she was making a difference with Trudy...

As they reached the last step, Trudy proceeded to flounce into the dining room. Bethany watched in dismay as the girl boldly approached the sheriff and began a conversation. Had she no shame? No fear? Trudy was certain to get her heart broken. Bethany sensed it coming like a brewing thunderstorm off in the distance. The men in Silverstone were not exactly refined gentlemen with whom a young lady could trifle in the parlor. No, they were hardworking river men, *vaqueros*, former soldiers, and, when it came to their land, their horses, and their women, these fellows were serious!

"Well, good mornin', Beth."

Startled from her musing, she looked to her left and found Luke leaning casually against the banister, wearing a rakishly charming smile—one that didn't seem to belong on a reverend's face.

Then, again, Luke was always charming, and they were merely friends.

"Morning, Luke."

"You look right pretty today," he drawled. "Can I escort you over to the dining table?"

"Yes, thank you." The compliment carried little weight. She knew Luke was just being his polite self. He'd been raised with the adage if you can't say something nice, don't say anything at all.

What's more, Bethany knew that if they were in Milwaukee or even back in Jericho Junction, Luke probably wouldn't give her a second look. He was, after all, a fine-looking man, strong, intelligent, and kind. She, on the other hand, was as plain as a field mouse. Her long hair was a nondescript brown and hung nearly to her waist, although she never wore it down. Her eyes were an average bluish-gray, like the sky on a misty morning, and her lips were just an ordinary shape. A smattering of freckles covered her nose and cheeks—her own fault, since she abhorred wearing a bonnet. She'd likely end up a spinster—a fate worse than death according to Trudy Winters. But so be it. Bethany felt sure she could be a respectable part of any community as an unmarried teacher...

Just not this community!

Luke slipped her hand around his elbow and guided her toward the dining room while Bethany gave him a furtive look. His hair was the color of wet sand, and his blue eyes were as clear and inviting as Lake Michigan on a hot summer day. Along his well-defined jawline a shadow of perpetual whiskers made the good pastor appear more like a shady outlaw. However, his rugged exterior cocooned a sweet disposition, and Luke's warm, friendly smile disarmed even the worst skeptics. His tall frame included broad shoulders, slim hips, and long legs, and many times during their journey, Bethany found herself admiring

God's messenger instead of listening to the message—a sin of which she was forever repenting.

But she'd gotten over that silliness now that they'd arrived in Silverstone. She simply refused to look at Luke while he preached on Sundays and, instead, forced herself to listen closely.

They reached the dining table, and Luke seated her politely before taking his place beside her.

"Good morning, Miz Stafford." Paden Montaño stood and smiled at her from across the table.

She inclined her head cordially. "Sheriff." She looked over at Jake, who had also stood when she'd entered. "Good morning."

"Beth." A smile warmed his brown eyes, although it never made it to his mouth. An onlooker might think Jake McCabe was terse and unfriendly, but Bethany knew from months of traveling with the man that he simply didn't show emotion like other folks. What's more, his bad leg pained him terribly sometimes. But far be it for Jake to let anyone know. He preferred to suffer in silence.

As everyone else took their places, Bethany allowed her gaze to wander around the table until it met the sheriff's brown eyes. He seemed to regard her with interest, and she shifted uncomfortably, lowering her chin and studying the plate in front of her.

"You look very rested, Miz Stafford." The sheriff spoke with a soft Mexican accent that Bethany found quite enchanting. And if she were completely honest, she'd have to agree with Trudy. Paden Montaño was definitely a "handsome curiosity." Today his shiny, dark hair had been pulled straight back and tied with a piece of leather string. His skin was tanned and clean-shaven with the exception of his sleek, black mustache. "I trust you are finding your stay here in Silverstone quite comfortable," he added, his dark eyes shining like polished stones.

Bethany hedged, not wanting to lie. She didn't dare say she hated the Arizona Territory with both Luke and Jake at the table.

"Everyone has been very kind to me thus far." She turned a smile on Mrs. Winters.

"Good, good…"

Mr. Winters gave a clap of his hands just then. "Let's ask God's blessing on the food and dig in." He sat at the head of the table and nodded at Jake. "Reverend Jacob, will you do the honors?"

"Of course." Bowing his head in reverence, he began, "Heavenly Father, we thank You for this beautiful day and the appetizing bounty You've placed before us. Thank You for the hands that prepared this meal. Bless it to our bodies, I ask. In Christ's name, amen."

Dishes were immediately passed around the table.

"So, Montaño, I hear you had some excitement last night." Mr. Winters forked a large piece of egg into his mouth.

"Excitement, indeed. Cattle rustlers hit the Buchanans' ranch. Clayt suspects the Indians, of course."

"Any truth to that?" Ed Winters smacked his thick lips together beneath his long, bushy, light-brown beard. "I heard there's a tribe living just north of here."

"*Sí*, but the Indian nations around here are not bloodthirsty. Nor are they interested in the Buchanans' cattle." Sheriff Montaño took a long drink of his coffee. He smiled at Doris Winters. "Ah, a good strong brew. Just the way I like it."

The older woman blushed, looking pleased. "I'll be sure to tell Rosalinda," she promised, referring to the grandmotherly Mexican cook.

"About that looting last night, Montaño," Mr. Winters continued, "you think us townsfolk have to worry?"

"No." He bit into his biscuit.

"Well, what are you going to do about it?"

"Watch. Keep my ears open." He paused to chew his food and then sat back in his chair. "I have a hunch it is the work of outlaws, but they will not get away."

From the sheriff's right side Trudy sighed dreamily. "You're so brave."

He gave her an indulgent smile.

"Well, I'd keep my eye on them Indians, if I was you." Mr. Winters snorted. "Can't trust them. I just wish the government would hurry up and take care of them."

Paden Montaño's face was devoid of expression, although his next words were deliberate and carried force. "It is a shame that most people feel as you do, *señor*, because in general the tribes are peaceful since the war in the fifties. But just like white men, they do have their outlaws and renegades." He looked over at Luke. "I'm sure the reverends would agree...God made the Indian as well as the white man. Isn't that right?"

"He did," Luke said.

Jake agreed.

"Well, even God makes mistakes," Mr. Winters grumbled.

"No, sir, He does not," Jake quickly replied. Leaning back in his chair, he folded his arms, and Bethany could tell he enjoyed the turn in the conversation. "The God of the Bible is perfect and does not err. He made man in His image. 'For God so loved the world that he gave his only begotten Son, that *whosoever* believeth in him should not perish but have everlasting life.' I reckon the words *world* and *whosoever* includes Indians, Mexicans, and every other kind of people there is."

"Thank you for the sermon." Mr. Winters arched a brow. "And it ain't even Sunday."

"Oh, now, Ed," Doris admonished her husband, looking chagrined. "Birds fly and pastors preach."

Next to Bethany, Luke chuckled. "Amen!"

Paden's mustache twitched slightly, indicating his mild amusement. Then he slid his chair backward, scraping its legs against the wooden plank floor, and rose. As usual, he'd dressed in a black shirt and trousers, but he'd tied a red bandana around his neck. "If it is any consolation, *Señor* Winters," he said, adjusting his gun belt, "I have every intention of finding those cattle rustlers, whoever they are. I gave Clayt my word."

The man nodded in satisfaction.

Sheriff Montaño turned to Mrs. Winters. "Breakfast was delicious, as always. Please compliment Rosalinda for me."

"I shall. Thank you, Sheriff."

With one last nod in Bethany's direction, he strode purposely for the door and out of the boardinghouse, leaving starry-eyed Trudy Winters gazing in his wake.

Bethany expelled a weary sigh. Would she ever be able to convince the girl to look beyond her romantic fantasies and see God's plan?

Just then, Ralph Jonas burst into the building wearing a determined expression, which skirted on desperation. His dismal gaze fell on Bethany.

She slowly stood, noticing the mat in his blond, scruffy beard. What did this man want with her now? She couldn't quell the aversion she felt at the very sight of him. He took care of his children little better than he cared for himself. Mr. Jonas's ratty, off-white shirt and knee-worn brown trousers looked as though they could use a good scrubbing—or burning.

"'Scuse me, Miss Stafford." The man sounded breathless. "But I need to speak with you. And, Preacher," he added, his gaze hardening and moving to Luke, "I'll thank you to stay out of my way."

Two

Luke rose from his chair. "Well, good mornin' to you too, Jonas."

"I mean it, Preacher. I come here to speak with Miss Stafford... privately. So mind yer own business!"

All humor slipped from Luke's expression. "Miss Stafford *is* my business. It's like I told you before. My brother Jake and I sponsored her—"

"I heard ya then like I hear ya now."

Jake pushed his chair back and stood. "Look here, Jonas..."

"Maybe Miss Stafford could speak to Mr. Jonas in the lobby," Mrs. Winters suggested diplomatically. A worried frown crimped her brow. "No need for anyone to lose his temper. We'll only be a few yards away."

"That'd be fine." Mr. Jonas thrust his ham-like hands into the pockets of his dusty coat.

"Providing Beth wants to talk to you," Jake added, a wary eye on the rancher.

"Beth?" Luke asked. "You want to talk to him?"

"Well..." Glancing up at Luke, she found his blue eyes staring back at her, his golden brows raised in question. She wanted to refuse in case Mr. Jonas proposed again, but then she wondered if there was a problem with one of his children. "I guess it's all right." Bethany's face flushed from being the center of such heated attention.

The muscle in Luke's jaw worked, but he didn't argue with her decision. His gaze moved to Mr. Jonas. "I won't be too far out of earshot."

Mr. Jonas grunted a reply, and Bethany followed him into the lobby, which really wasn't anything more than a small extension of the dining room.

He continued his grumbling. "I'm so tired of that man poking his nose into my affairs. This here's between you and me—nothing to do with him."

"Luke is merely protecting me."

"Ain't got nothin' to do with protecting." Mr. Jonas rubbed his stubbly face. "It's got everything to do with plain selfishness."

Bethany inhaled sharply at the remark.

"And that brings me to the reason for my visit. I need a wife," he blurted. "My children need a mama. The Winterses told me their daughter is too young to wed, and I reckon they're right. She ain't much older than my girl. The doc just turned me down, so you're the only one left."

"I'm flattered." Bethany couldn't keep the hint of facetiousness from her tone. Slowly she glanced over one shoulder.

"Luke?"

He stood beside her in a flash. "Trouble, Beth?"

"In a manner of speaking, yes."

"Ain't no trouble here." Mr. Jonas pulled himself up to his full height, which still came to just above Luke's shoulder.

Jake stepped to Bethany's other side. "What's this all about, Jonas?"

Before the man could answer, the door to the boardinghouse swung open, and Dr. Annetta Cavanaugh walked in. Her gaze flitted around the group. "Hello." Her tone sounded as arid as the desert wind.

The men inclined their heads politely, and Dr. Cavanaugh removed her sunbonnet, revealing her light brown hair. It was nearly the same color as Bethany's, but thicker and with a slight wave to it.

Bethany smiled. "Good morning, Dr. Cavanaugh."

"Miss Stafford." The woman's gaze briefly touched Bethany's before flitting to the dining room. "I hope I'm not too late for breakfast."

"Oh, not at all." Mrs. Winters stood from the table and strode toward the small group in the lobby. "Please come in and sit down, Dr. Cavanaugh. I'll ask Rosalinda to prepare you a plate."

"Thank you."

Bethany watched as the sturdy-framed physician came forward, but then paused in front of Mr. Jonas.

"If I advised you to take that child of yours home and put him to bed, what are you still doing here?"

"I'm a rancher." Mr. Jonas hardened his gaze. "Not a nursemaid."

"Little Jeb is ill again?" Bethany's heart sank. The toddler took ill quite frequently, and she'd taken a turn caring for him, Lorna, and Michael, the three children who weren't old enough to attend school yet.

"I'll arrange for some help," Luke promised.

"Sign me up." Bethany gave him a smile.

He winked. "You're top of the list."

"Just pack your bags and plan on staying, Miss Stafford," Mr. Jonas declared. "I believe it's God's will for you to be my wife. Why else would He have brought you here to Silverstone?"

"To teach school, for one thing." Luke folded his powerful forearms across his broad chest.

Bethany took a step closer to him. "I must properly refuse your...um, kind offer of marriage, Mr. Jonas. I'm sorry. But I feel I'm called to be part of the McCabes' ministry. It's an answer to my prayers as well as theirs."

"Doc, how 'bout you? Won't you reconsider? I'm a reasonable man at home. I promise."

"No!" Dr. Cavanaugh raised her chin.

"Look, Jonas," Jake said, "you can't just go around town asking women to marry you."

"Yer right, McCabe. Them women got hearts of stone." His beady eyes rested on Dr. Cavanaugh then Bethany, who resisted the urge to wither under his glower.

Dr. Cavanaugh obviously wasn't cowed. "The ladies in this town have been very generous. They've sacrificed time with their own families to tend to yours, Mr. Jonas. Now take that child home and try acting like a man and owning up to your responsibilities instead of looking for someone else to do it for you."

"Why, you..." Mr. Jonas lifted his hand, and Bethany was sure he'd strike Dr. Cavanaugh.

But then Jake stepped between them. "Don't you dare lay a hand on this woman."

"Get out of my way, McCabe. I don't care if you're a preacher or not."

Jake didn't budge.

Luke put his hands on Bethany's shoulders and steered her back into the dining room.

Dr. Cavanaugh followed Bethany.

"Trudy, run and fetch the sheriff." Mr. Winters stood with hands on hips, eyeing the men in the lobby area. "I don't want trouble here."

"Yes, sir." The girl quickly skirted around the men and ran out of the boardinghouse.

"Let's sit down and drink our coffee." Mrs. Winters's gaze moved to Dr. Cavanaugh. "While you were talking to Mr. Jonas, I spoke to Rosalinda, and she'll be in shortly with your breakfast."

"Thank you." Pulling out a chair, Dr. Cavanaugh sat down and arranged her dark brown skirt. Her blouse was an eggshell color with a high neck, and on it she wore a colorful broach. She appeared so calm while the trouble continued to brew in the lobby. Bethany couldn't help overhearing.

"I tell you that woman is nothing but trouble," Ralph Jonas said about Dr. Cavanaugh. "Hear how she spoke to me so disrespectful like? She needs a man to put her in her place."

Bethany's hand flew to her lips as Mr. Jonas attempted to enter the dining room. Jake stopped him easily enough.

"Why, I've never seen Ralph Jonas so prickly," Mrs. Winters remarked.

"Oh, he and I have gone around once before. In my office. He raised his hand to me then too, but he never struck me." Dr. Cavanaugh's hand shook slightly as she sipped from her porcelain coffee cup.

"What would you have done if he had?" Bethany couldn't seem to quell her curiosity.

"I would have probably shot him dead. I keep a small pistol on me at all times."

Mrs. Winters gasped.

"The sheriff can't protect me all the time." Dr. Cavanaugh pressed her lips together for a moment. "A woman has to learn to protect herself."

Bethany thought a shadow of fear had crept across Dr. Cavanaugh's features. What had happened in this woman's past to make her so…hardened?

"It's a good thing you didn't kill Ralph Jonas," Mrs. Winters said, "because I hate to think of all his children being orphaned."

"Might be better for them." Dr. Cavanaugh's cup rattled against the saucer as she set it down. "The man is an unfit parent."

Bethany silently agreed. The man's older children, particularly the boys, came to school unkempt. In many ways, Ralph Jonas reminded her of her own tyrannical father. He didn't have a nurturing bone in his body. Hard work meant everything—except when it came to Bethany's stepmother. She lounged around, reading books all day while Bethany served her, took care of the children, milked cows, mucked out the stalls, weeded gardens, canned preserves, cooked, cleaned…her chores were never-ending.

But then Luke came to Milwaukee to visit Sarah. He wanted to make Sarah the new teacher in Silverstone, but God orchestrated things so she had to remain in Milwaukee. Then, after meeting her at the Navises's farm, Luke offered the position to Bethany. It seemed like a dream come true.

Until she arrived in Silverstone and met the stark reality of her new existence. She breathed in deeply. Next spring couldn't come soon enough.

"Right now two-year-old Jeb lies in the back of Ralph Jonas's wagon, sick with a fever."

The physician's remark pulled Bethany from her thoughts.

Dr. Cavanaugh sipped her coffee again, and tiny creases formed around her hazel eyes as she frowned. "I checked on him before I came into the boardinghouse. He's sleeping, and the wagon is parked in the shade. I plan to care for him myself after I have a bite to eat."

"Mighty kind of you, Doctor." Mrs. Winters gave her an approving smile.

"But you see, I can't make caring for the Jonas children a habit, or I'll never get anything accomplished."

Bethany spoke up. "I'll help you once school is through today. Perhaps I can even dismiss the children earlier than usual."

"That would be a help, Miss Stafford. Thank you."

She smiled at the doctor.

Ralph Jonas obviously heard the offer from his stance in the lobby. "And plan on staying," he called. "Mebbe one of these preachers'll marry us after you make supper tonight."

Dr. Cavanaugh and Mrs. Winters both turned to Bethany.

She fought back the insult and disgust she felt at his crudeness. Slowly rising, she felt forced to take a stand. "I think not, Mr. Jonas. Thank you all the same. I will not marry you. Hear me? *I will not.*"

"That remains to be seen."

Bethany's shoulders sagged in a weary sigh.

"Obstinate old fool," Mrs. Winters muttered.

"Look, Jonas," Luke interjected, "under the circumstance, I don't believe it's a good idea for Beth to watch your kids and make your supper this evening after all." He faced Dr. Cavanaugh. "Sorry, ma'am, but I've got to be up at the Whitakers' today."

"I understand. I'll find another woman to help me today."

Gratefulness enveloped Bethany. She'd hate to be on the Jonas farm without another man's protection. No telling what Mr. Jonas was capable of doing in his desperate state.

She glanced at the timepiece pinned to her bodice. "I'm afraid you will all have to excuse me. I must run along or I'll be late, and that will set a bad precedent." She stood and glanced into the lobby. The sheriff had arrived, and young Trudy stood in the center of the throng.

Shaking her head, Bethany walked to the lobby and took hold of Trudy's elbow. "Time for school."

"Do I have to go?" She eyed Sheriff Montaño. "This is ever so much more interesting."

Bethany gave her a yank. "School."

"Mama!" Trudy looked for a backup.

"Mind your teacher, dear. I'll send Rosalinda with your lunch."

Bethany sent Mrs. Winters a grateful smile before propelling Trudy out the door.

Outside, the dusty air swirled on a light breeze. Bethany couldn't help but peek in on Jeb as they passed the Jonas wagon.

His eyes were closed, and he lay unmoving on a blanket. Lorna, his sister, sat holding baby Michael.

"You're doing a good job, Lorna."

A smile spread across the little girl's dirt-stained face.

Putting her hand on Jeb's chest, Bethany felt that he was still breathing. She placed her hand on his hot forehead and sent up a prayer that God would heal this little boy soon—and find him and his siblings a mother, one who could handle the likes of both them and Ralph Jonas.

Gathering her skirts, she moved away from the wagon, although it took every ounce of her will. She hated leaving the children alone in the wagon. But Mrs. Winters would likely come for them soon.

Meanwhile, Bethany's students awaited her. "Come on, Trudy, let's go or we'll be late."

"Hold up, Beth." Luke strode from the boardinghouse and ran down the steps from the porch. "I'll walk you and Trudy to the schoolhouse."

"Thank you, Luke." She glanced back at the wagon.

"And don't worry about the Jonas kids," he said as if reading her thoughts. "It'll work out."

Luke offered his arm, and his blue eyes met Bethany's gaze. Her heart did a little flip as she slipped her hand around his elbow. It occurred to her then that Luke McCabe would be the only thing she'd miss when she left Silverstone.

Annetta Cavanaugh tried desperately to quell the fear mounting inside of her. Memories flashed before her. Gunfire. Gregory lying dead near the brick fireplace. Then the blow across the face that knocked her senseless. The killer's leering grin. His hands on her body. Her screams that no one could hear splitting the night. *Oh, God! Oh, God!*

"Dr. Cavanaugh?"

Annetta wrestled from the grip of her past and stared into Mrs. Winters's surprised face.

"Are you all right, dear? Why, you're trembling."

"I–I'm fine. I must have caught a chill." She'd thought for sure she'd buried the past with Gregory and her dreams of becoming his wife. Then she'd sealed that coffin by coming out West to work as a doctor in Silverstone and starting a new life.

"Caught a chill?" Mrs. Winters eyed her speculatively. "Hmm…if you say so."

Annetta realized the folly of her remark. Not many folks caught chills in this dreadful heat, unless they were ill, of course.

She sighed and glanced over her shoulder. She wished Ralph Jonas would leave peaceably now. As much as she hated to admit it, he'd frightened her this morning with his forceful marriage proposal and then lifting his hand to her—

"*Señor*, you go now," the sheriff said. "These women here, they do not want to marry you. Do not humiliate yourself further."

Annetta winced. Would the sheriff's rebuff only anger Jonas all the more? She walked to the windows and stared through the stiff white café curtains at the dirt street. This town wasn't anything like Parkersburg—and that's what she'd wanted. A place where nothing and no one would remind her of the horrors she'd suffered.

Except one ornery man seemed to accomplish the feat in seconds.

"Dr. Cavanaugh?"

She felt a hand on her shoulder and whirled around. Her back to the windows, she found herself staring at a metal shirt button until she lifted her gaze higher and higher still. Suddenly she found Jacob McCabe's arresting brown eyes staring into hers.

"Pardon me, but…" He appeared chagrined. "Ralph left peaceably but asked if he could drop the boy off at your office."

Annetta willed herself to relax. She needed to remember she was the physician in this town. Unemotional. Detached. Competent. "Yes, of course. I'll care for Jeb today—as well as Lorna and Michael too, I suspect."

"Actually, Mrs. Winters said she could mind the other two if you'd tend to the sick boy."

"Fine." Rubbing her palms on her dark brown skirt, she wished the good reverend wouldn't stand so close, but, oddly, she felt safer than scared in his shadow. "Well, I'd best get back to the office if Mr. Jonas means to drop off his little boy."

"I'll walk over with you, seeing as I'm going that way anyhow."

"That's not necessary, Reverend."

"I know." A little grin tugged at his mouth. "But I aim to do it anyway."

"Suit yourself." It wouldn't do to let him know how grateful she was for his presence. She had to prove herself better than any man in this town, which meant she couldn't let memories disable her—

Not when her entire future was at stake!

The hot Arizona sunshine beat down on Luke as he and Jacob walked up the hill to their quarters, built right behind the church. The day promised to be a scorcher, and he almost wished he hadn't committed himself to working out on Harlan's ranch beneath the blistering sun.

"You know, brother," Jacob began, "there's been some speculating on you and our new schoolteacher. Truth is, I've done a bit of speculating myself."

"Well," Luke drawled, "you know I've always been fond of Beth, but last Christmas she managed to pique my interest. Traveling together, she earned my respect." He folded his arms and grinned, remembering back to when he'd first met her. "In the beginning she was so shy and melancholy that it was a challenge for me to even make her smile."

"Oh?" Jake arched a brow. "I make her smile all the time."

Luke didn't appreciate the remark. "Well, you're one laughing matter."

Jake chuckled. Then slowly his smile dwindled. He paused at the well and pumped some water, splashing it onto his face. "So? You gonna marry her?"

"Maybe. I mean, I've been thinking and praying on the matter. It's just that Beth doesn't seem very happy these days."

"I noticed the same thing." Jake wiped the dripping water on his chin with his sleeve. "I suspect Silverstone came as something of a shock to her. But she'll get over it now that school's started."

"I hope so."

"Maybe you should have a talk with her." Jake stepped into their small cabin.

Luke followed, breathing a sigh of relief to get out of the blazing sun. Jake had constructed the home, which contained one large, main room that served as both a sitting room and dining area. Two bedrooms had been built off the main room, and cupboards, counters, and a cast iron stove occupied the other end of the cabin. But neither Luke nor Jake cooked much, as Mrs. Winters offered them free meals on account of them both being ministers.

"Yeah, maybe I'll talk with Beth about a few matters," Luke said. And maybe he'd mention courtship too and gauge her reaction. Was she the one? Seemed he'd been dwelling on marriage a lot lately, so he'd been praying and asking the Lord to direct his paths in this matter. So far God had shown him Beth's courage, which Luke had observed more than once on the trail. Yet there were times when she seemed as vulnerable as a small, gray-eyed kitten. Or maybe it was her youthful innocence that caused him to want to protect her—share his life with her.

Did she want the same?

In the past, Luke suspected she had feelings for him, judging by the way she gazed up at him with something akin to adoration in her eyes. But would she marry him, or would she turn him down like she had Ralph Jonas?

"You scared to talk to Beth?" A teasing gleam entered Jake's eyes as he pulled out a chair and sat down at the large, square table near the stone hearth.

"No."

"Then you might make haste and propose marriage before someone else captures her heart—like the good sheriff."

"Montaño?" Luke waved a hand. "He's not a believer. Beth wouldn't marry a nonbeliever." He paused before adding, "I wouldn't let her!"

"Well, you know what they say about the love of a good woman." Jake tipped his head. "Haven't you seen the way Montaño's face lights up with interest when Bethany enters the room?" Luke didn't reply, but he'd seen it all right. "He's most likely intrigued with Beth because she's the only woman around who doesn't swoon over his good looks."

Jake grinned. "Now, I'd be inclined to think that remark stemmed from sour grapes on your part, Luke, except I've taken note of it myself. Beth doesn't bat a single lash at the debonair Paden Montaño."

"Aw, he ain't so debonair. And where'd you learn that word, anyway?" Luke thought of their sister-in-law. "You sound like Valerie."

Again, Jake chuckled. "Can't say I learned it from her, although she is forever using those fancy French words."

They shared a chuckle, and Luke recalled the day their oldest brother, Ben, had introduced him to his blue-eyed, New Orleans socialite wife—well, ex-socialite. That had been six years ago and just after Luke had gone missing after the first battle at Bull Run.

He'd been wounded and had lost his memory. Even now Luke only remembered snippets of the event. It took Ben months to find him. In that time, Ben had met and married Valerie Fontaine and helped her escape the city and wrongful allegations of treason.

"I know you're not asking for it, but as your older brother I'm giving you my advice anyhow. I think you'd better decide whether you're going to marry Beth or else stand aside and let other fellas have a chance at her hand."

"What are you talking about? There's no other fellas."

"Would be if you'd quit hovering over that young lady like, like…well, what is it like, Luke? Brother or suitor?"

Luke opened his mouth to reply, but no words came out. He didn't think of Beth in the same way he thought of his older sister, Leah, or younger sister, Sarah. And the thought of other fellas calling on Beth caused a painful knot to form in his chest.

"You've got a point. Maybe now's the time for action."

"I'm thinking so."

"Yeah?" Encouragement surged up inside of Luke.

"Yeah."

"Well…all right, then." Luke proceeded to collect a few things he'd need today and packed his saddlebags. Suddenly he thought he might prefer the blazing sun on Harlan's range to any kind of rejection from Bethany. "Guess I'd best pray about that today."

"Good plan. And will you join me in praying over someone else too?"

"Who's that?"

"Annetta Cavanaugh."

Luke glanced at his brother. "The new doctor?"

"Uh-huh. I saw something in her eyes this morning—like a real deep hurt."

"Maybe it was aggravation," Luke quipped, remembering Dr. Cavanaugh's scrape with Ralph Jonas.

"No, brother. It was pain. I know pain when I see it."

Luke wasn't about to argue. Ever since he got wounded, Jake struggled with that injured leg of his. Sometimes the intensity of the ache didn't allow him to sleep at night.

"All right. I'll pray for the doc." Setting his wide-brimmed hat on his head, he sent Jake a parting nod. "You've got my promise on that."

THREE

LUKE PAUSED ON THE RIDGE TO APPRECIATE THE SIGHT before him. Harlan Whitaker's ranch spread out as far as the eye could see, his crops to the east, and cattle on the western edge dotted the countryside. Luke suddenly longed for his own homestead but quickly reminded himself that covetousness was a sin and old Harlan deserved his acreage. After all, he had been one of the few settlers who'd stayed on after the army pulled out when the Civil War erupted. Most ranchers left their homesteads on account of renegade Indians and outlaws who were known for their thieving and murdering of not only whites but other tribes as well. However, Harlan refused to leave his land, even though it had cost him his oldest son and scores of field hands.

"Sure appreciate yer ridin' out here today, Preacher," the aging man told Luke as they met just inside the Whitaker property line. His dark, thinning hair was hidden beneath a red-and-white checkered bandanna, topped with a wide-brimmed hat. Leaning forward in his saddle, he added, "Hard to find good help these days."

Luke couldn't help a grin. It was said that a man took his life into his own hands when he set out to work for Harlan.

"Hope yer a good shot." Glancing at Luke's waist, he frowned. "No holster...gun?"

"I don't carry a gun on me—not since my time in the war."

"Are you crazy, boy?"

Luke ignored the remark. Harlan hadn't been the first to wonder if he was *loco* not to carry a pistol. However, Luke did pack a Winchester .44 Carbine in his saddle just in case he came face-to-face with a wild boar, snake, or sundry other nasty critters. He'd shoot them in a minute. But a human being...never. Never again. Luke made a vow to himself the day he arrived home in Jericho Junction with his older brother Ben that he'd never take another human life—even in self-defense. He'd rather die than kill a living soul.

"Now, Preacher," Harlan insisted, "you'll hafta carry a gun today. Just take one look at my hogs and you'll see why." Turning his horse, he led Luke around to the far side of his ranch and stopped near the hog pen. "Will ya look at that? And don't laugh, Preacher. It ain't funny!"

Too late. Luke chuckled at the sight. There before his eyes were hogs, all right, but several had arrows protruding from their thick skin, and they squealed loudly as they circled the pen.

"My wife says they look like four-legged pin cushions."

"I'd say that's about right."

Harlan shifted in his saddle. The leather creaked beneath his weight. "Indians come by almost ever'day and shoot arrows into my hogs. Then I've gotta butcher 'em. Guess there's another thing you can help me with later today. Now, about that gun...you can use one of mine."

"No, thanks, friend." Luke sent him a confident grin. "My God is bigger than all the Indians put together."

"Yer a fool, Preacher." Harlan shook his head.

Luke let the ridicule blow on by like the hot, dusty, desert wind. Still, it stung a little as it passed. But he'd made his decision, and he wouldn't go back on it no matter what anyone else might think.

"Well, I reckon I'll put you in the barn. You can repair a few harnesses. Can't rightly send you out on the range, seeing as yer being so mule-headed."

"Harlan, you want me on the range, that's where I'll go, gun or no gun."

"You got suicide on your brain this morning, Preacher? You can't ride the range unarmed."

Luke shrugged. "Choice is yours."

Harlan thought it over then slapped his hat onto his receding brown hair. "I reckon I got enough men out minding the cattle. You go on over to the barn."

"Be glad to."

After tethering his horse, Luke walked into the barn, thanking God that at least he'd work out of the sun most of the time. His eyes slowly adjusted to the darkness of the rough-hewn, square-shaped building. It smelled of dried grass, sweat, leather, and horses. Luke ran his gaze over the damaged harnesses hanging from large nails on the wall. With little effort, he pulled one down, inspected it, and got to work.

Hours passed, and the sun blazed mercilessly from its midday perch in the cloudless sky when something at the doorway caused the barn to grow unnaturally dim. Luke looked up and barely glimpsed a man's silhouette before a shiny object came hurling toward him. He tripped backward just as the knife's blade whizzed by, lodging itself in the splintering wall. Turning back at the entrance, he watched with a mix of horror and interest as an Indian brave stepped in.

Luke didn't utter a sound but stared at the expressionless coppery face framed in long black hair. His gaze moved over the long-sleeved white tunic, belted with ammunition, and sun-bleached britches tucked into leather knee-high moccasins. In his left arm, he cradled a rifle that Luke recognized as an old Henry .44, and suddenly he wished he'd taken Harlan's advice and packed a pistol. His next thought was imminent death. Oddly, a sense of peace enveloped his being.

The brave took another cautious step forward, eyeing Luke

as intensely as Luke had scrutinized him. Finally he spoke in broken English. "You no have gun."

He shook his head. "No. No gun."

The Indian narrowed his dark gaze then tipped his head in speculation before glancing over his shoulder warily. "Me kill you, white man."

"Yeah, I reckon that's the plan."

The warrior seemed perplexed by the quip and again looked over his shoulder. "Why you no have gun?"

"Don't need it." Luke glanced upward. "My God protects me."

The brave followed Luke's line of vision and studied the roof of the barn. At last, he pointed to it. "Your God?"

Luke grinned. "No, no, that is not my God. My God is the God of the Bible who lives in heaven...way up in the sky, beyond the moon and stars."

Obvious understanding washed over the warrior's face. "Ha! Your God not protect you from my gun!" He shook his rifle under Luke's nose.

"No, but if you kill me, I will be with my God in heaven."

The other man frowned heavily, and his jaw dropped in wonder.

"My God loves all men," Luke continued, figuring his time was short and he'd best get as much evangelizing in as he could before meeting his Savior. "He loves red men just as much as white men. My God sees no difference between you and me."

The tip of the rifle was suddenly thrust against his throat. "White men murder my people," the Indian sneered.

"And red men murder my people. But isn't it time we stop killing each other and live in peace?" Luke's eyes met the warrior's fearsome gaze. "Peace."

Slowly, the gun lowered from his throat.

"Hey, Preacher...?"

At the call outside, the brave startled and cocked his rifle, pointing it toward the door. Luke put his hand on the barrel. "No need for killing," he whispered. Then, persuading the warrior back into a darkened corner, Luke touched a finger to his lips, urging his uninvited guest to remain silent.

"Yeah, Harlan, go ahead."

"Carolyn's about got supper on the table," he hollered from outside, "and she don't want you eating with the hired hands on account of you being a man of the cloth and all."

Luke's gaze never left the Indian. "I appreciate that. Tell your wife I'll be along shortly. Just finishing up in here."

"Very good." The sound of Harlan's retreating footsteps reached them inside the barn.

For a long while, the two men stared at each other. Finally the brave said, "You, Preacher?"

He nodded. "Name's Luke McCabe."

"Preacher Luke McCabe," he said as if the three names were all one word. "Me, Warring Spirit," he stated proudly, thumping his chest.

Luke cocked his head. "I don't suppose you know anything about the raids around here."

"I know plenty." Warring Spirit put away his rifle. "But it is not my people who steal and kill."

Luke pulled the knife from the wall. "You were about to kill me."

Warring Spirit shrugged as he handed back the knife. "I more frighten than kill."

Luke wasn't convinced, but he wanted more information about the raids. "So you think it's outlaws, then?"

"Maybe...or maybe the bloodthirsty half-breeds."

Luke set his hands on his hips. "So they are Indians then..."

Warring Spirit snorted out cynical laugh. "The white men see only one kind of red men, but there are many. Me"—he drummed his fingertips against his chest—"I am Yuma. We hunt, fish, and grow our food from the land."

"Farmers?"

Warring Spirit gave a nod. "But there are white men who want us gone."

"Hmm...you've got a point. I know a few white men like that."

"Yes." The brave moved closer. "That's why I must protect my village. We are innocent of the raids you speak of."

Luke understood. After all, he himself had been guilty of lumping all Indians into one body of people.

"Warring Spirit, I understand, and I will pass on this informa-tion to our sheriff and some of the men looking for the raiders. I will do what I can to help you protect your village. I hate the thought of innocent people losing their lives."

The brave eyed him speculatively before he gave a nod. "Then I will call you friend, Preacher Luke McCabe."

Luke stuck out his right hand. "I wish you peace, Warring Spirit. Peace that comes from the one true living God."

Warring Spirit took his hand, and Luke gave it a shake.

"Peace," the brave said. Then he turned and left the barn, van-ishing as quickly as he'd appeared.

Having survived his encounter with Warring Spirit, Luke felt unusually courageous as he rode into Silverstone. So after he learned from Jake that Beth was still in the schoolhouse, he decided to pay her a visit. But taking two steps out of the cabin he shared with his brother, he soon realized he smelled about as ripe as a Missouri cornfield during planting season. He quickly adjusted his plans to include a quick dip in the cool Colorado River.

He turned tail and reentered the cabin. "I decided to take a swim."

"Good day for it. I'd be inclined to join you except I'm working on this week's sermon." Looking up from the scarred table on which his Bible sat, Jake grinned. "Either way, I imagine you deserve a bath, what with being out on the range all day."

"Actually, I was indoors all morning, making repairs. Then I helped Harlan butcher hogs. But I managed to meet up with an Indian brave just the same."

Jake sat back, wearing an expression of interest, and folded his arms. "You don't say?"

"Yep. And it's only by the grace of God that I'm alive to tell about it."

"Well, hallelujah!"

"Hand me that soap, will you?"

His older brother twisted around in his chair and grabbed the strong-smelling bar, tossing it in Luke's direction. "Since when do you need soap for swimming?"

"Since I decided to court Beth—starting tonight."

Jake let loose with a loud, "Whoo-wee!"

"Pipe down," Luke said irritably. "She's liable to hear you clear to the schoolhouse." He shifted. "And I'm liable to lose my nerve."

"I don't think you've got anything to worry about, Luke."

"I'm not so sure." He sensed something was amiss. Maybe Beth wasn't happy. Either way, he aimed to find out what was going on inside that pretty head of hers.

What a luxury to read! Bethany closed the book in her hands and stared at its cover. Back on the farm in Wisconsin, Bethany had been so busy she never had a second to herself. Her step-mother, on the other hand, read books all day long. Sometimes while Bethany prepared dinner, she'd share the story she'd been reading that day. While she listened, hot flames of jealousy licked at Bethany's soul. But she never exerted her will. Her father would have shown his wrath if supper wasn't on the table by the time he came in from working in the fields.

The wooden door on the schoolhouse creaked open, and Bethany looked up to see a tall shadow of a man. When he stepped forward, she smiled. "Good afternoon, Luke." Standing from where she'd been sitting on the floor, she then tried to hide the novel in the folds of her skirt. It wouldn't do if Luke suspected she'd been slacking on her responsibilities as a teacher. "I didn't hear you come in."

"Hello, Beth." He stepped forward, smiling, yet wearing a curious expression. "What are you reading?"

She grimaced, realizing he'd seen it. But she wasn't about to lie to him. "This is one of the books Mrs. Buchanan donated to the school this afternoon." She made a sweeping glance around her. "Look at all of this, Luke!" Crates cluttered the plank floor. "Mrs. Buchanan said she loves books and has dozens of them shipped from San Francisco twice a year. These are just some she felt she could part with."

Luke's gaze traveled quickly over the wooden containers before it came back around to hers. "That was mighty generous of Mrs. Buchanan."

"Indeed." Bethany watched Luke step closer until he stood right in front of her. Then he held out his hand.

"Let me see what book's got you so captivated."

Guiltily, she relinquished the novel.

Luke inspected it. "Hmm...*Mountain Mary*." He raised his blond brows in question. "A dime novel, Beth?"

"I'm doing research," she stated in her own defense. "I wanted to see for myself what the fuss is all about...in case one of my students has a penchant for these things. I wouldn't want to be ignorant."

"I should say not." The corners of his mouth lifted with

amusement. He handed back the novel. "And just what is all the fuss about?"

"Well, in this particular story, Mountain Mary is quite a fearsome lady. She can tackle a bear and fend off an entire band of Indians single-handedly. However, she's willing to give up her love of the mountains for the love of her life. It is quite the sacrifice for her."

"I imagine so." Luke seemed to hide his chuckles behind his amused grin.

"In any case," Beth said, feeling indignation coming on, "the story is very compelling."

"I reckon it is, from what I saw when I walked in. You seemed engrossed." Stepping backward, Luke took a seat on the corner of the long table in front of the room. All amusement vanished from his features, and he gave her a warm smile. "Did you have a good day?"

"I stayed busy. I helped Trudy with the mail earlier."

"Does that constitute a good day then?"

Bethany didn't know how to reply. How could it be "good" if she was miserable here in Silverstone? Except she didn't have anywhere else to go...

Luke leaned closer. "Homesick, Beth?"

Nibbling her lower lip, Bethany thought it over. "No, not homesick. Just...well, Silverstone isn't what I'd ever imagined. I feel out of touch with the entire world."

Luke grinned broadly. "Welcome to the Wild West."

Bethany didn't feel welcomed in the least. But she couldn't see how complaining would do her any good either. She set *Mountain Mary* on a stack of books. "Oh! I almost forgot...do you know what Mrs. Buchanan told me?"

Luke squinted. "No, what?"

"Her husband, Clayton, along with their son, Matt, are planning to take the law into their own hands and find the cattle rustlers who looted their ranch. I mentioned it to Mr. Winters, who seemed to side with the Buchanans. They think the Indians are the thieves, but I said I believe Sheriff Montaño's theory that it's outlaws."

"Oh?" He frowned. "Is the sheriff aware the Winterses and Buchanans plan to do their own avenging?"

"Yes. He rode by the schoolhouse just after Mrs. Buchanan had these crates deposited here. I told him, since it didn't appear Mrs. Buchanan would. She told me Sheriff Montaño is most unreasonable."

"Hmm…" Luke didn't seem pleased.

Bethany folded her hands in front of her and sighed deeply, regretfully. "I probably shouldn't have spoken out of turn, huh, Luke? Maybe there's really no cause for concern anyway. You know how Mr. Winters likes talking so smart…"

"No, you did the right thing, Beth," he assured her. "Besides, a woman needs to have some gumption out here, although"—his mood brightened—"*Mountain Mary* is a bit extreme."

"Oh, all right," Bethany teased, "I'll stop wrestling bears in my free time." Stooping to pry open another crate of books, she heard Luke's deep, hearty laugh, and it made her smile.

Peeking over at him, she thought he seemed awfully clean for having been on a ranch all day. His blond hair was parted neatly to one side, and his pants of cotton jeaning seemed as crisp as the tan shirt he wore, tucked in neatly at the waist. Did he have important business to tend to? Was he going somewhere this evening? Seeing someone?

Oh, it's none of my business!

One by one, Bethany lined up the books so she could tell Mr. Winters how much of a bookshelf she'd need. After all, the man enjoyed pounding furniture together, crude as it could be at times, and far be it from her to rob him of his fun.

Still, she was curious about Luke. "How was your day?"

"Quite interesting. I met a Yuma Indian by the name of War-ring Spirit. He snuck up on me while I was in Harlan's barn. Scared the liver out of me, but after we talked awhile, we shook hands in peace."

"An Indian?" Bethany straightened and sucked in a terrified breath. "Luke? You came face-to-face with him?"

He nodded. Then a little smile tugged at the corners of his mouth. "Would you miss me, Beth, if I'd have gotten killed this afternoon?"

"What kind of question is that?" Flustered, she turned her back on him, setting down another armful of books. Why would he ask her such a thing? But his steady silence caused her to realize he was actually waiting for an answer. "Of course I'd miss you," she stated quickly. "The whole town would miss you. If you were dead, Luke, who would preach to us on Sunday mornings while Pastor Jake rode his circuit?"

She picked up another book, opened it, and pretended to be suddenly very interested in its subject. Why did he say such things? He often remarked that she looked pretty, and now he asked if she'd miss him if the unthinkable occurred. Didn't he know a girl could get the wrong idea, what with all his winsome words?

"It's a nice evening, Beth. Care to take a stroll before supper?"

Turning on her heel, she fairly gaped at the man. A stroll? Then slowly it dawned on her that Luke was simply indulging her as he might his younger sister, Sarah.

Except she wasn't his sister, and the things he said were affecting her heart in the most unreasonable way.

"You know, Luke…" She sent up an arrow of a prayer for courage to speak her mind. She fingered the edge of the book nervously. "For a better part of a month now, I've been meaning to tell you something, but it's hard to say."

"Don't tell me you're interested in a young man here in town."

"Interested?" Her head shot up, and she peered at him. "Why, no."

He smiled. "That's good."

"Good?" Perplexed, she stepped closer. "Luke, if you talk to all women the way you talk to me, you're bound to have some angry husbands on your hands. Women just naturally take to those niceties, those compliments. Understand? I'm telling you this for your own good."

"Much obliged." His blue eyes seemed to watch her carefully. "But I don't flatter all women, and I'm especially careful around the married ones—well, I'm careful around the unmarried ones too."

Frustration flamed in her cheeks. "So let me get this straight. You only flatter your...sisters?"

He lifted one shoulder. "I suppose—"

"But I'm not your sister, Luke. I'm not even a relation."

"For which I am most thankful," he stated emphatically, wearing a wry grin.

"What?" Bethany shook her head, refusing to be deterred by his smart remarks. Obviously he thought himself amusing, but this morning's incident with Ralph Jonas showed her there was nothing amusing about the opposite gender getting the wrong idea about marriage!

"Luke, the way you've been behaving lately causes me to wonder if you're interested in me—romantically—which I know is not the case," she put in hastily. "And, just for your information, my mind has not been influenced by dime novels. I'm merely stating the facts from a woman's point of view. For your own good."

Luke blinked. "I see."

She nodded satisfactorily. Judging from his expression, he finally understood.

"But what if I am interested, Beth?" The sudden earnest look on his face made him appear almost vulnerable.

"Interested?" The word seemed to stick in her throat. "In me?"

He nodded.

"Why?" Her father's description of her stuck in her soul like bread dough on her fingertips. *You're as plain as a field mouse.*

Luke gave her an easy smile. "How 'bout we go for that stroll? It's awful stuffy in here."

Before she could utter a reply, he took her elbow and propelled her toward the open doorway. They descended the steps of the schoolhouse, and he looped her hand over the crook of his arm.

Was she dreaming? Had she imagined the last few minutes of conversation?

"You know, I think it's going to rain." Luke hung his head back, gazing up at the sky.

Bethany didn't reply. She felt dazed.

They stepped onto the boardwalk and passed the mercantile, Luke keeping a slow pace so Bethany could keep up with his long-legged strides.

"I heard a druggist from California has plans to set up shop right here in Silverstone."

"Yes, I'd heard that too." Bethany began to relax. The shock was wearing off.

"Now that the war is over, I imagine more folks will be coming out West. Those moving into California will likely cross the river at the Yuma Crossing, which means additional business for Silverstone, seeing as our town is right on the way."

"Yes, Mr. Winters said much the same thing, and he's even talking about opening a hotel."

"Is that so? What do you think he'll do with his boardinghouse?"

"Run it just as he is now, I would guess."

"Hmm…"

Bethany's tension had all but completely receded, and she found it quite enjoyable to stroll along beside Luke this way.

Then all too soon they arrived at the boardinghouse.

Luke paused on the porch before they went inside. "I think I'll say goodnight here. Don't worry about the schoolhouse. I'll close up for you on my way home."

"You're not eating supper here tonight?" Bethany couldn't mask her disappointment.

"Naw. I'm still full from Mrs. Whitaker's midday dinner. But I'll see you tomorrow at breakfast. Perhaps we can talk some before you have to be at school."

"As you wish." Bethany tamped down her impatience. She wanted to talk with Luke now. Ask him what he meant before. Did he want to court her?

Luke smiled. "G'night, Beth." Softness pooled in his blue eyes, answering at least one of her questions.

"Goodnight, Luke." She'd have to leave it at that, although her head was still in something of a fog as she watched him traipse back up the hill toward the church. How could it be that the man she thought most handsome, so kind, gentle—and, most of all, godly—could even think to court a plain-looking woman such as herself? He couldn't be teasing her. Luke would never joke about something so serious.

Turning the brass knob, Bethany entered the boardinghouse. She closed the door behind her, leaning against it, but too late she realized she'd walked in on some sort of meeting. The lobby was filled with men. A thin layer of gray smoke from their tobacco swirled near the ceiling, and since all eyes were riveted to Mr. Buchanan on the stairway, her presence went unnoticed.

"This here's a call to arms, men. Our families are at stake. Them Indians gotta be stopped. The government isn't doing its job, so we've got to take matters into our own hands."

Shouts of enthusiasm filled the room.

"Cattle rustling is a high crime, one that can't be allowed to go unpunished. If we let those savages get away with stealing our livestock, there'll be no telling what they take next. Might even be our wives and children."

The audience murmured in concern.

"So, are you with me?"

Loud, exuberant affirmations filled Bethany's ears, causing her to wince.

"Then, as soon as it's dark, we ride!"

More cheering broke out, and Bethany slipped back out the door. The sun had begun its descent in the western sky amidst ribbons of orange, red, and lavender.

She nibbled her lower lip, wondering what she ought to do about what she'd just heard—if anything. Looking down Main Street, she spied the sheriff's office. Did she chance it? Crossing over to the "bad side of the street," even if it was for a good cause?

Except how could she stay quiet? Innocent lives might be lost if she didn't speak out.

Decision made, Bethany made her way from the porch. Reaching the street, she looked this way and that, and praying no respectable persons saw her, she stepped off the wooden walk.

She'd only made it halfway across when suddenly someone grabbed her roughly around the waist. She tried to scream, but a gloved hand went over her mouth. Eyes wide in panic, she kicked and clawed, but she was no match for her assailant's powerful arms. He quickly lifted her up and around to the back of the Winterses' establishment.

Finally his low, husky, and very familiar voice reached her ears. "Miz Stafford, are you trying to get yourself killed?"

FOUR

ETHANY RELAXED, RECOGNIZING PADEN MONTAÑO'S deep, smooth voice. Slowly he lifted his leather glove from her mouth, and she turned in a whirl to face him.

"Sheriff, I was just on my way over to see you!"

Several inches taller, he smiled down at her, a curious look in his eyes. "Iz that so?"

She nodded, growing uncomfortable as the sheriff's dark gaze boldly assessed her face, lingering on her lips, while his muscled arm still held her captive. Bethany could feel the top of his ammunition belt pressing against her ribs. She hoped no one would happen to pass by and see them in this most compromising position. It could mean her reputation! Placing her hands on the sheriff's black leather vest, she tried in vain to create more distance between them.

"And what were you coming to see me about, Miz Stafford?"

"I need to tell you something...ooh! Let me go!"

Sheriff Montaño released her, and Bethany would have fallen backward from her efforts to dislodge herself had he not caught her elbow.

"I apologize for apprehending you that way, but the alternative would have resulted in your being run over by twenty exuberant cowboys on their way out of the boardinghouse." He raised his swarthy brows and looked as though he might chuckle. "But you have my undivided attention now, I assure you. What did you want to see me about?"

Pulling out of his grasp, Bethany gave him a quelling look.

"Those same men, the ones you claim would have run me over"—she paused to finish collecting her wits—"well, I overheard their discussion tonight. They're planning to ride—"

"*Sí*, I know all about their intentions." He wore a stony expression.

"But, the Indians…those men plan to kill them. Would those tribes really rustle cattle and risk breaking the treaty?"

"No. They would not. And I am aware of tonight's plans. But you, Miz Stafford, should not go about eavesdropping."

She replied with an indignant gasp. "I was *not* eavesdropping. I simply walked into the boardinghouse, and there they were, discussing their murderous plans."

"Hmm." The sheriff looked thoroughly amused, but in a patronizing sort of way.

"Oh, never mind!" She turned in a huff. Why had she ever thought this man was charming? He was positively maddening!

"Miz Stafford?"

She stopped and glanced over her shoulder. The sheriff stepped around, facing her once more.

"Forgive me, *chiquita*. I appreciate your concern. Very few Silverstone residents would care if Indians were murdered."

"I don't want anyone to be killed."

"I know. You are a very special young woman."

Bethany gave him a skeptical look before quizzing him further. "What are you going to do?"

The sheriff gave her a tolerant smile. "I will try to persuade the men of this unlawful posse to turn back and allow me to take care of finding the real thieves. After that, what more can I do?"

"Will they listen?"

He shrugged.

"But you're one man against so many."

"I will do what I can. Meanwhile, you mustn't worry your pretty head about such things. Go on inside." He nodded toward the back entrance of the boardinghouse, which led to the outside kitchen and a courtyard where clean laundry still hung from the line. The chicken coop was there too, along with a pathway to the stables. "I can still hear excitement in the voices coming from the front. It would not be wise for you to meet up with those ruffians right now."

The sheriff's expression appeared indiscernible, although his dark eyes seemed to plead with her until Bethany felt she had no other choice but to comply with his wishes.

"Very well. Good night, Sheriff."

Removing his wide-brimmed, black hat, he bowed gallantly. "Sleep well, Miz Stafford."

Hours later Bethany petitioned the Lord. She asked for Paden Montaño's safety when confronting the angry mob of men. She prayed about her upcoming conversation with Luke, scarcely believing that he could have taken a romantic interest in her. She entreated her Savior for wisdom concerning the forthcoming school year and her new students. "And please bless the Winterses, Dr. Cavanaugh, Jake, and all the McCabes. Be with Sarah and Richard. I know they love You and want to raise children who are serious about their faith—just as they are." She paused, thinking of her own family. Bitter resentment filled her belly. She hated her father for his mistreatment of her all these years. She hated him for his angry words. Now she worried about her siblings. But she couldn't be bogged down with worry. She could do nothing to change the situation. She needed to focus on her future. "Lord, keep me safe in this untamed land." She paused before adding, "Thank You, Jesus, for hearing my prayers."

Standing to her feet, she crawled onto her bed. The room was hot and motionless. Bethany knew in her heart that God had heard her prayer, and yet she couldn't help feeling He was as far away from her as her family and friends back home in Wisconsin. She had been struggling lately in her Bible reading but couldn't figure out why. She loved to read. Why not God's Word?

Some pastor's wife I'd make.

Turning onto her side, Bethany watched the moonlight stream through her muslin window curtain. *Certainly there's someone else more suitable for Luke. Someone more mature and godly…*

An instant later jealousy coursed through her at the idea of Luke marrying another woman. Jealousy and something else. Regret?

But I want to leave Silverstone. I can't marry him—therefore courtship is out of the question!

Suddenly Bethany knew she had to tell Luke of her plans to leave in the spring. After all, he'd paid for her to obtain her teaching certification in St. Louis, and then he sponsored her journey here. Didn't she at least owe him the courtesy of being honest?

However, the memory of his expressive blue eyes haunted her. Of course, the dime novel she'd been reading didn't help matters. Neither did Sheriff Montaño's earlier behavior. She'd never experienced a man holding her so tightly, and she imagined Luke's arms around her, his lips close to hers.

Bolting to a sitting position, she stopped herself. Such foolish dreams would never do. She'd never escape the Arizona Territory if she allowed herself to fall in love with Luke McCabe.

Stretching out on her bed once more, Bethany closed her eyes and tried to fall asleep. Thoughts crowded her mind, loud and demanding. Finally, when the first pinks of dawn lit up the eastern sky, she drifted off into a fitful slumber.

The morning sun poured relentlessly down on Annetta as she walked into the boardinghouse's dining room. Inside, she took a seat and realized she'd come in during the middle of a conversation between the McCabes and the Winterses, although it didn't seem private.

"It was them. I saw them both!" Trudy declared.

Annetta nodded at the maid, and Rosalinda poured strong-smelling coffee into her cup.

"*Gracias,*" Annetta whispered.

The sturdy, brown-skinned cook curtsied in reply then retreated to the kitchen.

"Now, Trudy, I'm sure you were mistaken." Mrs. Winters stared at her daughter, and Annetta thought she glimpsed a warning in the older woman's greenish-brown eyes.

"No mistake, Mama. I saw them with my own two eyes!"

Across the table, Annetta saw Luke McCabe shift uncomfortably in his chair.

"Our eyes can deceive us at times, Trudy," Pastor Jake said, sitting beside his brother. "Are you sure that's who you saw?"

"Positive. It was Miss Stafford and Sheriff Montaño. They were out back last evening. I watched them from my window. He had his arms around her. Why, I'll bet he was whispering all sorts of romantic things 'cause Miss Stafford looked like she was about to swoon!"

"Mercy!" Mrs. Winters put her hands on each side of her plump face.

"A shameless tryst," Ed Winters concluded.

Annetta couldn't believe her ears. Miss Stafford, the schoolteacher? And Paden Montaño? The thought amused her, and she laughed under her breath...

Until she caught Pastor Jake's dark stare.

"Please excuse my sense of humor. But I thought I heard Trudy just say she saw the schoolteacher in Paden Montaño's arms." Annetta laughed again.

"That's exactly who she saw, Dr. Cavanaugh." Ed Winters puffed out his self-important chest. "This is no laughing matter."

Annetta wasn't cowed. "I think you're mistaken."

"Are you calling my daughter a liar, Dr. Cavanaugh?" Mrs. Winters held her chin high and defiant.

"Of course not." She glanced at the young lady whose fat, blonde ringlets hung alongside of her round face. Then she looked over at her father. "But I think the situation bears investigation. Whatever Trudy saw out her window couldn't have been anything romantic—at least not on Miss Stafford's part."

"I appreciate your sticking up for Beth like that, Doctor."

Annetta met Luke McCabe's blue eyes. Gratitude shown in their depths. She gave him a curt nod in reply.

However, it appeared that Mr. Winters wasn't about to let the matter die an easy death. "I recommend we bring Miss Stafford before the school board and make her answer to these charges."

"And what charges would those be?" Pastor Jake's voice sounded a few octaves short of menacing.

Annetta sipped her coffee and found herself admiring the man. Broad shoulders, walnut-brown hair, a pair of brown eyes to match, and a kind of personality that allowed him to preach to gunfighters as well as girls Trudy's age. He seemed both rugged and gentle at the same time.

And right now he seemed like an unyielding advocate for Miss Stafford. The thought she was one lucky woman flitted across Annetta's mind. With the two McCabe brothers on her side, a woman couldn't go wrong.

"I'm referring to immorality charges, of course," Mr. Winters said. "We can't have Silverstone's schoolteacher consorting in the dark with our sheriff!"

Pastor Luke shot to his feet. "I'll talk to Beth. There's no reason to call a meeting of the school board members until I get her side of things."

"Won't change what my daughter saw."

Annetta watched as Pastor Luke turned and gazed at Trudy, noticing the way the girl refused to meet his eye and the way her chin dropped rather guiltily. Setting down her cup of coffee, Annetta shook her head. "Mr. Winters, Trudy is a child. Sometimes children see things, but out of context. They don't see the whole picture. Now I think you ought to let Pastor Luke talk to Miss Stafford and—"

"Enough!" Mr. Winters slammed his meaty fist on the table, causing the porcelain cups to clatter in their saucers. "My daughter knows what she saw last night, and I believe her!"

"Just like you believe the Indians are responsible for the cattle rustling, right?"

The man stood. "I will thank you, Dr. Cavanaugh, to leave my premises at once and never return."

Annetta grinned. *Until you have another one of your gall-bladder attacks and need my assistance.* She slowly dabbed the napkin at the corners of her mouth and then rose from her chair.

"Oh, Ed, there's no need to insist upon Dr. Cavanaugh leaving," his plump wife said. "She hasn't had her breakfast, and she's a good paying customer."

"Thank you, Mrs. Winters, but I have work to do anyway." Annetta met Mr. Winters's angry glare and promised herself she'd stall an extra fifteen minutes next time he summoned her for help with one of his gallbladder attacks. Sliding in her chair, she strode out of the room, through the small lobby, and out of the boardinghouse.

Outside on the dusty boardwalk the heat felt like a heavy drape. It promised to be another hot day, although it looked like rain was coming.

As she walked toward her office, she heard someone leave the boardinghouse behind her. She glanced over her shoulder to see one of the McCabe brothers following her.

"Dr. Cavanaugh. Hold up."

She paused on the plank and watched as the preacher hobbled toward her. Today he used his cane, but she'd seen him walking without it. Since her arrival in Silverstone a month ago, she'd often wondered what had happened to make him lame. Childhood fever? Accident? War injury?

He reached her, and she avoided his ever-probing dark-brown gaze.

"May I have a few words with you?"

"Of course, Reverend McCabe. Would you care to speak here or in my office?"

"Here's fine." He glanced around. No one else was about. The other side of the street was usually quiet this time of morning, and the row of businesses on this side had just opened for the day.

He removed his tan, wide-brim hat. "I wanted to thank you for standing up for Beth inside the boardinghouse just now."

Annetta laughed. "You don't have to thank me. Those fools in there"—she nodded toward the boardinghouse—"should know that Paden Montaño is a womanizer. I'm sure Miss Stafford is completely innocent of Mr. Winters's charges against her."

"I am too." Concern knit his thick brown brows together. "Dr. Cavanaugh, I hope the sheriff has been respectable to you at all times."

"Most times, yes. The other times I've managed just fine." Her hand touched the place where she'd strapped her pistol beneath the waist of her skirt. Drawing a gun on Paden Montaño could have gotten her killed, but instead she'd gotten her message across to him. She wasn't interested in his charm, good looks, and flirtatious manners. He hadn't tried any tricks ever since.

"May I walk you to your office?" The reverend dropped his hat back onto his head.

"No need. It's just two doors down."

"I insist."

Annetta shrugged before berating herself. How stupid could she be, taking a job in Silverstone, Arizona, where the men were plentiful and the women were not? She should have guessed that there would be wife-hunting going on. The last thing she wanted was a man's attention—and a preacher of all things!

Except this preacher, this man, had a way about him that seemed disconcerting—even threatening—and it caused Annetta to want to put as much distance between them as possible.

"I haven't seen you in church on Sundays since your arrival."

"And you'll never see me there either."

He replied with a crooked grin. "Never is a mighty long time."

Annetta hardened her expression. "Never."

"Well, all right," he drawled, sounding amused. "I won't ask again, but you've got a standing invitation if you ever change your mind."

"Look, McCabe, unless you're in need of medical attention, I'm not interested in you. I'm especially not interested in whatever religion you're peddling." Annetta pulled the office keys from her skirt's deep pocket.

"May I ask why?"

She paused, thinking she might sidestep the question. But then she thought twice about it. "I lost my soul a long time ago. Now if you'll excuse me, I have work to do."

With that she unlocked the door, walked in, and slammed the door on the reverend's astonished expression.

She leaned against it, willing the memories away. Her honest reply had somehow summoned the devil himself.

No!

She wouldn't think about the past. She couldn't! She'd worked too hard and come too far to be haunted by what happened ten years ago. She was a doctor now.

Gazing around the sparse office, she remembered that she had an order to fill. Mr. Titus at the mercantile would put it in with his order this morning, and hopefully she'd get her needed replenishment of medical supplies in the next month or two.

Annetta breathed in deeply.

There!

She'd successfully fought off her demons again…

This time.

FIVE

BETHANY TRIED TO STIFLE A YAWN AS SHE ENTERED THE dining room. All eyes turned toward her. "Good morning," she stated hesitantly. "Am I late?"

When the stares continued, she looked down self-consciously at her brown skirt and then glanced behind her, up the stairwell. "Is there something amiss?"

"I'll say," Mr. Winters groused.

Trudy giggled.

Luke cleared his throat and stood. "Excuse us, everyone. Beth and I are going to have a . . . conversation."

She looked at him askance. Was he angry? Luke rarely got angry.

"Shall I hold breakfast?"

"No, Mrs. Winters," he said over his shoulder. "Y'all go on and enjoy your meal." Taking Bethany by the elbow, he escorted her out of the boardinghouse.

"What's going on, Luke?"

He said nothing until they reached the boardwalk. The sky looked menacing, and the smell of rain hung in the air like an imminent threat.

"Why don't you tell me what's going on, Bethany Stafford?"

"Tell you what?" Bethany saw the muscle work in Luke's jaw, and it caused her stomach to knot. Most things rolled right off his back. He never took things to heart and stewed. "Are you angry?"

He stopped abruptly. "Should I be?"

She blinked. "I don't know."

They resumed their stroll, and Bethany felt the tension mounting between them. This never happened before. Luke had an endless amount of patience. What had she done to displease him so?

At the end of the boardinghouse, Luke steered her down a wheel-rutted road that Bethany hadn't ventured on before. With each step, they left Silverstone farther behind.

"I'd like to hear your version of what took place last night," Luke finally said. They came to the end of the road where a steep, craggy bluff plunged downward into an equally rocky valley. Taking a seat on one of the large, red, flat stones on the ridge, but well away from the edge of the cliff, he motioned for Bethany to sit on the ledge across from him.

"Last night?" She wondered if the sheriff had spoken to him about her "eavesdropping." However, she wasn't about to incriminate herself and suggest it.

Luke got right to the point. "Trudy Winters said she saw you and Sheriff Montaño last night engaged in a ... well, let's call it an intimate discussion."

Bethany's hand flew to her mouth, but she wasn't successful in stopping the horrified gasp. "She saw us?"

"Aw, Beth..." Luke winced. "So it's true?"

"Sort of."

Luke leaned forward, his hands resting over his knees. "Beth, I asked if you were interested in someone yesterday when we spoke in the schoolhouse, remember? Why couldn't you be honest with me?"

"But I'm not interested in Sheriff Montaño."

"Trudy said he had his arms around you."

"Yes, but..." She stood, shaking her head vigorously. "Luke, this isn't what you think. Please let me explain."

He inclined his head.

"Last evening, after you left me at the door, I walked into the boardinghouse in time to hear some men talk about taking their revenge out on the Indians. I left to tell the sheriff, but he'd been listening to them plot and pulled me around back so I'd escape injury when the men left to saddle their horses." She hoped Luke believed her. "He quietly berated me for eavesdropping, but I explained that I hadn't done such a thing. I merely walked in on the conversation."

Luke didn't seem pacified. "He had his arms around you?"

Bethany swallowed hard. "In a protective manner, yes." She shifted, knowing the sheriff had been quite flirtatious about it.

He shook his head. "I think it's a whole lot more on his part."

She swallowed hard. "Luke, you know how the sheriff is. He's charming to every woman in Silverstone. That's all—"

He raised a hand, preventing further explanation. "I believe you, Beth." He inhaled deeply then expelled a long, slow breath. "Except I don't know if everyone else will see it that way. Mr. Winters is talking about bringing you up in front of the school board. Many of its members might find Trudy Winters's version more…*interesting*, and that's not good. The Christians in this town wanted a schoolteacher above reproach."

"I meet those qualifications, Luke. It's not as if I allowed it or met the sheriff secretly in the back of the boardinghouse. God forbid I should ever do any such thing!"

Luke stared at her for a long moment then sighed again. "Aw, I know it's not your fault, Beth." He stood and kicked a stone over the cliff's edge.

"Are you sure? You seem doubtful."

"I believe you." He stared across the valley. "I just got stirred up, is all."

"Then let Mr. Winters bring me in front of the school board if it'll make him happy. Perhaps Sheriff Montaño will agree to testify on my behalf."

"Perhaps." Luke looked at her. "Unfortunately, he's not sheriff of this town on account of his impeccable character. He's a fast draw and communicates with the Indians. He's also unafraid to deal with outlaws."

"You once told me he's a fair man. Surely everyone in town agrees."

"For the most part. But is that enough to save your reputation from the town gossips?"

She rolled a shoulder, feeling guilty for disappointing Luke this way. He and Jake had worked hard to gain the trust of the people in Silverstone. They were seen as men who grew their congregation by leading others to the Lord, not by making false promises or accepting bribes. Folks respected the McCabe brothers. However, this scandal was sure to disgrace them, Luke especially.

"You could send me back to Jericho Junction." Hope suddenly soared within her. "If you arrange it today, I might catch the last wagon train out of Santa Fe."

"What?" Luke brought his chin back, looking stunned.

"It's just a suggestion." Bethany tried to take back some of her enthusiasm. "I mean, sending me away would satisfy both the gossips and the school board."

"Send you away…" The rest of the words died in his throat. He narrowed his blue eyes in a way that made Bethany avert her gaze.

"Is that what you want?"

"Well…" She hedged and studied her folded hands. "It doesn't really matter what I want. Your ministry is more important."

Luke crossed the distance between them until he stood only inches away. Then he hunkered down in front of her. One knee of his black trousers brushed against her skirt. He cupped her chin, forcing Bethany to look into his face.

"Could you leave Silverstone and never look back, Beth?"

"Oh, I'd look back." She wetted her suddenly parched lips and swallowed. *At you!*

Luke moved his hand away and then draped it across his leg. "You're not happy here, are you?"

Slowly, Bethany wagged her head. "But last night's got nothing to do with it—or with anything."

"I know. I've suspected you haven't been happy for quite a while."

"I tried to hide my feelings. I apologize for not doing a better job."

His gaze captured hers. "You're doing a fine job, Beth, both at teaching and fighting your feelings of discontent. You never complained. It's just that I know you so well." He gave her a warm smile. "We met more than a year ago at the Navises's. Remember? I walked you and your sisters home, to your family's farm next door, and a storm came up on us fast."

"A tornado." Bethany recalled how frightened she'd felt at that moment when the dark funnel cloud roared toward them. Thankfully Luke kept a cool head, which calmed Bethany's nerves. Together they took hold of her little sisters' hands and ran to the house. They were able to warn all of her family and take shelter before it hit.

Fortunately, the twister missed their farm and the Navises, but it damaged several others in the area.

"I knew right then you belonged in Silverstone. You've got a soft way about you and an inner strength I've grown to admire."

"Thank you, but..." Bethany hated to disappoint him. "Luke, I hate it here."

"What specifically?" He leaned his head closer.

Bethany thought he'd be more shocked or even angry. His easy manner allowed her to be honest. "It's so primitive here—and so brown. I'm accustomed to lush green farm fields and the colorful seasons in Wisconsin. I'm also used to a cooler climate. The heat here is unbearable."

"I'd have to agree with you there, but darlin', you haven't even been here a whole two months." Luke tone exuded patience. "The improvements will come. As for the desert, there's beauty in all the brownness. I'll show it to you, Beth." He sat forward and took her hand. "But I think you'd do well to focus on the townsfolk. We're here to help them spiritually and intellectually. I trust you'll educate the children while helping other ladies realize their own dignity in Christ. The people here…they're why we came."

Bethany bobbed out a reply. Maybe she hadn't given Silverstone a chance.

"Now, by next spring, if you still want to leave"—Luke released her hand—"I'll take you home myself."

She swallowed a bitter laugh. She'd never go home. Never. Not to Wisconsin. But Luke didn't have to know that.

"In the meantime, we've got a situation. What are we going to tell the school board?"

"The truth." Bethany squared her shoulders.

"They won't believe it. Besides, we can't count on Montaño coming to your defense. He'd likely describe a scene from out of those dime novels of yours."

"They're not mine."

Luke fought back a grin.

"And nothing could be further from the truth."

"In your mind—but maybe not in Paden's."

Every muscle in Bethany's being wanted to scream in frustration. "Do you see how close-minded these people are, Luke? First they jump to conclusions and blame the Indians for any trouble that comes along, then when the sheriff grabs me, they immediately think the worst of *me*!"

"God can open their eyes and change their minds. Meanwhile, there is one thing we can do."

Bethany sat forward. "Yes? What is it?"

"It'll shut the mouths of the gossipmongers, no doubt about it. You'll be able to teach school, and no one will have a single qualm about sending children into your classroom." He grunted out a laugh. "It'll also take care of Jonas's pleadings once and for all."

"Great. What do you have in mind?"

He removed his hat and slid to his knees. Then he took her hands. His blue eyes darkened with earnestness. "We can get married."

"Married?" The suggestion knocked the breath out of her. "You mean, as in... you and me?"

"Yeah." He drawled the word slowly. "I told you yesterday I wanted to court you, Beth. It's really just the end result coming more quickly, that's all."

She was still in shock about the idea of Luke courting her. But marriage?

"Why?" she asked. "Why do you want to marry me? I'm a plain old field mouse."

"On the contrary. I see a young woman who can support my life's work. That's important to a man."

She supposed it was.

"If I'm not mistaken, Beth, you're not averse to the idea of marrying me."

He'd noticed? Her cheeks flamed. "No... no, I'm not." But then a shadow of sadness crept over her. "It's just that..." *Where are the words of love?*

"What, Beth?"

"Oh, I guess it's all just happening so fast. I never dreamed you'd want to marry me." Except she'd dreamed about him, all right!

"Well, I'm askin'. Will you be my wife?"

Her gaze locked with his. Marrying Luke meant she'd be a

McCabe. Truly part of their family. Not merely a friend, but a member. Of a new family. A much better one than she left in Wisconsin.

"Yes, I'll marry you."

SIX

WELL, THAT WAS THE SHORTEST COURTSHIP I EVER saw!" Jake snorted a laugh from where they both sat at the rough-hewn table, two tin cups of coffee in front of them. "Twelve hours...and you slept through six of them!"

Luke shrugged off his brother's amusement.

"Do you love her?" Jake's brows knit together.

"More than I loved any woman. I guess I just didn't realize it until earlier this morning when I heard about Montaño's little stunt."

"You sure you're not just reacting to pangs of jealousy."

"Oh, I'm reacting, all right." Luke wanted to punch the sheriff in the jaw. "But I've got enough sense about me to know I want to make Beth my wife."

"OK, then." Jake's smile widened. "I reckon congratulations are in order."

Luke grinned too and gazed around the little cabin in which they now sat. Small but efficient, it provided easy access to both the church and schoolhouse, and he felt certain that with a little imagination Beth would get this place feeling like a home. A table and four chairs occupied a good amount of space on one side, and the stone hearth, which could be used for cooking, had been built into the middle of the far wall. Two rough-hewn wooden beds with straw mattresses occupied the two bedrooms, but pushed together, Luke decided they'd accommodate a newly married couple just fine—namely himself and Bethany.

He chuckled, looking back at his older brother. "So, when did you say you're moving out?"

"I didn't." Jacob arched a brow. "When did you say you're getting married?"

"As soon as you'll conduct the ceremony. How's this afternoon sound?"

Rubbing his thumb over his lower lip, Jake shook his head. "Nope, sorry, brother."

Luke pulled his chin back. "Huh?"

"This is all sounding rather impulsive to me."

"Jake, remember what Pa used to say? Long engagements aren't always a good thing, especially when two people love each other. You've seen how Beth looks at me."

Jake shrugged.

"And think about Ben and Valerie. They're about as happy as our folks."

"Yeah, except I listened to that woman's doubts about her marriage the whole time Ben was gone looking for you. She was afraid Ben had just married her out of guilt." Jake shook his head. "Don't do that to Beth. Give her an engagement period—so she can back out if she comes to her senses." Jake grinned.

"Thanks, brother." Luke shot a gaze upward. But then he got to wondering if maybe Jake had a point. Beth seemed a bit thunderstruck when they returned to the boardinghouse. She only picked at her breakfast and said nothing as they walked to school afterward.

Luke chuckled inwardly. The best part had been watching Ed Winters eat crow when he announced their engagement. The man might be quick to make judgments, but he knew Luke would never marry a woman with questionable morals. Winters finally agreed that the incident last night might have been a tad exaggerated by his daughter. Beth would not be brought up before the school board.

"Besides," Jake continued, "it'll take me a couple of months to build myself a new place."

"You've got a point there. Where are you thinking of building?"

"Not sure. But the other side of the church comes to mind."

"That'd be good enough." Luke figured his brother would be plenty far away from him and Beth and yet close enough if either needed the other.

"Mind if I change the subject?"

Luke knew his brother's tone meant serious business. "Go ahead."

"It's about Dr. Cavanaugh. I followed her out of the boarding-house this morning and thanked her for sticking up for Beth."

"I appreciated it too."

"Well, she's a hard woman." Jake wagged his head. "When I mentioned church, she said we'd never see her there and that she'd lost her soul a long time ago."

"Lost her soul?"

"That's what she said."

"Hmm..." Luke rubbed his palm across his shaven jaw. "What do you make of it?"

"She's in pain. Emotional pain. I can see it on her face. I know that look. There are great pools of sadness in those big hazel eyes of hers."

Luke mulled over what his brother just said. Something stood out more than Dr. Cavanaugh's spiritual problem. It wasn't like Jake to notice the specific color of a woman's eyes—and Jake had worked with a lot of women. Their folks had a ministry in Jericho Junction. They helped women escape from the bondage of prostitution and go on to lead successful lives in the Lord. When Jake returned from the war, wounded for life, he began working with Pa.

"What do you plan to do about it?" Luke asked.

"Nothing I can do now—except pray." Jake heaved a sigh. "She doesn't want any help, especially from me. It's like her troubled spirit knows I have the key to unlock it, because I know Christ. I'd venture to say Dr. Cavanaugh is as scared of me as she might be of any war-painted brave."

"Well, brother, we're in a war, all right. A spiritual war."

"I know it." Jake slid his chair back and stood. He walked to the doorway and tossed out the remainder of his coffee. He leaned against the wood frame and stared outside, toward the center of town.

"I'll pray for her, Jake."

He turned, met Luke's gaze, and grinned. "I knew I could count on you."

Bethany felt as though she might scream if silly Trudy didn't stop her overzealous ramblings. And she still hadn't completely forgiven the girl for defaming her character before breakfast. But Trudy decided to adhere herself to Bethany's side after school, and the girl's excitement grated on her nerves.

"Oh! I just knew you and Reverend Luke were meant for each other! And to think you forced his hand by leading us all to believe you and the sheriff were romantically involved. How clever you are, Miss Stafford!" Trudy sighed dreamily. "Reverend Luke is so in love with you that he couldn't bear the thought of you in Sheriff Montaño's arms and had to claim you for his own. Soon you'll be his wife."

"Stop it, Trudy." Bethany gave the girl a hard stare as she turned the key and locked the schoolhouse's door. "And I'll thank you not to go around repeating that nonsensical story." She paused to keep herself from spilling out the truth. Luke was marrying her to save her reputation and his ministry in this small, dusty, Western town, and love had nothing to do with it.

She and Trudy strolled up Main Street, toward the mercantile.

Bethany needed material for a few new dresses. Since she no longer worked so physically hard, like she had at home, she'd been steadily gaining weight. Mrs. Winters had offered to sew them for her.

Her thoughts wandered back to Luke. A loveless marriage—like so many others. Her heart ached. She'd wanted love. True love. Except she couldn't do better than marry Luke McCabe. Bethany had the utmost respect for him—and feelings for him too. Feelings she could now permit to grow. And, perhaps, if she loved him enough, he would, in time, return her affections. Hadn't he said last night that he was "interested"?

But interest wasn't the same as love. Of course she supposed she could approach him and ask, "Do you love me, Luke? Do you care for me in that very special way?" However, the idea of confronting him about such a particularly crucial matter of the heart caused Bethany a good deal of trepidation. She'd never been good at revealing the deepest, most tender parts of herself. Life with her father had taught her to keep those parts hidden away, where they could not be hurt.

"Oh! I'm so happy for you," Trudy continued. "May I be in your wedding, Miss Stafford? I've never been in a wedding—not in my whole life!"

"We'll see," she hedged. "I'm not certain of the details yet."

"I can't wait. I love weddings!" Trudy's fat curls bounced as she skipped down the warped boardwalk.

However, Bethany felt miserable, and the light rain falling from the overcast sky only added to her gloom. She glanced around, but she didn't catch sight of Luke anywhere. Usually he walked her to the boardinghouse after school. But something must have tied up his attention today.

"And just think," Trudy persisted, "before Reverend Luke rode over to Harlan Whitaker's place this morning, he wired your father and asked permission to marry you." Suddenly she stopped short and covered her mouth. "Oops."

Bethany too paused in her tracks. "Luke did...what?"

"It's supposed to be a surprise."

A lead weight dropped inside of Bethany. *Luke sent a telegraph to Papa?*

She slowly took a step forward. Then another. She recalled how her father had ordered her out of the house before she departed Milwaukee for Jericho Junction. He said she'd never be welcomed in his home again. But she hadn't told anyone, only wrote about it in her journal. She didn't think any of the McCabes would understand. They were a family-oriented people, closely knit in a loving way.

But Papa—he was different. Hard, stern, unyielding, except when it came to Bethany's stepmother, Maribel. Ever since they met, Papa treated the woman like a fragile little flower that would break if she had to lift a finger around the house. Bethany had been making supper since she was eight. She worked in the barn and the fields. Then when her siblings began coming, Bethany cared for them too, so the strain of raising children wouldn't be too much for Maribel. And when she displeased Papa, she endured the whippings, although she'd only suffered them a few times. She soon learned to avoid them. On the contrary, her stepmother never endured a cross word from her husband. Bethany remembered how she sobbed the night Bethany left.

Of course, Maribel was losing her maid and nanny...

Trudy suddenly gasped, startling Bethany into the present. "Your father won't deny Reverend Luke's request, will he?"

"I'm sure he won't. He met Luke last summer and thinks very highly of him." In fact, Papa probably wouldn't respond at all.

Would Luke marry her without her father's consent?

"That's good." Trudy sighed, and then another giggle escaped her. "Oh, Miss Stafford, we'd best get sewing on your wedding gown!"

Bethany groaned inwardly as they resumed walking. It suddenly dawned on her that soon she and her dearest friend, Sarah, would be more than sisters in Christ. They'd be sisters-in-law! The idea brought a small smile to Bethany's lips. *I'll have to write Sarah another letter and tell her I'll be a McCabe.*

The very idea almost made her willing to stay in this godforsaken town. Still, her heart longed for the family she'd never had—a warm, loving mother like Rebecca McCabe, a kind and wise father like Reverend McCabe, and siblings her own age that she didn't have to diaper or feed or raise. All that was back in Jericho Junction. Not here.

Reaching the mercantile, they entered and were immediately greeted by the proprietor's wife, Mrs. Titus.

"Miss Stafford and Reverend Luke are betrothed!" Trudy blurted.

Bethany sent her a heavy frown. After all, it was her news to tell.

"Oh, I heard this morning, Trudy. Your mama told me."

Bethany rolled her eyes just as Mrs. Titus fixed her ginger-colored gaze on her. "Congratulations."

"Thank you."

"Do you plan to continue teaching after you're wed?" The woman gave her dark-brown bun at her nape a pat. "We all hope so. You're doing a good job, learning our young'uns."

"Thank you. And, yes, I intend to keep teaching."

"But what if you find yourself in the family way?" She wiped her large hands on her white apron. "Then what will we do? What will our children do? They won't have a teacher. We'll be right back to square one."

A heated blush spread across Bethany's cheeks. *The family way?* She hadn't got that far in her thinking yet. "Well, I...I guess we'll just have to trust the Lord to give me children in His timing."

"Hmpf," the woman snorted in reply, although she soon nodded in agreement.

Relieved by the outcome, Bethany inspected the bolts of material set out in rows on a large table. There were plenty to choose from, thanks to the freighting that took place on the Colorado River. Silverstone wasn't as primitive as some towns in the Territory, but it wasn't as sophisticated as Arizona City. In any case, both towns were still recovering from the devastating blows inflicted upon them by the Civil War. In essence, they were just now coming back to life.

The tiny bell above the door jangled, signaling another patron's entrance, and Trudy gasped.

"Don't look now, Miss Stafford," she whispered loudly, "but it's one of the girls from the brothel! Why, it's a wonder Mrs. Titus allows her in here with other respectable customers."

"Her money is just as good as yours, Trudy," Mrs. Titus retorted, obviously having overheard the remark. "My husband and I are in business, after all, and it's none of our concern where the funds originate."

"Yes, ma'am." Trudy gave Bethany a skeptical glance.

The woman from the brothel stepped farther into the store and began quietly browsing at the next table. Bethany watched her curiously. She'd never known someone in that profession before, and, amazingly, the young woman didn't look much older than herself. She had a flawless peaches-and-cream complexion and her hair was a dark honey-gold. She looked up guardedly, and Bethany saw her sad, pale blue eyes.

Bethany kept looking at the material while making her way over to the next table. A kind of boldness settled in her heart, one she'd never experienced before.

"Hello, my name is Bethany Stafford, and I'm the new school-teacher in town."

"I'm Angie Brown," the woman replied.

From behind Bethany, Trudy inhaled sharply.

"Miss Stafford, you ought not talk to the likes of her!"

"It won't hurt anything to just introduce myself," she said over her shoulder before turning back and giving Angie an apologetic grin. She knew all about the McCabe's ministry in Jericho Junction.

"I'm telling Mama!"

Trudy fled the mercantile, leaving Mrs. Titus frowning in her wake. The proprietress then turned her glowering countenance on Bethany. However, Bethany suspected both Luke and Jake would approve of her actions here.

"You'd be wise to mind your own business, Miss Stafford," Angie warned. "You wouldn't want to lose your teaching position on account of me."

That did it. Bethany didn't want to spark any more gossip about herself. It could affect Luke's and Jake's ministry here. And wasn't that why Luke wanted to marry her in the first place? To quell the gossip surrounding her and the sheriff?

Bethany nodded reluctantly and returned to her task of selecting fabric, except she couldn't seem to rid her mind of Angie's haunted eyes. But, at last, she made her purchases and left the store. On the way to the boardinghouse, she grimaced at the thought of what Trudy might be relaying to her mother.

Bethany only prayed that Luke would find it in his heart to understand her side of the story.

SEVEN

WHEN BETHANY RETURNED TO THE BOARDINGHOUSE, she fully expected a reprimand for speaking to Angie Brown. But to her surprise, the Winterses, including Trudy, were so engrossed in conversation that they scarcely noticed her entrance.

Eyeing the man they talked to, Bethany realized she'd never seen him before. With his brown, shaggy hair framing a ruddy complexion and his wiry frame, he appeared to be no more than fifteen years old, although there was a wild look in hazel eyes—a look that didn't belong on a man so young.

"You say it was an ambush, son?" Ed Winters asked. Worry lines etched his face at the sides of his eyes and around his mouth. "Tell us what happened."

"Yes, sir. Whole lotta men were hurt too. Best as we can figure, someone tipped off the Indians." The young man paused, shaking his head. "No good Indians were waiting for us." He gulped.

Mr. Winters wagged his head from side to side.

"An Indian attack!" Mrs. Winters declared.

"All those men injured…why, I'm going to cry for a week!" Trudy exclaimed dramatically.

Bethany stood by, feeling stunned.

It was then that Doris Winters noticed her presence. "Why, Bethany, did you hear? This is Nate Lowel. He said some of Silverstone's finest men were attacked last night while performing their civil duties."

"Yes, I heard." She wondered if those same men were the ones plotting against the Indians at the boardinghouse last night.

"Some are saying the sheriff informed the Indians," the young man stated, "but he's got an alibi—says he was at Chicago Joe's all night, and one of the working girls backs up the story."

"Merciful heavens!" Doris exclaimed. "And here I thought that man had some scruples."

Bethany's reaction mirrored Mrs. Winters's, although she kept silent.

"But Mr. Buchanan swears he'll find the man who sided with the Indians and see that he hangs. Meanwhile, another ranch got raided last night and a field hand got killed—got an arrow right through the heart."

"Them Indians gotta go." Mr. Winters stared at the plank floor and shook his head.

Mrs. Winters walked over to the young man and placed a motherly arm around his drooping shoulders. "Come on over to the table, and I'll have Rosalinda fix you up a good hot meal."

"Thank you, ma'am."

Trudy bounced along in their wake.

Mr. Winters followed while Bethany took in the scene before her, unsure of what to think. Was Sheriff Montaño really involved? Had his alibi been a fabrication? On the other hand, she couldn't condemn him if he'd merely alerted the Indians. But was he directly responsible for the ambush?

The sound of wagon wheels coming to a halt outside the boardinghouse captured Bethany's attention, and she turned to see a man climbing down from his perch, grabbing hold of a bundle from in back of the wagon, and heading toward the door. He wore a blue army uniform, and after he entered, he dropped the package on the floor.

"This here's some mail that should've got delivered yesterday. Came to Fort Yuma by mistake."

"Thank you, soldier." Mrs. Winters returned to the foyer. "I'll see to it from here." Her voice was polite yet held an unmistakable crispness.

The man tipped his hat and left. Trudy ran to the window and watched him climb back up into the wagon.

"Oh, aren't those Union soldiers a handsome lot?" She sighed dreamily.

"Trudy, really!" Mrs. Winters appeared horrified. "I will not have you ogling a Yankee!"

"Yes, Mama." Wearing a pout, the girl stepped away from the window.

"The war is over." Bethany eyed both women. "There's no Union and Confederacy, just one United States Army."

"That's right, Mama," Trudy stated hopefully. "Could be that man was a Confederate before the war."

"Quite unlikely."

Bethany was somewhat taken aback by the anger in Mrs. Winters's reply. A moment of strained silence passed, and then the older woman seemed to snap out of whatever bothered her.

Glancing at Bethany, she said, "I never did say congratulations on your engagement."

"Thank you." It still felt so surreal. After a moment, Bethany thought she should at least try to explain her side of things. "Mrs. Winters, about last night. Trudy didn't lie, but it wasn't what it seemed. The sheriff and I were not meeting secretly or shamefully."

"Of course you weren't. Why, I know that, dear."

Bethany sighed with relief.

"Reverend Luke wouldn't have asked you to marry him if he thought you were a woman who carried on with a man."

Consolation quickly turned to disappointment as Bethany realized how right Luke had been about her reputation being so easily soiled. She'd been redeemed in the eyes of the Winterses now, but only because of his marriage proposal.

"Reverend Luke is one of the finest men I know. He suffered a head injury in the war and wound up in some dirty Union camp until his older brother rescued him."

Bethany gave a slight nod. "I know the story well."

"Why, if my son were alive today..." Mrs. Winters swallowed hard, her usually jovial countenance masked by sorrow. "I'm certain that if my son hadn't been killed by Yankees, he would be as much a gentleman as either of the McCabes."

Bethany's heart grew heavy. "I'm sorry. I had no idea you'd lost your son in the war."

"We don't speak of John's death often." Trudy sniffed and pulled out her hankie. "It's too sad for words."

"I'm sure it is." Bethany set her arm around the girl's shoulders. She suddenly understood Mrs. Winters's infuriation just minutes ago.

"Yes, but we cannot dwell on the past, Trudy."

"Yes, Mama."

Bethany patted her shoulder.

"John knew and loved the Lord Jesus. He's with Him today." After a deep breath Mrs. Winters looked at Bethany and pushed out a grin. "Besides, we've got a wedding to plan!"

Trudy turned so her round face was just inches from Bethany's. "Oh, please can I be in your wedding, Miss Stafford?"

Bethany gave both women a weak smile, wishing this event were occurring out of Luke's love for her instead of some measure to ensure her good reputation and solidify his ministry in Silverstone. Then at last she relented. "Yes, Trudy. You can be my bridesmaid."

~eeexeee~

Shrieks bounced off the walls of the boardinghouse, but it wasn't a renegade's attack; it was just Trudy throwing a veritable temper tantrum when her father ordered her to sort the mail.

"Go to your room, young lady." Mr. Winters puffed out his chest and pointed up the stairs. "You'll stay there for the rest of the evening and eat dinner up there by yourself. Understood?"

After a stomp of her foot, Trudy ran up the steps with fists clenched.

"Mr. Winters, I'll sort the mail." Bethany really didn't mind and actually hoped she'd discover a letter from the McCabes in the bundle.

"Well…"

"Really. I've nothing better to do at the moment."

"All right then." He looked embarrassed, likely by his daughter's disobedience. "Much obliged."

Bethany dragged the mailbag into the parlor and thought that if she'd ever behaved as Trudy just did, her father would have given her a sound whipping. Bethany vowed right there that she'd never discipline her children in rage and with physical violence.

She shook her head at herself for already thinking about children.

On the settee, she deftly sorted the envelopes, creating piles according to the names of the addressees. She'd learned that folks here in Silverstone knew to check their mail slots whenever they came into town. Bethany noted that Sheriff Montaño had received a couple of very official-looking envelopes. Soon she found a fat packet addressed to Reverend Jacob McCabe that appeared to be from St. Louis. Bethany was certain it'd be a welcomed surprise.

Picking up the very last letter, she hoped against hope it would be for her. Instead the name read, *Miss Angela Brown.*

"Angie Brown." She realized it belonged to the woman she'd met in the mercantile an hour or so ago.

Staring at the letter, Bethany nibbled her lower lip contemplatively. Should she personally give Angie her mail? She'd just been embroiled in a scandal, so she couldn't very well knock on the front door of the brothel without causing quite a stir.

But what if she delivered the sheriff's mail and slipped out the back door of his office? Anybody watching would just assume she had business with the sheriff and that's all. Besides, she was engaged to Luke McCabe. No one would question her motives now. As for the sheriff's back door, Bethany knew of it because rumor had it the sheriff often used it to access Chicago Joe's.

Bethany thought on it some more. Her plan might work. And perhaps in doing this small favor for Miss Angela Brown, she'd befriend the young lady and gain an opportunity to share Jesus. Bethany couldn't help but believe that both Luke and Jake would approve of her intentions. In any event, neither of them was here in town to ask.

She'd do it!

With her mind made up, Bethany gathered the mail. "I've got an errand to run," she called to Rosalinda, who was dusting the furniture. "I'll be back shortly."

The Mexican woman nodded, and Bethany left the boarding-house.

Outside, the October day felt like a hot oven against her face. In Wisconsin the weather might be some thirty degrees cooler. The leaves would be turning beautiful colors of reds and golds, but here in Silverstone, there was only brown and more brown to see. Bethany didn't think she'd ever adjust to life here.

She stood at the edge of the boardwalk. After several wagons rolled past, she crossed Main Street and quickly entered the sheriff's office. It was dark but cool inside the adobe building, and

Bethany found the tan-skinned man reclining lazily in his chair, his feet up on the desk. He glanced at her and grinned.

"Miz Stafford," he drawled, "to what do I owe this unexpected pleasure?"

"No pleasure," she quipped, "I'm simply distributing your mail, and I need to use your back door." She plopped his two letters on the desk and then strode purposely past the jail and up a few wobbly wooden stairs to the back entrance.

"Hold it."

Bethany paused, turning. "Yes, Sheriff?" She prayed he wouldn't interrogate her.

He swung his booted feet off the desk and stood. As he walked slowly toward her, Bethany was reminded of a sleek black panther she'd once read about, stalking its prey. He stopped just inches away. "What are you up to, *chiquita*?"

"I'm not doing anything against the law," she assured him. "I'm simply delivering a letter to Miss Angela Brown."

Paden Montaño looked at her askance. "Angie Brown? Who is that?"

Two steps up, Bethany stood eye to eye with the sheriff and marveled at his dark, penetrating gaze. She felt somewhat intimidated, yet she refused to back down. "Angie lives a couple of doors away," she said vaguely. "I've got a letter here for her."

"She is one of Chicago Joe's working girls, eh?"

Bethany frowned. "Is Chicago Joe a real person or just the name of the saloon?"

"A real person." Paden Montaño's thin black mustache twitched with something of a smile. "Her name is Josephine Martin and she originates from Chicago, or so the story goes."

"She?" Bethany felt her jaw go slack.

"*Sí*. She enlisted her, uh, talents in the war and kept up the soldiers' spirits. How fortunate we are," he stated with sarcasm, "that she decided to settle in Silverstone and take in young women who have nowhere else to go."

"She takes in young women?"

Paden inclined his head slightly. "But in exchange they have to work for her. It's hardly a charitable act. Chicago Joe is making a fortune, and her girls are dirt poor."

"That doesn't seem very fair."

He chuckled at her statement. "Life is not fair, haven't you learned that by now?"

She had. "But God is fair. Always. He only allows certain things to enter our lives for our good."

"Hmm..."

Bethany felt her face warm with a sudden flush as she recalled that the sheriff had frequented the disgraceful establishment last night. She couldn't get herself to meet his gaze. "Well, I...I just want to deliver a letter, that's all. I won't be long."

"And what do you think the good pastors will have to say about your mail service?"

"Back in Jericho Junction their parents minister to working girls," Bethany retorted, lifting her chin but still avoiding the sheriff's dark eyes. "Besides, they're both out of town, and Miss Brown should have her mail."

"I see." The sheriff smirked then lifted his hands. "Well, I think your plan is unwise, but I will not stop you."

"Thank you, Sheriff." With that, Bethany turned on her heel and left his office. After a few short steps, however, she could see the wisdom in his words.

All around her, the alley was littered with broken glass and empty liquor bottles. An unkempt man lay off to one side, either sleeping or dead, steeped in his own filth. Bethany grimaced. Looking back over her shoulder, she spied Paden Montaño at the doorway and felt somewhat comforted by his presence. She watched as he lit a cheroot, a sure sign that he'd be there awhile.

Whirling around, she quickly walked the rest of the way to the brothel and knocked.

The back door opened slowly, cautiously, revealing a woman wearing a stained, red, satiny robe. Her eyes were puffy and her cheeks slightly swollen, and Bethany wondered when she'd last had a good night's rest.

"What do you want?" The woman's tone was razor-sharp. She patted her matted dark brown hair.

"I'd like to speak with Angie Brown, please."

"Angie? What do you want with her?"

"I...I have something that belongs to her."

The hard-faced woman held out her hand. "Give to me. I'll see Angie gets it."

Bethany shook her head. "No, thank you. I need to give it to her myself, if you please."

The door slammed in her face, and she nearly gave up trying to speak to Angie, when it opened again and there she stood.

A frown creased her golden brows. "What are you doing here?"

Smiling, Bethany held out the letter. "This came for you today in a packet of mail that accidentally got shipped to Fort Yuma. I had a feeling you'd want to see it right away."

"Oh?" Angie took the proffered envelope and then gasped. "It came! She answered my letter!" Angie clutched it to her heart. "There is a God after all."

"Of course there is." Pausing, Bethany pointed at the letter. "Is it from home?"

"Sort of. I contacted my stepsister in San Francisco, never really expecting a reply. We were never close."

Bethany nodded mutely.

"But it's important to me just the same." She met Bethany's gaze. "Thank you so much for risking your good name to bring me this letter."

"You're welcome. But I was just trying to be a good Christian woman."

Angie snorted contemptuously. "This town is full of 'good Christian women,' and their good Christian husbands come and visit me after they get paid." Her laughter rang out on a note of contempt. "Hypocrites, that's what Christians are."

"Some, yes, but not all." Bethany had known a few herself. "And the Lord Himself is certainly no hypocrite. He is the same yesterday, today, and forever. Perfect and loving."

Angie lifted a doubtful brow. "Well, maybe He is, and maybe you're different. You sure did take a chance coming over here today."

Bethany smiled, feeling hopeful. "Do you like to read?" As the question rolled off her tongue, she wondered where it came from, and she felt momentarily embarrassed for asking.

However, Angie's reply alleviated her chagrin. "I love to read." She rolled a slender shoulder. "But I don't have any books. None of the other girls own many, and what they've got I've read."

"I have a lot of books. They were donated to the school, and many of them aren't fitting for children, but they're fine for adults. I'd be happy to share."

"Would you?" Angie's face gleamed.

"I'll gather together a few volumes and bring them by tomorrow. Is that all right?"

"You're comin' back here?" Angie shook her blonde head.

"I'll try."

"You're crazy." Angie pulled her shoulders back. "Something tells me you won't be teaching school here for long—not if you keep company with me."

"No one has to know." Bethany held out her right hand. "Friends?"

"Are you loco? You can't be friends with me."

Bethany stood undaunted, her hand outstretched.

Finally, Angie acquiesced. "Friends...at your own risk, mind you."

"See you tomorrow."

Smiling, Bethany turned and made her way down the alley. Sheriff Montaño still leaned against the door frame, waiting for her.

"Your good deed for the day is now done." His dark eyes glimmered with amusement.

"Something like that. Thank you, Sheriff."

Without so much as a backward glance, Bethany left Paden's office and crossed Main Street. Several passersby called greetings to her, and she politely acknowledged them. Oddly, the heat didn't seem quite so stifling anymore.

She entered the boardinghouse and left word that she'd be at school for a while. Leaving the Winters's establishment, Bethany quickly set out to select some books for Angie.

EIGHT

ANNETTA'S LIMBS ACHED FROM THE DAY'S BUSYNESS. JUST after she returned to her office this morning, three men burst in, bloodied and in need of her attention. She'd dug an arrowhead out of Miles Lohan's shoulder. She'd set Jim Tucker's arm. Pete Littleton had a nasty gash on his head that Annetta stitched. But none of the men would say what happened.

Then Tom Richter hobbled into the office with the help of his wife, Ruth. He had a broken leg and some minor contusions. He'd muttered his injuries were a result of an Indian attack and that he was just lucky to be alive.

Indians?

After that, Annetta had to tend to Ruth Richter, who'd fainted from sheer fright.

What a day! But at last her patients had gone home to recuperate. She locked her office door and started toward the boardinghouse but noticed a faint light coming from the school. She wondered why Miss Stafford would be there this late in the evening.

A moment's deliberation, and then Annetta strode toward the schoolhouse. That naïve teacher probably had no idea a threat of an Indian attack hung over the town like a fog.

Reaching the plank door, she knocked before pushing it open.

Miss Stafford startled. "Dr. Cavanaugh?" She sat on the floor with piles of books surrounding her.

"It's getting dark, and I saw the lamplight shining from the window." Seeing Miss Stafford's wide, bright eyes, Annetta decided not to worry her. "We'll have to hurry if we hope to make it to the boardinghouse for dinner. Mrs. Winters closes the dining room at seven."

"Oh, dear, I must have lost track of time." The slender, yet shapely, teacher stood to her feet and stretched. She surveyed her books. "I'll have to come back early tomorrow morning and finish my project."

Annetta smiled. "Shall we go?"

"Definitely. I'm famished."

Miss Stafford turned down the lamp, and outside she locked the door. Peering around the structure she looked back at Annetta. "It doesn't appear that Luke and Jake are back from the Whitaker's ranch yet."

"It's quite the ride out. I'm sure they'll be back soon." Annetta narrowed her gaze, curious. "Are you worried about them?"

"Maybe just a little. I dislike the thought of them riding home in the dark. I heard the sheriff tell Luke that not all *vaqueros* are friendly, especially if they've been tipping the bottle, if you know what I mean."

"I most certainly do." Annetta locked elbows with the younger woman. "And for the same reason we ought to make haste to the boardinghouse."

They quickened their steps down the warped boardwalk and arrived without incident. Once inside, delicious smells assailed Annetta. She inhaled deeply, and her stomach rumbled in antici-pation of being fed. As they entered the dining room, she was surprised to see the Winterses and Paden Montaño still sitting around the table. Usually at this hour the room was deserted except for the servants clearing dishes.

"Please join us, ladies." Mr. Winters stood.

Paden pushed to his feet as well. He smiled at Annetta and winked at Bethany, who quickly lowered her gaze.

Annetta narrowed her eyes at the man. Would he ever cease

his philandering ways? He'd already gotten tongues wagging about Silverstone's new teacher.

She and Bethany were seated, and Rosalinda carried in two servings of beans and rice and a plate of warm flour tortillas. Annetta waited to eat until Miss Stafford had finished her silent prayer and ignored the pinch of guilt. She no longer believed there was a God in heaven. If He truly existed, He wouldn't have allowed her to suffer such pain and sorrow—the kind that left emotional scars and wounds that never healed.

Miss Stafford lifted her chin, and Annetta shook off her demons before lifting her fork.

"Isn't it marvelous news?" Mrs. Winters gasped with happiness.

"What news is that?"

"Why, about Bethany and Reverend Luke getting married?"

"Oh? I hadn't heard." Annetta glanced at Bethany, who lowered her gaze. "Congratulations, Miss Stafford."

"Thank you," she murmured.

"Yes, Miz Stafford, congratulations." Paden wore a wry grin beneath a hooded glance, and Annetta thought she wouldn't mind slapping that smug expression off his tanned face. "Reverend Luke is a lucky man."

Again, the schoolteacher uttered her thanks, and Annetta wondered why she wasn't filled with wedding plans and giggles. The night she and Gregory became engaged, Annetta had wanted to shout it from the mountaintops.

Stop it! Don't think about Gregory.

Annetta mentally gripped her wayward thoughts and tossed them aside. She had purposely tried to kill those memories and bury them in Hamilton County before she'd taken the train to Pittsburgh and attended school—all very far away from Silverstone, Arizona. This was her life now.

"Where's Trudy this evening?" Annetta forced herself to ask so she could steer her mind clear of her past.

"Up in her room," Mr. Winters replied. "She's to remain there for the rest of the night."

"Yes," Mrs. Winters chimed in. "Our daughter's behavior required some modification, and spending time by herself will help bring it about."

"I'm sure you're right." Annetta pushed out a polite smile before her gaze landed on Bethany Stafford again. Curious, she studied the young woman. With head lowered, Miss Stafford picked at her meal. The features on her slender face appeared to slant downward, an indication she wasn't happy. Instead she seemed...humiliated. But then one glimpse of Paden's grinning face across the table and Annetta put the pieces together.

So that was it. The reverend felt obligated to marry the sweet schoolteacher in order to save her reputation since the sheriff's actions and young Trudy's tongue had brought it into question.

Thinking it over, Annetta took a bite of her rice, flavored with peppers, onions, and tomatoes. A taste of sweet and spicy exploded in her mouth and left her hungry for more. She ate another forkful and recalled how Miss Stafford had always seemed very close to the McCabe brothers, comfortable in their company. She'd traveled from Missouri with them. In Annetta's opinion, marriage to either one of the brothers didn't seem like the worst that could happen to a woman here in the Territory. Good heavens! Marrying Ralph Jonas would be far more terrible.

So why the long face?

At that moment the door of the boardinghouse opened, and the sound of boots scraping against the plank floor reached the dining room. A thumping sound followed, and Annetta turned to see who walked in. The topics of her thoughts strode across the lobby and stopped, looking like two redwoods as they stood in the threshold. Both men sported damp hair, and Annetta wondered if they'd jumped into the river for a quick washing before coming to dinner. If so, she silently commended their efforts.

Then suddenly a pair of blue eyes landed on Miss Stafford while a shining brown gaze met hers.

She looked away.

"Told you we'd make it back in time for some dinner," Reverend Luke said, clapping his brother on the shoulder. "Oh ye of little faith."

"Of course you're in time," Mrs. Winters announced with relish. "Come in and sit down." She swiveled the upper half of her torso so she faced the doorway to the outer kitchen. "Rosalinda! Another two plates, if you please!"

"Looks like you're right again, little brother."

Annetta felt a presence behind her and then froze as Jacob McCabe claimed the chair next to hers. She noticed he used a cane today and his limp seemed more predominant.

"Good evening, everyone...Dr. Cavanaugh."

"Reverend." She inclined her head. To her right, Annetta saw Luke McCabe bend at the waist and whisper something to Miss Stafford before he took the place directly across from her and beside the sheriff.

The schoolteacher replied with a timid smile and blushed to her hairline.

Annetta grinned inwardly. It didn't appear that Miss Stafford minded her intended one bit, and she wished the couple all the happiness in the world. At the same time, she fought off the regret filling her heart. She had once been young and innocent, but then—

She blinked, forestalling the memories. It seemed to be a minute-by-minute feat these days. But why? Why now?

"You missed the excitement, gentlemen." Sheriff Montaño's gaze slid from Jake to Luke McCabe.

"Indians ambushed some of Silverstone's finest men," Mr. Winters interjected.

"Ambushed?" Jake McCabe sat forward.

"That remains to be seen," the sheriff said. His dark eyes narrowed in a menacing way.

The conversation lagged when Rosalinda walked in carrying two plates. She set one down in front of Luke first and then Jacob. She glanced around, wiping her large brown hands on her white apron. Seeing that no one needed anything, she returned to the kitchen.

"I'm sorry to hear about the ambush," Reverend Jake said. "Anyone killed?"

Annetta turned to watch him as he spoke.

"None killed. Several hurt, though," Mr. Winters said.

"I treated several men who were victims of the attack." Annetta didn't know why she decided to add that piece of information.

"Who were they? What was the extent of their injuries?" Mrs. Winters's greenish-brown eyes were round with curiosity.

Annetta shook her head. "I'm afraid I can't say. I believe in confidentiality between a doctor and her patients."

"Oh, of course." The older woman appeared contrite.

Glancing down at her meal, Annetta found herself wishing Silverstone had a hospital—a hospital, and perhaps another doctor or two. While it was true that some days Annetta had very little to do, medically speaking, on other days she felt overwhelmed.

Like today.

"Many Indians were hurt in the, um, *ambush* as well," Paden said. There was little mistaking his take on the incident.

Mr. Winters's face reddened with anger. "Some say you were the one who tipped off the Indians." He ground out each word.

The sheriff appeared unaffected. "People talk. You know how it is." He slowly slid his chair back and stood. "One cannot believe gossip. I'm sure everyone at this table would agree, would they not?"

"That's right, Sheriff," Jake drawled his words. "But is there any truth to this particular piece of hearsay?"

"None whatsoever, Reverend. However, there is likely another informant, because the Indians were in the right place at the right time. They knew when the vigilantes were riding for their camp." He straightened his black vest, and his silver badge caught a speck of candlelight from the table. "But I must admit, I cannot blame the Indians for wanting to protect their women and children from being slaughtered."

"I can't either," Annetta said boldly.

"I agree." Bethany Stafford bobbed her head.

Beside her, Jake sat back in his chair with a slow, easy move. "Those men were wrong to take the law into their own hands and go gunning for Indians when we're not even sure they're responsible for the cattle rustling."

"Sí. My sentiments exactly, Reverend." Paden nodded his thanks. "And I can assure all of you that I will do my best to find the culprits."

"Seems I heard that promise before." Mr. Winters looked none too impressed.

"And I make it again, Señor. Now, if you will excuse me..."

Stepping around Luke's and Mrs. Winters's chairs, the sheriff left the dining room. The heels of his boots echoed in the lobby, and then the front door opened and closed as he left the boardinghouse.

Mr. Winters muttered under his breath, "That no-good sheriff..."

"Seems to me, folks need to set back and let the man do his job." Reverend Luke forked a bite of food into his mouth and chewed.

Annetta had to smile at his boyishness.

"I met an Indian when I helped Harlan yesterday," Luke commented.

Annetta sat back in surprise, and her gaze flitted to Bethany. She didn't appear disturbed by the remark in the least. Annetta wondered if her intended had already told her about the incident—and if he did, it added to the proof in Annetta's mind that Luke wasn't marrying the schoolteacher out of obligation.

"He was fierce-lookin'," Luke continued, "and I gotta admit that I thought he'd surely kill me. But when he found out I was a preacher, he let me live."

"This happened on Harlan's land?" Mr. Winters brought his shoulders back.

"Yes, sir."

"Just proves that those Indians are the culprits. It ain't too hard to figure out." Mr. Winters rose quickly from his chair and stormed out of the dining room.

"Ed!" Mrs. Winters stood. "Where are you going?"

"To talk some sense into that sheriff."

With that he left the boardinghouse.

Luke sat back and shook his head. "I likely said too much. I had only hoped to make the point that there's a chance we can befriend the Indians."

"You did fine, Luke." Next to Annetta, Reverend Jake wiped his mouth with his napkin. His eyes moved to the proprietress. "I hope your husband won't go off half-cocked, Mrs. Winters. He's liable to get himself killed."

Doris Winters's hand trembled slightly at her throat while she sat back down. "I believe my Ed has enough sense not to do anything foolish."

"I sure hope so," Jake said. "There aren't enough guns in Silverstone to defend this town, should the Indians decide to attack—that is, if we give them good reason to attack."

Annetta heard the sarcasm in his voice. But then she thought of the scores of wounded men she'd have to treat. This town definitely needed a hospital and a second physician.

"What do you suggest, Reverend?" Mrs. Winters paled.

"We watch and pray, asking God to spare our town. It was founded on Christian principles, and it's His."

"Why don't we all bow our heads and pray right now," Luke suggested. He and Bethany both reached for Mrs. Winters's hands.

Annetta decided to take her leave, but then Jake's large hand found hers. He gave her a smile before lowering his head.

A pool of warmth spread up her arm, and Annetta chided herself for feeling anything at all as this reverend began praying. This wasn't an intimacy.

Then why did she feel like it was?

Annetta shook herself. Well, in any case, she didn't want any of it—beseeching God or holding hands—none of it!

Worming her way out of Jake's grasp, she quietly excused herself and left the dining room. She did her best to be quiet, but her skirts still rustled and heels of her leather ankle books clicked on the tile floor as she made her way through the small lobby. Reaching for the door, Annetta opened and stepped out, closing it softly before turning on the boardwalk. She paused to check the dainty gold watch with its mother-of-pearl face pinned to her bodice. Eight o'clock.

Glancing around she saw that darkness had fallen on this dusty town, and the night air felt cool against her face and forearms. Across the street the saloon and brothel lamplight shone from each of the many windows, indicating they were open for business. With cynicism filling her heart, she wondered if the reverends prayed for God to take care of the working girls and their patrons as well as the Indians. She doubted it.

Smiling rather cynically, Annetta turned and walked toward her office. Her quarters were located above it.

"Dr. Cavanaugh. Wait up."

She turned on her heel to see Jake McCabe limping toward

her. She steeled herself as he neared. "I thought I might walk you to your door."

"No need. I don't need any protection." The truth was she'd never had it. "I can take care of myself, thank you."

"Now, slow down there. I wasn't thinking you needed protection. I thought maybe you could use a friend."

"A friend? You?" Indignation griped her. No man would ever be her friend. "I'm afraid not." Wheeling around, she strolled toward her office again.

"Hold up a minute."

She paused and allowed him to catch up. But only too late she realized how much his nearness troubled her. He stood mere inches from her on the boardwalk. A faint scent of leather mixed with masculinity reached her nose. It wasn't unpleasant, but Annetta backed away just the same.

"Dr. Cavanaugh, did I offend you somehow?"

She hardened her heart, reminding herself that his entire gender offended her. An angry, murderous man killed the love of her life before physically overpowering her, violating her, and leaving her for dead. Pompous, arrogant men had belittled her as she struggled to become a doctor so she could help others. Sweaty, dirty men treated her with little respect as she walked beside a wagon filled with her belongings, including her beloved rolltop desk all the way from Missouri to this nothing town in the Territory.

Friends? Hardly!

"What do you want with me, Reverend McCabe? Are you looking for another convert? If so, I'm not the one you seek. I told you this morning that I'm not interested in your church—or you. So leave me alone."

"Forgive me, ma'am." No strains of insult or irritation were evident in his tone. "I just thought with you being a doctor and me being a minister of Christ, our paths might cross in the line of duty. Wouldn't hurt to get to know one another."

She tipped her head. "What do you mean?"

"Well, there might come a day when a patient of yours asks for a minister. I want you to know that you can call on either Luke or me anytime, day or night."

Annetta found herself unable to lash out at him again as it appeared the good reverend was simply being nice. "Thank you." It was all she could muster for now.

Spinning on her heel, Annetta hastened to the front door of her office, unlocked it, and entered. All the while she knew Jacob McCabe watched her every move.

NINE

SITTING ON THE LONG BENCH OUTSIDE THE BOARDING-house, Luke watched his older brother walk back from the doc's office. Jake's gait seemed more unsteady than usual, thanks to riding hard from Harlan's place this afternoon. Across the street, raucous singing came from the saloon, accompanied by someone playing a squeezebox. Luke got a remembrance of his wartime days when he and other soldiers sat around in tent cities, waiting on their next orders.

How these folks in Silverstone need Christ. Luke closed his eyes and prayed for wisdom. How could he reach them? He'd already gone over and preached a sermon right in front of the brothel. He figured if they didn't come to him at church, he'd go to them. Luke ended up in a brawl with three drunken men. Pa always said never run from a fight—and he didn't. Walked away from that one too, although he was mighty banged up. But that was during his last stay in Silverstone, before Bethany came to town. He figured she wouldn't appreciate looking at him with two black eyes and a busted nose these days.

Luke stretched out his legs, wishing he sat on one of Jake's pieces of furniture instead of this flimsy piece of plank. Jake's carpentry work couldn't be compared to the nonsense Winters came up with—like the desk he attempted to fashion for Bethany before Jake stepped in to do it. What a sorry sight that was!

"Howdy, Preacher."

Luke barely made out the lone figure of a tall, lean man. He inclined his head. "Evenin'." Next he watched with disappointment as John Dempsy turned out into the street and made his way to the saloon.

Shaking his head, he swung his gaze to the boardinghouse door. Bethany had gone in to fetch her shawl as the temperatures plummeted after the sun set. Luke wished she'd hurry back out. He hadn't seen her all day and wanted to tell her that he'd sent a telegram to her father. He hoped Mr. Stafford would give his consent and wire back soon. He felt confident Bethany's father would be pleased with the match. Maybe he even expected it.

Jake finally reached him and claimed a place beside Luke. "She's a hard one, all right."

"Who's that?"

"Dr. Cavanaugh."

Luke thought a moment. "Why do you suppose that is?"

"Don't know." Jake worked to get comfortable on the hard piece of wood. "I imagine it could be any number of things."

"Reckon so." Luke watched the door of the boardinghouse, anxious for Bethany to return. He sincerely hoped his older brother would mosey on back to their cabin when she came out. Luke intended to spend some precious few minutes alone with his bride-to-be.

"But I'll say this much..."

Luke turned to Jake.

"Annetta Cavanaugh came a long way to be unfriendly to an entire town." Jake gave his head a slight wag. "Doesn't make sense."

"You know as well as me that since the war, thousands of people have headed West for new beginnings. Maybe Dr. Cavanaugh is just one of them."

"Maybe."

Luke could practically hear the gears of his brother's mind cranking. He grinned, and seconds later Bethany finally stepped from the boardinghouse.

Luke stood and reached for her hand. She looked awfully fetching in the moonlight.

She smiled at him then turned her gaze toward the inky-black sky. "Look at all those stars."

"There's a mess of 'em, all right," Jake replied.

"Who asked you?" Luke glanced over his shoulder. "Sorry you have to go home now, brother." He gave his head a jerk in the direction of their cabin.

"Well, now, Luke, a little constellation-watching might be just the thing I need before calling it a night." A wide grin stretched across Jake's face.

Luke forced himself not to react to his older brother's goading and turned his attention to Beth.

"The sky looks close enough to reach out and touch." Her voice contained enough awe to encourage Luke.

"I'll take you on a picnic near the canyon sometime." Luke tucked her hand under his arm. "The sky looks really close from up there."

"I'd like that." She smiled up at him. "It would be nice to see something besides the flat and barren desert."

"You can see the mountains on the horizon. They aren't but a day's ride away."

Bethany rolled one shoulder. "The mountains might be inspiring...if they were closer."

"You make Silverstone sound awful, Beth," Jake remarked from his perch.

Beneath the moon's glow, Luke saw her press her lips together. His heart sank at her unhappiness. "You haven't seen much of the area," he said hopefully. "There's a lot of beauty here. Just have to look for it."

He felt her stiffen beside him.

"You enjoy teaching here, don't you, Beth?"

"Well, yes..."

That was *something*.

"I sent a telegram to your father today, asking for your hand."

"I know."

"What?"

"Trudy told me."

Luke gnawed the corner of his mouth, wondering how Trudy found out.

"Yeah, well, her pa runs the post office," Jake muttered, as if divining his thoughts.

"I had hoped to tell you myself." Luke strained to see Beth's face. "I wanted it to be a surprise."

"Luke," she whispered, "what if my father doesn't reply?"

"Why wouldn't he? You're his daughter, and he loves you."

"Well, yes..."

Luke opened his mouth to say more, but before a word could form on his tongue, two men burst out of the saloon and onto the boardwalk. The music stopped, and women's screams followed as the men continued their fight.

"Come on, Beth." For her own safety, he steered her back inside. Once they stood in the dining room, he motioned to the sheriff, who had returned to the boardinghouse to debate the Indian situation with Ed Winters over a cup of coffee and pie. "Fight goin' on outside, Sheriff."

Montaño slowly stood, graciously thanked his host, and then made his way to the door. Luke disliked the way he bowed in front of Bethany before he secured his hat on his head.

"Until we meet again, Miz Stafford."

"Goodnight, Sheriff." She didn't meet his gaze, for which Luke was grateful. However, the way her cheeks pinked forced him to quell the urge to sock the suave Mexican in the jaw.

Flexing his fist, he watched the man head for the fight. Jake trailed, and Luke figured he'd better get out there and help. Already more men had joined into the brawl.

"I'd best say g'night, Beth. I might be needed outside." Luke stared into her kitten-gray eyes. "You go on upstairs, all right? I want you to stay out of harm's way."

She nodded, but as she pulled her hand from around his elbow, she clasped his hand. "I'll be praying you're not hurt tonight."

"Much obliged."

"And then I'll see you at breakfast, right?"

"Right." He gave her a smile then bent to place a quick kiss on her cheek. But since she hadn't been expecting it, she moved and Luke's lips caught the corner of her mouth. A thrill ripped through him like a hot lead ball, and if he thought he'd seen Beth blush moments before, he'd been sore mistaken. However, the crimson stain creeping up her neck and face...now *that* was some kind of a blush.

An overwhelming desire to kiss her senseless caught him by surprise. He blinked. Time to flee temptation. "G'night." Luke turned on his heels and strode from the boardinghouse as fast as his legs would carry him.

He might as well do his part to break up the fight before half the town's men got involved. At least it would keep his mind busy. But even as he stepped forward, the memory of kissing Beth's lips, even though it had been accidental, remained foremost on his mind. He knew without a shadow of a doubt that Bethany Stafford was the woman for him.

The next morning, Bethany stared at her reflection, wishing her eyes didn't appear so red and puffy. She'd cried all night, recalling how Luke fled from the boardinghouse after he'd accidentally kissed her. Was she that repugnant to him? Oh, why did she ever hope that Luke had fallen in love with her—the way she'd fallen in love with him.

Moving away from the looking glass, Bethany finished

dressing in a plain brown skirt and ivory blouse. She recalled her father's reaction when he'd learned that Richard intended to marry Sarah.

"I always thought the two of you would marry," Papa had said as he mucked a stall in the barn. "A shame it won't happen. Half the Navises' farm could have been ours if you'd turned out pretty instead of plain." Papa then heaved a sigh. "Looks like you'll live out your days with us. Plenty of work here to keep your mind off of being a spinster. It's just a good thing you don't eat much."

Even now his words stung. But the longing to prove him wrong and throw his insults right back in his face fueled her determination to succeed as a teacher—and a wife to Luke McCabe. Papa would never have to know the situation behind Luke's marriage proposal.

But how could she go from her father's low opinion of her to Luke's lack of attraction?

Bethany sank into the nearby wooden chair and stared out the window. But perhaps she was looking at her circumstances all wrong. She'd never find a better man to marry than Luke McCabe. He was kind and gentle. She'd never have to worry about Luke mistreating her, and she wanted nothing more than to be part of his family...

A knock sounded. Then the door creaked open before Bethany could voice a reply, and Trudy's round face appeared.

"Mama says breakfast is ready."

Determination sprouted inside Bethany. She raised her chin. She was a respectable teacher, engaged to a handsome, honest man of God. So what if he didn't love her? What was love anyway? Certainly not what was found in those dime novels Mrs. Buchanan donated.

Bethany made note to give them back at once. It wouldn't do if some of the older girls, like Trudy, got their hands on those romantic stories. Just look what they'd done to her!

Luke ran a hand over his stubbly jaw as he watched the school-children playing in the yard beneath the late afternoon sun. Funny how the heat didn't seem to affect the young'uns. Boys chased each other round, while four girls jumped rope. Only a few others sat in the shade of a mesquite tree listening to Beth read.

He pursed his lips, pensive. Ever since this morning at break-fast Luke noticed Beth seemed downright miserable. Come to think of it, ever since he'd proposed, she hadn't quite seemed herself. Didn't she want to marry him? Had he been presump-tuous in his asking? Impulsive?

Confused, he ambled back through the sanctuary, toward the small podium where he'd been working on his message for Sunday morning. Once he stepped behind the square, wooden stand, he gazed out over the benches on which his congregation sat. A sense of need enveloped him. Silverstone's townsfolk had been spiritually neglected until he and Jake arrived. But now God was using them to reach men and women alike, turning their hearts toward the Lord. As a minister of Christ, Luke couldn't ask for more.

If only Beth would realize the positive impact she could have on the next generation.

The school bell clanged loudly, pulling Luke from his thoughts. He closed his Bible and left the church, intending to walk Beth to the boardinghouse when she was ready. He'd hate for her to happen upon an Indian brave the way he had come face-to-face with Warring Spirit the other day on Harlan's ranch.

Luke reached the yard as the kids sprang from the small, one-room school. He smiled and watched as they scattered in all directions. None wore shoes, but that didn't seem to slow them down.

Suddenly the tantalizing smell of roasting poultry met his senses. He glanced toward the boardinghouse and saw a haze of grayish smoke rising from behind the structure. Seemed Rosalinda had begun dinner preparations. Luke's stomach rumbled in anticipation.

He walked into the school and found Beth standing behind her desk.

"Howdy." Luke took a few steps toward her. "Did you have a good day?"

She looked up at him with a tentative smile. "Yes. Everything went fine."

As the school's disciplinarian, Luke was glad to hear it. To date Beth hadn't summoned him once. "It appears the kids have taken to you. They all looked happy as they left school."

Beth's smile widened. "Every child is happy when the school bell rings at the end of the day. Teachers too." She sighed. "I'm exhausted from this heat."

"You'll get used to it. And it should be cooling off any day now." Wearing a grin, Luke moved forward and sat on the corner of the desk. Jake had made it so it was a sturdy piece of furniture. "You ready to head over to the boardinghouse?"

"Not quite. Give me about a half hour."

"Sure." He watched her busily collecting the children's slates. Her movements were quick, and it was obvious she avoided meeting his gaze. "Beth, is something wrong?"

She paused momentarily then continued on. "No..."

He waited, but when she didn't offer more, Luke decided not to press the issue. Perhaps she'd like some time to herself. He'd head back to the church and work on his sermon.

But then thirty minutes became an hour. Donning his black, wide-brim hat, Luke walked the dusty path to the schoolhouse again. However, this time Beth was nowhere in sight. Traipsing around back, Luke called her name and looked for her near the outbuilding. She wasn't there. His heart hammered at the thought of Beth abducted by some ruthless man.

Jaw clenched, Luke ran to the boardinghouse. His boots skidded on the plank walk as he reached the door. Pulling it open, he stepped inside and nearly collided with Beth in the lobby.

"Where've you been?" Luke's breath came fast as he removed his hat.

"Well, I..." She smoothed down the fabric of her brown skirt while giving him a nervous smile. "I've been helping Mr. Winters sort mail."

"You were supposed to give me a holler when you finished at school."

"But when I came to the door of the sanctuary you seemed so engrossed. I didn't want to bother you."

Luke rubbed the back of his neck and sighed. "You're never a bother, Beth. And I worry about you when you go off on your own like that."

"I was perfectly safe." She squared her shoulders. "Besides, I've walked home from school before when you've been away or busy."

"I know, but—"

"I'm not a child, Luke."

He narrowed his gaze. "Seems I've heard that before—from my baby sister, Sarah, who got herself into a fine mess last year."

Beth stepped closer to him. "I'm not your baby sister either, Luke, so I would thank you to respect me as the grown woman and teacher that I am."

Luke considered her as she stood before him with her freckled, upturned face and gray eyes staring back with fierce determination. Her pink mouth was pressed into an unyielding line, but the thought of kissing it still crossed his mind.

"I don't think of you as a child, Beth—or my baby sister,

either." He reached out and brushed a few strands of light brown hair off her cheek. "Nevertheless, I aim to protect you, and there's a threat of an Indian attack looming over this town. You can't take that lightly."

Her features relaxed. "I suppose you're right." She lowered her gaze. "Forgive me for being so stubborn."

Luke took hold of her chin, bringing her gaze back to his. "Nothing to be sorry for." He suddenly wished they were married right now so he could take her in his arms and kiss her, tell her he loved her...

He loved her!

"Beth, I..." Suddenly he knew this wasn't the time or the place for admissions of the heart.

Questions pooled in her eyes. "Yes, Luke? What were you about to say?"

Luke dropped his hand and glanced around the lobby. His gaze halted on Trudy standing several feet away giggling behind her hand.

"I think we'll talk later." He inclined his head, and Beth whirled around. The hems of her skirt brushed the tops of Luke's boots.

"Why, Trudy Winters." Beth put her hands on her hips. "Have you been eavesdropping?"

The girl grew wide-eyed then took off toward the dining room.

Beth glanced at Luke, who shrugged. Wasn't the first time he'd heard a giggling girl, and it wouldn't be the last, no doubt.

"Can I help you sort the last of the mail?"

Beth shook her head. "I'm finished."

"Good. How about we partake of an early supper? I feel half starved."

As Luke reached for her arm, Dr. Cavanaugh entered the boardinghouse. She gave a curt greeting to both him and Beth before making her way to the dining room.

"Goodness, my guests are arriving early this evening." Mrs. Winters appeared pleased nonetheless.

"I think you've got those good smells coming from the kitchen to blame." Luke held out the chair for Beth before seating himself. Dr. Cavanaugh had seated herself. Mrs. Winters remained standing.

"I don't usually roast chickens midweek, but earlier today some soldiers from Fort Yuma came to town. They met with the sheriff this afternoon regarding the cattle rustling and the Indian attack. They'll be staying the night in our boardinghouse, and I aim to give them good, home-cooked meals before they ride back."

"Why, Mrs. Winters..." Luke couldn't help teasing her. "You mean what you've been serving up lately isn't home-cooked?"

Across the table, Annetta smiled at the glib remark.

Mrs. Winters folded her arms and arched a brow. "For a preacher, you've got one sassy tongue."

"And a powerful hungry stomach."

Beside him, Bethany nudged him with her elbow. Had he embarrassed her? Mrs. Winters didn't seem to mind the teasing.

She put hands on her hips while amusement danced in her hazel eyes. "I reckon I'd better feed you before someone loses a limb." She turned and walked toward the back of the boarding-house and the kitchen area.

"Where's your brother this evening, Reverend?" Dr. Cavanaugh didn't look at Luke when she asked. Instead she slowly unfolded her napkin.

"He's fetching supplies in Arizona City, and he'll most likely spend the night at a hotel there." Luke took his napkin and gave it a shake before setting it across his lap. "If a spiritual need has risen, I'm happy to help in his absence."

"Oh, no, no..." Dr. Cavanaugh motioned with her hand. "I was just curious. That's all."

Luke made a mental note to tell Jake she'd asked about him.

Mr. Winters sauntered in and sat down. He asked Luke to pray over their meal. When grace was said, Rosalinda carried in supper plates of roasted chicken, baked beans, and biscuits.

"A small package arrived from Prescott for the sheriff," Ed remarked. "I had expected him and those soldiers from Fort Yuma to be here for dinner by now. Wonder what's keeping them?"

"Could be they're in the saloon," Dr. Cavanaugh remarked. "It would seem rather typical that a couple of soldiers would enjoy drinking, playing cards, and the company of cheap women to one of Mrs. Winters's home-cooked meals."

Luke winced, but he had hoped the men were of a higher caliber.

Beth suddenly pushed her chair back and stood. "Please excuse me. I just remembered something that needs my immediate attention."

Luke pushed to his feet as Beth ran from the room, through the lobby, and up the steps. But if he'd felt bewildered by her odd behavior, he was even more perplexed when she reappeared with an armful of books.

"I've got a few errands to run," she announced, suddenly looking bold and determined, "so I'll take this package to the sheriff. I'll eat my dinner later, if you don't mind."

"Well, that's mighty considerate of you, Miss Stafford, but—"

Before Ed Winters even finished his sentence, Beth had grabbed the package and rushed out the door.

Glancing at the confounded expressions around him, Luke stood, smiling politely to conceal his chagrin. "'Scuse me, folks."

Following Beth, he got as far as the edge of the sun-blanched boardwalk when he saw her enter the sheriff's office. His blood began to brew. Had she been carrying on with Montaño after all?

Just looking for an excuse to see him? And using her engagement to him as a cover for the scandalous relationship?

That didn't seem like the Beth he knew and loved, but had he been blind to this other side of her?

The muscles in his limbs contracted with frustration, but Luke forced one foot to follow the other and crossed the street. No wonder Beth looked none too pleased to see him this afternoon. She'd been hoping for a chance to rendezvous with Montaño.

Except his mind had a hard time grasping that reality.

Luke entered the sheriff's office and found Paden Montaño, his back to him, standing at the back door, holding his package in one hand and his gun in the other. "Touch that woman and it's the last thing you will ever do, *amigo*," the sheriff said to someone outside, his voice filled with a venomous warning that stopped even Luke in his tracks. Then he added, "Make haste, *chiquita*; I have work to do."

"What in the world is going on here?" Luke moved forward.

Montaño turned and grinned wryly. "Ah, Reverend, nice to see you again."

"Where's Bethany?"

Montaño flicked his dark gaze toward the alleyway. "She is just now knocking on the brothel's back door."

"What?" Luke felt dumbstruck.

"Seems she has befriended one of the prostitutes." Montaño looked over at him, his grin broadening. "But I will let her explain."

"And she will, trust me." Luke sauntered farther into the office. "Mind if I wait here?"

"Be my guest." Gazing back out the door, the sheriff let out an irritable-sounding sigh. "You might want to inform our little schoolteacher that this time of day is not so good to use the alley, particularly for a woman. The establishments next door are starting to get busy, and it's filled with drunk men and desperados."

"I'll be sure to tell her." *Along with a few other choice words,* he added silently. Settling into the wooden chair in front of the desk, Luke did his best to quell his anger, confusion, and impatience and waited for Beth to return.

TEN

"YOU CAN'T KEEP COMING HERE," ANGIE SCOLDED, STANDING at the unpainted back door of the brothel.

"But I've brought you some books, just as I promised."

"I appreciate your gesture, but...well, it's too dangerous for you to come here."

"Sheriff Montaño is guarding me."

"Yes, I see." Angie glanced down the alley. Then bringing her vacant blue eyes back to Bethany, she added, "But you're still asking for trouble, if not from the despicable characters back here then from Chicago Joe. She won't like it that we're keeping company."

"Can you and I meet somewhere else?"

Angie shrugged. "I don't know..."

"Please? I need a friend, and I think maybe you do too."

Angie laughed. "There are plenty of other women who'll be your friend, little Christian girl. Now go. And leave me alone."

Bethany felt crushed by the rejection. Yet she could hardly force a friendship. "Well, all right." She swallowed hard, willing herself not to cry. But the truth was she did need a friend— another woman her own age with whom she could converse, someone she could trust. And there was just something about Angie Brown that tugged at her heart and caused her to believe that beneath the hard veneer lay a soft, lonely heart in need of companionship and God's love. But there wasn't much she could do about it if Angie refused her efforts. "I'll be on my way."

Angie tipped her head. "Want your books back?"

"No, you may keep them."

Bethany turned and began to take her leave when Angie's voice halted her steps.

"Do you know where the eastern ridge is?" she called out.

Turning, Bethany shook her head.

"Well, ask somebody for directions. I go there every morning about sunup to clear my head and think."

Smiling, Bethany nodded then continued on to the sheriff's office. Progress!

"Thank you for the protection, Sheriff," she stated, slipping past him.

"My pleasure."

His husky tone caused Bethany to bristle, but she proceeded down the rickety stairs without further comment. Five steps later, she looked up and gasped with horror. "Luke!"

He lifted his blondish-brown brows, and a hint of irony crossed his features.

"Seems you have some explaining to do, *chiquita*." Sheriff Montaño sounded thoroughly amused.

She cast him an annoyed glance before returning her gaze to Luke's. "I'm not doing anything wrong."

"I'm glad to hear that." Luke's tone was as flat as a hotcake.

The sheriff chuckled once more, much to Bethany's aggravation. Then Luke stood and held his hand out to her. She strode forward and took it. Luke led her out the door and across Main Street. Reaching the other side, they walked down the boardwalk, and Bethany had to fairly trot in order to keep up with his long strides. As if sensing her efforts, Luke slowed his pace, although he didn't release her hand. Was he angry? He looked angry.

Bethany kept silent all the way through town and even held her peace after they reached the little road, which took them out to the exact spot where he'd suggested they get married. Only then did she speak up.

"Luke, hear me out. Please. I can explain."

He dropped her hand. "Glad to hear it. Have a seat."

Sitting on a large, flat rock near the bluff, Bethany couldn't tell if he'd stated the remark sarcastically, but she hoped he'd listen.

He lowered his tall frame down beside her. "All right." He let out a long breath. "Let's have it."

To the best of her ability, Bethany explained how she'd met Angie Brown in the mercantile and how she felt burdened for her. She told him how she'd used the excuse of delivering mail yesterday to talk to Angie and that she devised the plan of going through the sheriff's office as a means to get to the brothel unnoticed.

"But I won't have to do that anymore because Angie said I could meet her at the eastern ridge. Will you tell me how to get there?"

"It's right where we're standing." Luke's voice sounded calm. "But let me ask you this. Did you ever consider how it might look like to anyone else watching you enter the sheriff's office and not coming out for a good measure of time?"

Beth stiffened. "I thought our engagement solved that problem."

Luke sighed heavily.

"Luke, forgive me, but I just don't think that way. I don't have a suspicious mind."

"I know," he replied on a softer note.

"All I could think of was talking to Angie again. There's something about her, Luke, that makes me think she's desperate to leave the brothel. I want to help her in some way."

"Very admirable." He took her hand once more and held it between both of his much larger ones. "You're young—sometimes I forget that I'm eight years your senior. You're very mature for a woman of only eighteen years old. Even so, you tend to believe the best of folks—and I'm not saying that's bad. But trust me, the world is rude and unkind, and many times Christians are too."

Bethany decided she much preferred Luke's talking-to than her father's horsewhip. The gentleness in Luke's voice seemed to reach in to touch her very soul. "I'm sorry, Luke," she whispered.

"No harm done, although you need to promise me you won't do anything to help Angie escape, if that's her intention, without talking to me first. I'll help you, Beth, but you're not to act alone. Will you promise?"

It seemed a reasonable request. "I promise."

"And now, I aim to ask you one more thing." His tone hardened. "I want you to give me an honest reply."

"All right." She waited apprehensively for what he might say.

Luke paused, looking momentarily pensive. "Do you have feelings for Paden Montaño?"

Startled, she looked up at him. "What kind of feelings? I mean, I do find him rather irksome. I suppose that's a feeling, although I did appreciate his protection while I visited Angie."

"Beth, I'm supposed to do the protecting, not him. And it bothers me that you didn't give me a yes or no answer just now." He searched her face, and Bethany felt her cheeks warming to a blush from the intensity of his gaze. "Let me rephrase the question. Are you in love with the sheriff?"

Bethany gasped. "No!" She pulled her hands from his. "I already explained about the other night when…"

"I know, Beth, but I had to ask. Don't you see?"

She rolled a shoulder, still uncertain of his motives.

"And I'm glad to hear you don't harbor feelings for him."

"How can you even ask me such a thing?"

Luke raked a hand through his sand-colored hair. "Because I'm a jealous fool, Beth, that's how."

A surprised laugh made its way from her throat, nearly choking her. "At least you're an honest one." Her smile broadened.

Luke smiled too.

Bethany stood, picked up a stone, and tossed it aimlessly over the cliff. The arid breeze blew strands of hair onto her cheek as the sun continued its descent across the canyon. If Luke felt jealous, that meant he cared...didn't it? She wanted desperately to know.

"Luke, I don't want us to marry just to cease the gossip in this town about me." She faced him. "I don't care what people say about me." Come spring, she was leaving anyway, if she had any say in the matter.

"Are you saying you don't want to marry me?"

"No." She tried to quell her sudden nerves by smoothing her hands down her skirt. "I just want us to marry for the...the right reasons."

An easy grin crossed his handsome face. "I've prayed about us, Beth, and I truly believe you're the one God has chosen for me. Why, I have every confidence you'll help move my ministry forward. You're a hard worker, kind, sweet-spirited, patient..."

"I'm not very patient with Trudy Winters."

Luke smiled. "I would have never guessed."

Bethany continually tried to hide her irritation with the girl.

"We'll work out the rest together." Luke stood and walked toward her. "All right?"

She bobbed out a reply, wishing he'd be more specific.

Luke's hands enveloped hers again. "We'll be happy, I promise." The same smile on his lips sounded in his voice.

Bethany met his gaze. "You're sure? You really want to marry me?"

"Never been more sure of anything in my life."

She wished she could say the same. "What if we don't hear

from my father, Luke? There's a good chance he won't respond to your telegraph."

"We've got to give him more than a couple of days, Beth."

She sighed, but she couldn't get herself to tell Luke that she'd gone against her father's wishes when she left Milwaukee. Maybe life in Silverstone was her punishment. Glancing at the sand and dirt beneath her boots, Beth suddenly felt like crying.

"Come on." Releasing her, Luke offered his arm. "Let's walk back to town and eat supper."

Shaking off her melancholy, Beth slipped her hand around his elbow, and they ambled back to the boardinghouse, looking every bit the adoring couple. But all the while, Bethany longed to ask Luke the foremost question on her mind, except she couldn't seem to force it past her lips. *What about love, Luke McCabe? Do you love me?*

Her heart sank inside her. Without love, she might as well be marrying Ralph Jonas!

Annetta arrived too late for the regular mealtime and was waiting for her dinner to be heated when two uniformed soldiers entered the boardinghouse. They looked dusty but quite official, and Annetta felt her heart crimp as memories of Gregory surfaced. He'd been a Federal sergeant, home on leave over the Christmas holiday.

No! Don't think of Gregory! Don't think of the past!

She listened as the soldiers reported meeting an injured man on a wagon heading into town. Mr. Winters turned to her. "Doctor Cavanaugh, that sounds like a patient needing your attention. Go ahead, and we'll keep your dinner for you when you're finished."

Annetta nodded and excused herself, glad to leave the soldiers behind. She strode through the lobby and left the boardinghouse.

No sooner did Annetta's leather boot touch the wooden walk when she nearly slammed right into Jacob McCabe.

"My apologies, Dr. Cavanaugh." His hands gripped her upper arms so she didn't lose her footing. "You're just the one I'm looking for. I've got an injured man in my wagon."

"I thought you were in Arizona City overnight," she said as he steered her toward the road. Again she noted Reverend McCabe's unsteady gait.

"I got loaded up right away and decided I could make it back to Silverstone by nightfall. Then I happened on this man."

They'd reached the wagon, and placing his hands on Annetta's waist, the reverend lifted her into the back. There amongst freshly cut lumber lay an unconscious, burly, bearded man with a growing bloodstain in the middle of his shirt. She quickly checked for a pulse.

"Still alive?" Reverend McCabe leaned over the side of the wagon bed.

"Barely. Do you know what happened?"

"He claims an Indian shot him with a bow and arrow. He managed to escape his attacker, but when he started having breathing problems, he pulled the thing out of his chest. He lost consciousness just after I helped him into the wagon."

"Pulling that arrow out may have cost him his life."

"I told him as much."

Annetta met Reverend McCabe's gaze. "I need to get this man into my office at once."

The reverend looked toward the other side of the street and blew out a shrill whistle that left Annetta's ears ringing. "I need some help over here. Got an injured man!"

Annetta tore her patient's blood-soaked shirt and packed his chest wound, hoping she could slow the bleeding. But already the man appeared diaphoretic, and the faint pulse he had was racing. To sum it up, he was about to bleed to death.

Four men showed up, and Reverend McCabe explained the situation to them. Then he turned to Annetta and held out his arms. "Why don't you go on ahead and open the door and ready anything you'll need to treat his wound."

Nodding, she placed her hands on his broad shoulders and felt his hands on her waist. In one fluid move he lifted her down and set her feet on the plank walk. Annetta fumbled in her skirt pocket for her keys, wondering why her face flamed. Back in Philadelphia, scores of refined, educated men had helped her down from carriages and the like. Why in the world was Jacob McCabe having such an effect upon her sensibilities?

And why was she thinking about him now when she should be focused on a dying man?

Annetta found the key and opened the door. She walked through the sitting room, then the library, and finally back to the examination room, which doubled as an operating room. Oh, if only there was a hospital in town!

The men came in right behind her, and Annetta instructed them to lay the patient on the clean sheet-covered wooden table. They obliged her.

Afterward, they stood back.

"Let's leave Dr. Cavanaugh to her work." Reverend McCabe shooed the men out of the clinic. He paused before following them out. "Would you like some assistance? I don't know a lot about doctoring, but I can—"

"I can manage. Thank you."

Without another word, the reverend turned. The footfalls of his uneven gait filled Annetta's ears until they stopped, probably in the sitting room. She figured he'd wait for word about her patient, and somehow knowing he was out there comforted her.

She washed her hands and donned a black apron before inspecting her patient. A bluish shadow had crossed his face. Death lurked nearby. She removed the pieces of his shirt to inspect the chest wound more closely and realized then that there was nothing she could do.

Only seconds later, the stranger was dead.

Annetta stitched up the wound in case the man had family and wanted a funeral. Once the task was completed, she strode to the washbasin. As she soaped up her red-stained fingers, memories surfaced of Gregory, lying by the hearth, mortally wounded. She hadn't been able to help him either.

Why? Every muscle in her body tensed with anger. She hated death's brutal mockery.

Slipping out of her apron, she placed it in a basket of other soiled items needing to be laundered before making her way to the front to tell the reverend the news. She was surprised to see Sheriff Montaño beside him.

Both men stood as she entered the room.

"I did all I could." She lowered her gaze. "But he didn't make it."

"I had a hunch he wasn't going to." Reverend McCabe held his black hat in front of him with both hands.

Annetta shrugged at his remark.

"May I see the victim of the alleged Indian attack?" The sheriff stepped toward her.

Nodding, Annetta led him to the back. Reverend McCabe followed.

After a ten-second inspection, the sheriff's features contorted into a heavy frown. "Him." He said the word like a curse. Then he lifted the dead man's head up by his dirty brown hair. "Wally Hankins."

"You know him, Montaño?" The reverend set down his hat and put his hands on his hips.

"*Sí*, I know him. He is a wanted man. A murderer and a thief." He dropped the man's head unceremoniously, causing Annetta to wince when it bounced on the metal table. "Little wonder why the Indians killed him. If he'd lived, he would have hanged."

Paden Montaño's dark eyes moved to Annetta. "I am sorry you wasted your time, Doctor."

"Time spent saving a life, no matter to whom it belongs, is never wasted."

"Hmm..." Montaño shrugged. "You are very gracious." He bowed then turned around and searched the dead man's pockets. "I will bring over the wanted poster, and the two of you can verify and attest to Hankins's identity." Finding a gold pocket watch, he turned and handed it to Reverend McCabe.

"WH," the reverend read. "I reckon this is another proof positive the man is Hankins."

"*Sí*. And I will notify *Senōr* Rivers. He will come for the body." Jake nodded.

Annetta knew of him, Billy Rivers. She'd made his acquaintance numerous times. Mr. Rivers was the town's wagon-maker and blacksmith, and he also ran the mortuary. An odd side job, perhaps, but a very necessary one in this town.

The sheriff took his leave, and Annetta covered the dead man with a sheet.

"Are you all right?" Jake asked.

"Of course." She felt insulted that he would ask. As a trained physician she saw people die often enough. Besides, her well-being was none of his business.

Ignoring him, Annetta strode to the large rolltop desk she'd managed to bring with her from Pennsylvania. She took out a piece of parchment and dipped the pen into the inkwell, preparing to write the death certificate.

"Well, I'll be leaving now. Have yourself a good rest of the night."

Annetta stiffened. "You also, Reverend McCabe."

She listened to his footsteps and finally the opening and closing of the door. Her conscience pricked for her rudeness, but the fewer people who liked her in this town, the better. She was far too busy to make friends and get involved in their lives, and she certainly didn't want anyone in her life.

Suddenly Annetta realized ink had been dripping from her pen and spreading a black stain across the parchment. She set the pen aside and stared at the inkblot. It resembled a heart. Annetta looked closer. And sure enough, it was breaking.

Eleven

A N HOUR LATER THREE HARD KNOCKS SOUNDED AT THE door. Annetta set aside Mr. Hankins's death certificate, which she'd finished penning. Mr. Rivers and an assistant had come for the body a half hour ago.

She stood and straightened her dress and made her way to the front of the building. Another few raps and Annetta reached the latch and pulled. There on the boardwalk stood Reverend McCabe, his brother, and Miss Stafford. Each held a linen-covered basket.

"What can I do for you?" Her gaze flitted back to Reverend Jake.

"I reckon it's what we can do for you, Dr. Cavanaugh." He wore a wry grin. "You see, none of us had our supper yet, and we have it on good account that you didn't eat much yourself before you were called into duty. So we brought chicken, biscuits, and corn in hopes of sharing them with you."

Annetta opened her mouth to refuse the offer, but then her stomach protested loud enough for at least him to hear. Her face flushed with embarrassment.

He laughed and pushed past her. "I'll take that as a yes."

The other two smiled and followed him.

"Please, come in." Annetta spoke the words after the fact. She felt her resolve crumbling like stucco. There was just something about that man and his charm and persistence. "My quarters are upstairs." She motioned toward the back and grabbed the lamp off the wall. "Follow me."

Annetta led the trio to the stairs behind the clinic to the narrow stairwell that led to her apartment. She unlocked the door and stepped aside so her guests could enter.

"It's not fancy." Annetta hated the apology in her tone. "However, I do have a nice table at which we can all sit." She set the lamp down, found another, and lit that one too.

When they reached the dining area, which served as a parlor of sorts, Annetta gathered four chairs while the baskets of food were unpacked. Cool night breezes blew in through the opened windows along with strains of bawdy music from across the street.

"How nice that we can share a cozy dinner tonight," Miss Stafford said, "instead of sitting at a crowded table at the boardinghouse."

"Crowded?" Annetta knitted her brows. "Since when?"

"Since a couple of soldiers came from Fort Yuma today," Reverend Luke replied. "A lot of townsfolk decided to take advantage of their time and bend the officers' ears about the Indian situation."

"It doesn't help," Reverend Jake added, "that news is circulating about the outlaw's death. No one seems to care about who Hankins was, just how he died—from an Indian's arrow. The sheriff is there too, defending the Indians, which is causing more of a stir." He held out a chair. "Have a seat, Dr. Cavanaugh."

"Thank you."

Reverend Luke politely held Miss Stafford's chair. Then both he and Jake sat down. As Annetta reached for her napkin, her elbow bumped Jake's.

He fixed his brown eyes on her. "It's cozy all right."

Annetta smiled. She couldn't help it. Something about his glib remark struck her funny bone, if there ever was such a thing.

"Let's pray." Reverend Luke bowed his head, and the others followed suit.

Annetta sat by and mentally distanced herself. She'd given up on God a long time ago and didn't see any point in thanking Him. Once grace was said, she reached for the biscuits.

"You know, Dr. Cavanaugh," Jake started off, "you're real pretty when you smile. You ought to do that more often."

"Well, perhaps I will if there's ever something to smile at."

Beside her, she felt rather than heard Jake's chuckle, but she glimpsed Luke's amused grin.

"Woe abounds. Nothing to smile about here in Silverstone." Reverend Luke's mouth split into a grin. "Except for maybe Mrs. Morchunk's new hat. She wore it last Sunday."

Miss Stafford looked like she fought to conceal a smile. "That's not nice, Luke. She made that hat herself by dipping fruits and berries in wax then adhering them to her straw bonnet."

"Well, I got hungry just looking at it."

Miss Stafford rolled her eyes.

"I'll bet you McCabe boys were a handful when you were growing up." Annetta glanced at the schoolteacher. "Would you agree, Miss Stafford?"

"Oh, please call me Bethany, and, yes, I would agree."

"Now you just hold on, honey." Luke pointed his fork at her, feigning indignation. "I was a good kid."

"And that's why you put frogs and other reptiles in your cousin's bed when she visited?" Bethany lifted a piece of chicken to her lips.

"Not me. It was Jake who did that."

"Why am I not surprised?" Annetta retorted. True, she didn't know these men well, but somehow she could envision a younger Jake McCabe pulling all sorts of pranks. Maybe an older one too.

He chuckled before biting into a biscuit.

"I was a perfect child," Luke stated dramatically, "looking up to my older brothers for example—and finding none."

Bethany sent him a skeptical stare before smiling and taking another bite of her chicken.

"Hush, Luke, before I give all your transgressions away." Jake sent him a hooded glance.

"You wouldn't!" He looked aghast.

"Sure would." Jake pushed the remainder of his biscuit into his mouth.

"See? Some example you are."

Bethany laughed and gave Jake's shoulder a playful shove.

Annetta grinned, thinking the McCabe brothers were quite entertaining. And as much as she hated to admit it, there was something that drew her to them, Jake McCabe in particular.

"Do you mind if I ask how you injured your leg, Reverend McCabe?"

He met her gaze. "I'd be obliged if you'd call me Jake."

"All right." She didn't see any harm in it. "You may call me Annetta." She glanced around the table. "All of you."

A moment of silence passed. "Back to your question about my leg, I rode with McCulloch's Army of the West and got wounded at Wilson Creek. Lead ball shattered my leg. It never healed properly."

Annetta felt her throat grow dry. "McCulloch?" A Southern general. "You're a…a *Confederate*?" Another reason not to like Jacob McCabe.

"I hope that's not a problem," he said with a lazy drawl.

She clenched her jaw, unable to trust the next words from her mouth.

"War's over, Annetta." Jake helped himself to chicken. "I had my reasons for fighting with the South."

"You believe in allowing one man to own another?"

"No. I believe in the Constitution of this country and states' rights. I also didn't appreciate the heavy taxes the North imposed on Southern farmers, shippers, and other hardworking men.

However, I am opposed to slavery." He grinned wryly. "In fact, most of the soldiers I fought beside never owned a single slave."

Annetta replied with a dismissive roll of her shoulder and trained her gaze on Luke. "How about you? Are you a Confederate as well?"

"No, ma'am. I decided to remain neutral, being a chaplain and all. Then a funny thing happened at the first Bull Run. I got hit in the head with something, maybe a lead ball. I lost my memory and wound up with a Northern regiment until my brother Ben found me. I'm told I fought alongside them, although I don't exactly recall if I did or didn't."

"Really? A head wound?"

"Yes, ma'am."

Curious, Annetta turned to Jake. "And how does it make you feel that your own brother fought on the opposing side?"

"Well, it didn't start off that way. Both Luke and Ben thought both sides had good points. Both hated war, but Ben felt called to photograph the war as it happened and Luke felt called to share God's Word with the soldiers." Jake wagged his head and grinned. "Didn't bother me. I'm glad we all came home alive."

"Amen, brother," Luke said.

Annetta couldn't share their joy and relief. She'd lost her brother and…Gregory.

"Jake's always been interested in politics and community events. That's why he's on the Silverstone's advisory board. He'd be mayor of the town except he keeps returning to Missouri to recruit new residents."

Jake chuckled softly.

"My brother wouldn't tell you this because he's much too humble…" A facetious note rang in Luke's tone. "Seriously, Jake is a fine carpenter and was instrumental in helping rebuild Arizona City. You see, the town was nearly wiped out in the flood back in sixty-two. With the war and all, the rebuilding took years."

"That it did," Jake said. "I was happy to help."

"Some residents here in Silverstone were flooded out too," Luke added. "Folks still talk about it."

Annetta lifted a shoulder and shook her head slightly. "I haven't heard about it yet, but it sounds terrible." She eyed Jake more closely. "You're a carpenter?" She suddenly imagined a hospital at the end of Main Street, adjacent to the church.

"Yes, ma'am." He met her gaze. "Do you have a project in mind for me, Annetta?"

"Perhaps…in the future." Did she dare reveal her idea to him? After all, Jake was a town board member and had probably hoped for a male doctor.

"So you like it here, Annetta?" Jake reached for a chicken leg. "Think you'll stay?"

"I'm adjusting, and I plan to stay—unless city officials drive me out." She gave Jake a pointed look.

"I don't think there's cause for concern there."

Annetta pulled her gaze from Jake's. "What about you, Bethany? It seems you've adjusted well enough in Silverstone. And now you and Luke are going to be married. How nice for the both of you."

"Yes, it's nice." She pushed out a polite smile while Luke turned and seemed to study her every move.

"Beth is still…adjusting too." Luke stretched his arm out on top of Bethany's chair. "Wouldn't you say?"

"Yes, that's right."

Her eyes met Luke's for the briefest of moments, and Annetta had a sense that her first inklings had been correct. Bethany wasn't excited to get married.

"So when is your wedding?" Annetta pressed.

"As soon as Jake builds his own cabin and will marry us."
Luke wore a wide grin.

"I can start, now that I've got lumber."

"Well, I thought we'd be married in the spring." A frown furrowed Bethany's brow as she gazed at Luke. "In Jericho Junction. So your entire family can all attend."

Silence fell over the table, and Annetta watched the interesting dynamics around her. Bethany looked wide-eyed and hopeful while Luke appeared pensive and rubbed his shadowed jaw. Jake narrowed a puzzled gaze at his brother.

"I know Sarah will want to come for the wedding with Richard and their little one." Bethany sounded like she tried to convince him. "Leah, Jon, and their children. Valerie, Ben, and their brood. And Adalia and her husband...why, they're part of the family too. I imagine your father officiating the ceremony." She swung her gaze to Jake. "No offense intended."

"None taken." He still stared at Luke.

"Your father's a minister also?" Annetta glanced from Jake to Luke and back to Jake again.

"That's right." Jake pulled his gaze from Luke and gave his attention to Annetta. "We're from Jericho Junction, Missouri. It's a small town, just west of St. Louis."

"Yes, I'd heard you were Missourians." Annetta looked at Bethany. "And you're from Wisconsin, correct?"

She nodded.

"And what about your family, Bethany?" Annetta couldn't help asking. "Do you have relatives who will want to attend your wedding ceremony?"

She shrugged. "Perhaps my brothers and sisters...there's a chance my father will let the older ones come with Sarah and Richard. But he and my stepmother..." She paused and her eyes flitted to Luke, then Jake. "I doubt they'd be able to leave the farm for that long."

Then all at once Bethany sat back in her chair. "My, but this is a good supper. Mrs. Winters outdid herself again."

"Hits the spot, that's for sure," Jake conceded.

"You really want to wait until spring to get married?" Luke brought the subject back up despite Bethany's efforts to change it. He stared at her with what Annetta thought was a wounded expression. "I'd hoped by Christmas."

"Well..." Bethany shifted uncomfortably.

"Why don't you two discuss this later?" Jake took a long drink of his tea.

"Later is all right." Luke's tone was light, but determination darkened his eyes.

Bethany's gaze dropped to her plate.

Annetta knew at once there was trouble in the McCabe camp.

Twelve

Journal entry: *Thursday, October 10, 1867*

Many exciting things have taken place in the past few days. I have become engaged to Luke, although I worry that he's marrying me only to preserve his ministry and my reputation here in Silverstone. Sheriff Montaño was a bit forward on Monday evening and Trudy Winters saw us together. Before the talk could reach many ears, Luke proposed to me and I accepted.

But it doesn't feel real. I liken the situation to a play and I'm merely acting out a character's role. I think once some time passes and the threat to my reputation is over, he'll change his mind about marrying plain old me. And if he decides he wants to stay in Silverstone, I don't know if I'll marry him!

I'm not feeling sorry for myself. Very simply, I know the way it is with men. They always get what they want. And they want women who are beautiful. My father became enthralled with my stepmother because of her beauty. I bore his abuse because of her lack of interest in being a keeper at home. Then Richard preferred pretty Sarah to me. I'm no longer bitter. I have accepted this truth as painful as it is.

If that's good news, then the more is that I made a new friend and this morning Luke is walking me to the ridge so I can visit her. I must stop writing for now. I don't want to be late.

Bethany set down the pen and capped the ink well. Then she plucked her shawl from the wooden peg near the door and quietly made her way downstairs to the lobby. She prayed Trudy wasn't yet awake. The last thing she needed was for that girl's inquisitiveness to put an end to her meetings with Angie Brown before they'd even begun.

Seeing the lobby was empty, Bethany walked outside to wait for Luke. The early morning air smelled sweet and reminded her of a warm fall day in Wisconsin. A gentle breeze teased the rim of her white bonnet.

A movement suddenly caught her eye, and Bethany gazed to her left to see Luke making his way toward the boardinghouse. He made an imposing figure in his black trousers and matching vest, his white shirt covered mostly by a black jacket. The brim of his dark leather hat shadowed his rugged features, and if Bethany didn't know Luke and his gentle nature, she'd run back inside for fear a gunman approached.

A gunman minus a gun belt and weapon. Bethany grinned and supposed Luke didn't resemble a questionable character after all.

Luke reached her and slid his hat off his head. The way his sandy-brown hair lopped over his collar was an indication that it needed a trimming. "Mornin', Beth."

"Good morning, Luke." She smiled.

He offered his arm and she took it. They set off down the boardwalk. "It's shaping up to be a beautiful day."

"I suppose it is." She tried not to sigh as she glanced around at all the unpainted buildings.

"I think you're more homesick than you realize."

"Perhaps you're right."

"It'll pass."

Bethany had her doubts. She hadn't experienced a single pang of homesickness in Jericho Junction.

"You know," he drawled, "I was thinking about last night."

"Oh?"

"Yeah." Luke paused for a couple of steps. "You see, Jake, being the good older brother he is, was quick to point out a couple of my shortcomings after we left Annetta's. I got to thinking maybe he's right and I haven't been all that sensitive about our getting married."

Bethany listened closely. "Go on."

"Jake said most women start planning their wedding day as soon as they're old enough to understand the concept."

Bethany squinted beneath the sunshine as she glanced up at him. "I suppose that's true. I mean, what girl doesn't fancy herself a bride someday?"

"Honest, Beth, I had no clue." He stopped, bringing her to a halt also. "Tell me how you envision your wedding day."

"Happy. With lots of people in attendance." She smiled and stared off into the distance. "I always dreamt the day would pass in waves of white silk, satin bows, and lace." She looked back at Luke. "But I'm aware that's not reality."

He lifted his eyebrows. "White silk and satin bows, huh?"

"And lace."

His brows dipped inward. "Hmm…"

Bethany giggled at his perplexed expression. "Seriously, Luke, I'd be happy with a simple gown."

He turned, and they continued walking. "You'll need time to sew a wedding gown. I didn't consider that."

For a man who just confessed to being insensitive, Bethany found Luke very understanding now. "You know," she began, "ever since I was young, my father told me I'd marry Richard." She caught Luke's frown and rushed on to explain. "It was Papa's dream to combine the farms through the marriage."

"Hmm…and how'd you feel about it?"

"I always found Richard to be polite and nice. I guess I just accepted it. When he met Sarah, I thought I'd be heartbroken, but the truth was, I didn't feel badly. I didn't love Richard. In fact…" Bethany had to laugh. "I was more interested in making friends with Sarah than pining for Richard."

"Glad to hear it." Luke flexed his arm and gave Bethany's hand a gentle squeeze.

"But it dashed my father's dreams."

"God has a way of doing that sometimes, Beth. Our goals have to line up with God's will." A few seconds of silence passed. "You wouldn't be walking here next to me if your pa had had his way."

"You make a good point." Bethany hadn't realized the spiritual element. Which brought her to a second confession. "Luke, sometimes I get so busy I don't read my Bible as I should. How will I ever make a good pastor's wife?"

"Now, Beth, everyone gets distracted now and again. The important thing is that we get right back to it once we realize that's what happened."

Seemed logical. And obviously her perception of pastors and their wives had been skewed. Bethany knew nobody was perfect.

They strolled in silence for a while. Then Luke chuckled.

"Remember that time on the trail when Don Thorton fell over a big ol' tree root in the mountains? We all thought he was going to sail right over the ledge, but praise God he didn't. When we all got through holding our breath, we laughed till our sides ached and poor Thorton felt so embarrassed, he wished he would have tripped over the side of the mountain."

Bethany grinned. She remembered.

"You know," Luke stated thoughtfully now, "there's something about traveling with people that makes them grow closer. Like you, Beth. I feel like I've known you half my life. I reckon that's why I sprung a marriage proposal on you like I did." He shrugged, looking sheepish. "Then again, Jake is fond of saying I'm as impetuous as the apostle Peter."

Her smile broadened. "I rather agree with Jake."

Luke gave her a good jostling in payment for the glib remark.

"Stop, Luke, you're going to shake my brains loose." But Bethany's protest got lost somewhere between their laughter.

Suddenly the ridge came into view, and their playfulness ceased.

"That must be Angie, huh?" Luke nodded toward the lone figure of a woman, standing in the shadows of the early morning.

"That's her. Shall I introduce you?"

"Please. And afterward I'll make myself scarce." His eyes still twinkled from their merriment, yet he looked at her so hard it caused her to blush.

Bethany lowered her gaze, deciding instead to watch her gait for a few paces. Nearer to Angie, Bethany called out a greeting. The willowy-framed young woman turned toward them, casting a suspicious glance at Luke.

"This is Miss Angie Brown," Bethany began. "Angie, please meet my, um..."

"Intended." He removed his hat.

Bethany thought it sounded too good to be true.

"I'm Reverend Luke McCabe. Pleased to meet your acquaintance."

Angie pushed several strands of sun-kissed blonde hair from off her face and gave him a quick nod in reply.

"Well," Luke drawled, his gaze moving to Bethany. "I'll leave you ladies to your visit, but I won't be too far off."

With a slight incline of his head, he strode off along the stony trail. For a moment Bethany and Angie faced each other, saying nothing.

"The weather is cool this morning." Bethany stated at last, making herself comfortable on one of the rock formations.

"Usually is this time of day." Angie cast a look in Luke's direction. "I've heard about him."

"Oh?"

Angie nodded. "Talk is that he'll preach anywhere and to anyone, and he can fight just as good as the best."

Bethany chuckled. "Luke doesn't fight. Since the war, he doesn't carry a gun."

"I mean fistfight."

"Luke?" Bethany shook her head in disbelief.

"He's some kind of man." Angie smiled and lowered her head. "You're lucky."

Prickles of discomfort ran up Bethany's arms, and she decided to change the subject. "I prefer this cooler weather to the dreadful heat." She sighed. "I wonder if I'll ever get accustomed to Arizona."

Angie considered her momentarily. "Where are you from?"

"Wisconsin."

"Mmm…"

"How 'bout you?" Bethany tipped her head.

"Virginia."

So far away. "How did you get here? To Silverstone?"

"My stepfather. He met my mother on business out East, married her, and moved us all to San Francisco." Angie turned and sat down across from Bethany. "He was a gambler and gold digger. Never did strike it rich, but he traipsed all over the region testing his luck. Found he didn't have any. So he turned to drinking, and my mother fretted herself right into the grave. Then one night he came home and said he'd been gambling and lost me in a poker game. Can you believe it? A poker game?" Angie wagged her head and a look of sorrow entered her blue eyes. "He said I belonged to a woman named Chicago Joe. Just like that, like I'm nothing and nobody. He left me here to…to rot."

Horror gripped Bethany. What sort of a monster could do such a thing? "I–I don't know what to say."

Angie gave a toss of her head. "Well, it's because of him that I am in this business, and I curse my stepfather's name with every breath I take." She arched a brow. "Still wanna be friends?"

Bethany squared her shoulders. "Yes. What happened to you is not your fault. You were wronged in the worst way."

"That I was." Angie nodded toward the path Luke had taken. "What about your fiancé? He's a man of the cloth. How can he allow you to associate with me?"

"Because he knows, just as I do, that there is a God in heaven and He is the lover of our souls."

"I don't feel very loved."

"But you are, Angie."

An awkward silence grew between them, and Bethany felt a lump of pity and anger forming in her throat. "I understand about fathers not acting very kind and loving. Mine isn't."

"No?"

Bethany stared down at her hands. "My father whipped me a couple of times. I felt humiliated and disgraced and...completely unloved."

"I can imagine. But did you deserve to be punished?"

Bethany thought it over. "I deserved to be disciplined, but not whipped." She thought of the scars on her back that had taken months to heal. She'd had to take precautions at school so the other students would not see them.

"Well, I didn't deserve to get left behind by that no-good gambler." Angie made circles in the sand with her dusty boot. "And I dreamed about killing my stepfather for leaving me here." She stared out into the vast shrouds of jagged ridges. Her voice crumbled. "Now I'd rather be dead."

Bethany moved to sit beside the young woman with the vacant blue eyes. Compassion brought tears to her own eyes as she set her arm around Angie's slender shoulders.

Angie said softly, "Sometimes I come here and think about throwing myself off the ledge over there. But I'm too scared."

"And you should be." Bethany's nerves fluttered inside her midsection just imagining it. "Everyone is appointed to die, and after that comes the judgment. Will you meet Jesus Christ as your Savior or your judge?"

Turning, Angie gazed into Bethany's face. "Meet God? No. I won't meet him. My soul will plunge straight to hell when I die. Look what I've done!"

"Everyone will meet the Lord after this lifetime. Even those who won't be in heaven. But, Angie, it's not too late to change the course of your eternal resting place."

"So you preach just as good as your fiancé, hmm?" With hands clasped behind her back, Angie walked in a small circle. Her eyes narrowed distrustfully. "Don't you understand what I am?"

"Yes, but Mary Magdalene was a…well, she had the same profession as you do."

"Who's that?" Cynicism laced her tone. "Mary…who?"

"Magdalene. She lived a sinful life. But then she met Jesus of Nazareth, the Messiah. He's God's only begotten Son and was sent from heaven nearly two thousand years ago, clothed in humanity, to save those who'll repent of their sins and believe in Him." She paused. "Mary Magdalene was saved from eternal damnation, and you can be too!"

Angie sat there with a stunned expression. "Where'd you hear all that?"

"It's in the Bible, and…well, Luke preaches it all the time."

"The Bible?" Her eyes widened slightly. "It mentions *working girls* getting…*saved*?"

Bethany nodded. "Would you like to read it for yourself? You can borrow my Bible."

The nod was ever so slight, but visible enough to encourage Bethany.

Angie suddenly stood. "I need to get back. Chicago Joe will be wondering where I am."

"I'll bring my Bible tomorrow morning." Bethany rose from the boulder. "Is she truly from Chicago? That's not far from Wisconsin."

"What?" Angie regarded her as though she'd sprouted antlers. A moment later she shook her head in wonder. "You know what you are? You're like sugar. You make even a bitter pill taste sweet. 'Not far from Wisconsin,'" she mimicked in falsetto. Then she laughed softly. "Looks like you and Chicago Joe have something in common, eh? Lake Michigan!"

Bethany forced a smile, not quite sure if she'd just been insulted. "Well," she finally stated on a careless shrug, "I'm certainly impressed by your geographical knowledge."

Angie's laughter escalated until she had to sit back down. She laughed so hard that tears streamed from her eyes. "Oh, sugar," she said breathlessly, "I haven't laughed like that in a hundred years."

Bethany rolled her eyes. "Really, Angie, you can't be more than twenty-five."

"I'm nineteen," she corrected, the last of her mirth dying. "But I feel like I've lived a lifetime."

Staring into her eyes, Bethany almost believed her. "I'll be nineteen in January."

"I guess we have that in common."

A long moment passed, and then Angie pushed to her feet.

"I have to get back."

"Same time tomorrow?"

"I suppose so." Whirling around, Angie quickly made her way back to the brothel.

Luke felt proud of Beth for reaching out to one of the working girls the way she did. He knew his folks in Jericho Junction would feel the same. "You don't have to give her your Bible. Jake and I brought extras for just this very thing."

"Oh, good."

They continued their walk back toward the boardinghouse.

"Angie said you're a good fighter. She laughed at me when I told her that you're not the brawling kind."

"Now, Beth…" Luke glanced into her upturned face with its smatter of freckles across her nose and cheeks. Her innocent, gray eyes were wide with concern. "Out here a man's got to be able to protect himself. But honestly, darlin', I don't go looking for trouble. So you're right."

"Oh." She accepted the reasoning. "I guess that clears things up."

Luke grinned.

They reached the boardinghouse, and Luke's mouth watered when he smelled empañadas. Removing his hat, he and Beth entered the dining room, and the same two soldiers he'd seen last night sat at the table now with Ed Winters. Politely the men stood, and Luke held Beth's chair while she sat down.

"G'morning, Reverend." Winters smiled. "We were discussing the ambush that took place earlier this week."

"Which reminds me, I'm meeting with several folks who got hurt that night." He gave his head a wag. "A real shame."

"Sure was. But them boys had every right to—"

"No." Luke had to speak up. He'd held back for days now, wanting to learn the truth before he said anything. "Sounds to me like it was an illegal posse." He took a seat and tried to ignore Beth's incredulous stare.

"Sir?" A shaggy-haired soldier addressed him. "You take the sheriff's story over Ed Winters's?"

Luke eyed the stripes on the man's sleeve. "I don't see it as taking sides, Sergeant. And I think many of those men were just out to protect their ranches. Their hearts may have been in the right place, but I believe they should have left the situation to Sheriff Montaño."

"He didn't act fast enough." Winters slammed his fist on the table while his face turned as red as a radish.

"Perhaps I should go see if Mrs. Winters needs help." Beth moved her chair back to get up.

Luke reached for her hand. "No need, Beth. I'm happy to change the subject."

A look of relief spread across her face while the other men wore expressions of chagrin.

"You have our apologies, ma'am," the sergeant said.

Beth sent them each a gracious smile before lowering her gaze.

Just then the boardinghouse's front door opened and closed with a bang. Suddenly one of Ralph Jonas's young'uns appeared at the dining room entryway.

"Pardon me, but I'm lookin' fer the doc." His chest rose and fell as he fought to catch his breath. "My pa done tol' me to fetch her."

Bethany turned in her chair. "What's wrong, Nathan?"

"It's the little ones. All of them's sick real bad. Pa says he's got all he can do right now."

Standing, she moved toward the lanky boy. "I'll help you find Dr. Cavanaugh." She glanced at Luke.

"Go on." He inclined his head. "I'll ask Rosalinda to wait on your breakfast."

"Thank you." With an arm around Nathan's narrow shoulders, Bethany led him out of the boardinghouse.

Luke watched her go, wearing a grin. He had a feeling that Beth cared for the folks in this town a lot more than she let on.

Thirteen

Saturday arrived, and after Bethany helped Mrs. Winters and Trudy wash and hang clothes, she accepted Luke's invitation to ride out to the Jonas place. The children were still sick, and Mr. Jonas had gotten behind in his chores. Luke had offered to bring some charitable donations and supplies, and Bethany figured she could help with cooking, housecleaning, and caring for the children while Luke worked on the farm with Mr. Jonas.

Luke helped her into the wagon and then climbed in and took the reins. As he urged his team forward, Bethany considered him. He'd kept to himself the past day and a half.

"Is anything wrong, Luke?" The bumpy road leading to the Jonas farm threatened to uproot Bethany from the wagon seat, but she held on tightly. She never knew three miles in a buckboard could feel so uncomfortable—and it wasn't just the ruts in the road, either. Luke's silence was unnerving.

"Well," he drawled, "I've been doing some more thinking about our getting married."

"Oh?" Had he changed his mind? Bethany's heart beat a little harder, and she steeled herself for the worst.

Luke slowed the wagon to a halt in the middle of the seldom-traveled road. The morning sun beat down on them, and the air felt still and hot against Bethany's already flushed cheeks. Her sunbonnet proved little use today and more of a nuisance.

She gazed around. Not a soul could be seen for miles across

this desolate stretch of land, although she knew the Jonas farm was just over the hill.

Luke sat forward, his forearms resting on his knees. His shoulder muscles moved beneath his tan shirt as he shifted his weight. "I know family means a lot to you, especially at our wedding, so I'm willing to get married in Jericho Junction next spring. But you need to know that I plan to turn around and return to Silverstone." He paused and glanced around him. "This is my home now. Reaching the people here and encouraging their faith is my calling."

Bethany gazed at her hands, folded over the skirt of her russet-colored dress. Returning to Silverstone as Luke's wife defeated the purpose of traveling to Jericho Junction in the first place.

"I love the Territory, Beth. I sense the great need out here to share God's truth." He paused. "My heart is here."

"Your heart?" That meant she'd never own it. But hadn't she known that all along?

"That's right." He paused. "Looks like you've got a decision to make."

"I've already made it. I want to move back to Jericho Junction." Bethany forced herself to look at Luke.

His blue eyes darkened. "Now why do you have to be so stubborn? Can't you agree to at least pray about this?"

"Why should I?" Her ire flared. "You don't seem too interested in my opinion anyway."

"Well, you can't live in Jericho Junction and be my wife at the same time."

"Don't patronize me, Luke. I realize you're giving me an ultimatum."

"I don't see it as such." He adjusted the brim of his tan hat. "I just want to be honest with you from the git-go."

"Thank you very much." Bethany's jaw tensed, and she trained her gaze on the road ahead.

Luke slapped the reins and the wagon jerked forward. He gave Bethany a sideways glance. "I always hoped that the right woman would be willing to follow me anywhere."

"Maybe you need to keep looking for that *right woman*."

"Oh, now, Beth—"

"Figuratively, the Territory *is* your woman." Bethany hated the feeling of playing second fiddle. "After all, you can't share your heart with someone if you've already given it away."

"What?" He shook his head. "That makes no sense." He snorted indignantly. "*Figuratively*."

"The word means not literal, like a metaphor or figure of speech."

"I know what the word means." A knifelike sharpness edged his reply.

Bethany pressed her lips together. She saw no point in arguing.

The horses' hooves kicked up dust from the road as they trotted onward. Bethany suddenly recalled the times she'd sat next to Luke on the trail. But instead of gazing over horses, it'd been oxen pulling a covered wagon. She and Luke would talk or sometimes sing to pass the time. It felt uncomfortable not to be speaking to each other now.

Bethany tried hard to focus on her surroundings. What did Luke see in this dusty, brown desert dotted with brush and rock?

Within minutes she got what seemed like a divine reply. The road made a bend and ran parallel to the river. Then Luke steered his team across a narrow, wooden bridge, and suddenly lush, fertile land stretched out before them. Rivulets from the Colorado ran through it, dug in for irrigation purposes. Bethany had been here before and thought the Jonas farm was more pleasing to the eye than the desert. However, that didn't change Bethany's opinion of the Territory.

The silence between them continued the rest of the way to the Jonas farm. When they arrived, Luke slowed the horses to a halt and wrapped the reins around the brake. Bethany moved to climb off the wagon, but Luke stepped over her and jumped down first. He stretched out his arms to assist her, and she had no recourse but to comply, except he didn't remove his hands from her waist after her booted feet touched the dirt.

He leaned so close that the brim of his hat shadowed her face. His eyes flicked over her mouth before traveling up and meeting her gaze. "You gonna stay mad at me all day?" His voice was but a whisper.

"N–no." Suddenly his nearness had an unsettling effect and caused her to forget what had angered her in the first place.

"Glad to hear it." He stared at her hard, and Bethany suspected he was about to kiss her. But then he stepped back and took her hand. "Let's both pray on the matter, and we can talk later. All right?"

"All right." But neither prayer nor discussion would ever change her mind about staying here in Silverstone!

The incessant hammering distracted Annetta from penning in her medical log for the umpteenth time this morning. She rose from her desk and strode to the front windows, wondering who was building what. Unable to see anything except a few of the town's soiled doves wearing brightly colored dresses at the far side of the saloon, Annetta decided to investigate.

Leaving the clinic, Annetta walked in the direction of the pounding. The sound ricocheted off the wooden buildings she passed. As she came up to the church, she could see Jacob McCabe working with the load of lumber he'd picked up days ago. Two Mexican men assisted him. Then all at once Annetta realized they were the object of the prostitutes' ogling.

She set her jaw, and her fists clenched in irritation as her gaze darted between the women and Jake and his crew. Next the hope that Jake would never succumb to such temptation rose up inside of her. But why should she care? She didn't want to, and yet this morning she wished she had awakened in time to have breakfast with him at the boardinghouse. Since their impromptu dinner Wednesday night, he'd permeated her thoughts more than Annetta cared to admit. She hated to think that she might actually be attracted to the ruggedly handsome reverend.

The hot sun bore down on her as she stood there battling her emotions.

"Good mornin', Dr. Cavanaugh."

Hearing his voice, she snapped to attention in time to see Jake lift a hand in greeting. She gave him a nod. Glancing across the street, she spied the women's glare, and somehow their interest propelled Annetta forward. Lifting her hems, she stepped off the boardwalk and picked her way toward Jake.

He straightened, hammer still in hand. "What can I do for you this fine morning, Annetta?" he asked when she reached him.

"I couldn't help hearing you working over here and got curious." She eyed the spot where she'd been thinking a hospital would fit nicely. It appeared that dream got dashed like all her others. "What are you building?"

Jake's brown eyes twinkled. "Can you keep a secret?"

"Of course." Annetta kept many, many secrets.

"Well, Luke thinks I'm building myself a little cabin so he and Beth can live in the one behind the church. But I'm surprising him by building a formal rectory. He and his bride will have a brand-new home—and a larger one."

"How nice." Annetta folded her arms, impressed by Jake's benevolence.

"My wedding present to them."

"Very generous of you. I'd say Luke and Bethany are a lucky couple."

Jake smiled and then spoke broken Spanish to his helpers, telling them to take a break. They seemed to understand and dropped their tools to go sit in the shade of the mesquite tree near the schoolhouse.

Jake set down his hammer and limped to a nearby bucket. Reaching inside, he brought the dipper to his lips and swallowed several gulps of water.

"Is your leg bothering you today?" Annetta had noticed his uneven gait seemed more predominant this morning.

"No more than usual." With his back to her, he took off his hat and splashed his face.

Annetta sensed that her question embarrassed him. "Forgive me for noticing such things. I'm a doctor." Immediately she thought that quinine might ease any discomfort he experienced.

"No harm done."

Jake turned and made his way toward her. Perspiration and some of the water from the bucket stained much of his tan shirt, and woodchips stuck to his dark brown trousers. But even in his work-worn state, Annetta found him appealing. Masculine and yet harmless and...safe.

She pulled her gaze away. What minister of God would want her if he knew the truth?

"Annetta, you seem troubled. What's wrong?"

She shook her head. "Nothing. I'm perfectly fine. I just wanted to see what you're building out here." She rolled a shoulder. "Consider me a nosey neighbor."

Jake chuckled. "All right, I will."

The sound of his laughter caused her to smile—until she caught another sight of the prostitutes still standing beneath the overhang of the saloon.

"And I guess I'm not the only nosey one in town."

Jake squinted off in the prostitutes' direction, and an expression of sorrow fell over his face. Not of interest, Annetta noted, but of pity. "God help them, every one." His gaze returned to Annetta. "Back in Jericho Junction, my folks made a point to rescue women out of the bondage of that lifestyle."

"Oh?"

"Uh-hmm. You see, a lot of working girls believe they don't have other choices—until they let the love of God enter their hearts, souls, and minds." He inclined his head and flicked another glance toward the painted trio. "Seems to me I've talked to those three already."

"You...what?" A wave of shock went through her.

"Talked to them. Shared the gospel."

"You deigned to speak to...to women of ill repute?" Annetta had thought Jake would shun them. "What do the good citizens of Silverstone say about that?"

"I'm very careful how I approach those ladies. I keep a respectful distance at all times." Jake's tone was steady and sincere. "I think folks around here know Luke and me well enough and figure we're just doing our jobs."

Annetta felt repulsed. Imagine the Reverends McCabe consorting with that ilk! She imagined the sorts of diseases women in such an industry contracted. But before she could shudder at the thought, another notion formed. Diseases. She was a physician. Hadn't she sworn to treat everyone, no matter what their race or creed?

Slowly she looked from the women near the saloon to Jake. "I must say, you are truly an inspiration, Jacob McCabe."

"Oh?" He arched a brow.

"Yes." She turned to go, but remembered the quinine. "Will you be at the boardinghouse for dinner this evening?"

"I can be." He seemed a little puzzled.

"Good. I have something for you. And now if you'll excuse me, I have a job of my own to do."

Annetta strode back toward the clinic. Horse-drawn wagons

rattled up and down the street, but as soon as an opening pre-sented itself, she crossed the street. From a distance she heard Jake call her name and acknowledged the warning in his tone. How-ever, she refused to be dissuaded from her mission. If her par-ents hadn't been wealthy enough to fund her medical schooling, Annetta might be a woman of...of no choices too.

Determination guided her steps as she approached the three women. Their faces registered their amazement.

"Please allow me to introduce myself." Annetta squared her shoulders and paid no attention to the burly man who'd just stepped out of the saloon. "I'm the new doctor in town, and my clinic doors are always—"

Suddenly an all-too-familiar *click* sounded close to her ear just before she felt the barrel of a gun jab into the base of her skull. In that second Annetta knew she'd made a deadly mistake.

FOURTEEN

A HAND CLAMPED DOWN HARD OVER ANNETTA'S MOUTH. Panic rose inside of her. Had the nightmare returned? Only this time it wasn't just another bad dream!

Deciding she'd rather die than suffer at the hands of a strange, unkempt man, Annetta worked her teeth into his beefy palm and bit down hard, while jamming her elbow into his midsection.

"Ow!" He removed his hand. "You little she-cat!"

He released Annetta with a shove, and she stumbled, falling onto the dirty boardwalk. Bawdy female laughter followed her. Annetta's stomach lurched at the smell of stale whiskey, tobacco, and human vomit.

She squeezed her eyes closed, expecting to hear gunfire at any moment and then a lead ball piercing her flesh.

"You sure got a way with women, Crawford."

Hearing the familiar voice, Annetta looked to see a pair of dusty black boots before two strong hands gently gripped her arms and helped her to stand.

"Jake." Relief flooded her being.

"You all right?"

She nodded.

"I got ammunition enough to kill you too, Preacher," Crawford growled.

Prickles of foreboding ran down her spine. Something about the unshaven, pot-bellied man seemed oddly familiar. Perhaps it had to do with his icy-blue eyes. They were unnaturally bright.

However, their diabolically evil gleam caused Annetta to lower her gaze.

Crawford spit toward the street. "You know what Chicago Joe said about you do-gooders stayin' away from her girls."

"I just came to collect Dr. Cavanaugh." Jake pulled her behind him. "She's new in town. She didn't know better." He glanced over his shoulder, giving Annetta a stern look. "But now she does, so it won't happen again."

"I only wanted to introduce myself." A portion of Annetta's determination returned. "In case of a medical emergency."

"Well, it's a real pleasure ta meet ya." A blonde, wearing the greenest dress Annetta had ever seen, sashayed toward them. She gave Jake an appreciative glance before her gaze settled on Annetta again. "Next time we'll have a regular tea party."

The woman broke out in raucous laughter. Her friends did the same. Crawford stood by and snickered.

Annetta let out a long, slow breath. Her dignity had been bruised, but her conscience had not. She'd at least tried to reach out to these women, and perhaps if they found themselves needing medical advice, they would cross the street to the clinic or send for her.

"Hey!" An ebony-haired woman stuck her head out the opened, second-story window. "You girls get back to work! The saloon's pretty-near empty."

They scattered like leftover confetti.

"And Crawford," she bellowed in a deep, masculine voice, "I want to see that doctor up here in my room."

Jake turned to her. "You don't have to go, Annetta."

"Really?" She couldn't help her sarcastic tone. "If you haven't noticed, we have a gun pointing in our direction."

"I noticed. But my God is bigger than Dirk Crawford's gun."

Annetta marveled at his confidence and peeked around him to stare up at the window.

The barrel of a gun appeared. "Don't make me kill you, Preacher. If I miss, Crawford won't."

"Is your God bigger than two guns?"

"Yes, He is." Jake set his hands on his hips and faced his adversaries straight on. "She's not coming up."

Crawford took aim at Jake.

Annetta cringed, waiting to hear the gunfire. Around them, a small crowd gathered. Wagons halted in the middle of the street. An eerie hush seemed to fall over the town as if the townsfolk held their breath.

Panic rose inside of Annetta. Would this evil man shoot and kill Jake—like the renegade who murdered Gregory?

She moved to clutch the back of Jake's shirt, and her fingers fell over, and briefly lingered, on the gun tucked into its holster. She had her pistol. Maybe together they could—

"Don't even think it, Annetta," Jake muttered over his shoulder while slowly raising his hands in surrender.

Making a fist around the fabric of his shirt, Annetta held on tightly. She could barely breathe. But as the seconds ticked by, she started feeling safe with Jake. Somehow she knew he'd win this standoff. Besides, if Crawford meant to kill them, he would have pulled the trigger already.

So what hindered him?

"I said send 'er up, Preacher," the woman bellowed from the window.

"I'll go talk to her," Annetta whispered to Jake. Anything to make these fools lower their weapons.

Jake ignored the offer. "Now, Miss Josephine, I thought the two of us had an understanding."

"We did. So what are you doing on my side of the street?"

"I came to fetch Dr. Cavanaugh. She's new in town and—"

"We know who she is," Crawford said.

"That's right." The woman poked her head farther out the

window, and Annetta glimpsed her doughy-white skin, dark hair, and menacing gaze. "She's a doctor. That's why I want to talk to her. Now, quit your jabbering and send her on up."

Did the woman have a medical problem that required a physician? The last of Annetta's fear began to abate.

"Jake, I'll go talk to her." She stepped around him.

"Not a good idea." He caught her by the elbow. "That's Chicago Joe up there in that window." His lips were close to Annetta's ear. "She's infamous in these parts, known for killing men over minor disagreements. It's also a fact that she mistreats the women who work for her. All along she's maintained that the town of Silverstone belongs to her. The rest of us citizens are wont to argue that point."

"None of that matters right now." Annetta wetted her suddenly parched lips. "Chicago Joe is a woman, and she might need medical care." She peered deeply into Jake's eyes and watched his expression soften.

"Against my better judgment, I'll give you fifteen minutes. After that, I'll fetch the sheriff and—well, I can't promise the outcome."

Annetta knew her decision meant someone might get injured—or worse. It might even mean losing her own life. But, strangely enough, she knew she had to go.

She discreetly touched the handle of the gun she kept tucked into the waistband of her skirt. Then she gave the black, silk embroidered vest she wore a gentle tug to ensure her weapon was hidden from view.

"Is it agreed then? Fifteen minutes?"

Annetta gave Jake a nod. "Fifteen minutes."

He slowly released his hold on her.

Annetta swung her gaze to the woman, half-leaning out the window. "I'm coming up...but only on one condition."

"And that is?" The woman's features contorted into an unbecoming mask of incredulity and impatience.

"Call this man off." Annetta's gaze briefly flicked to Crawford. "Tell him to put away his gun."

"Oh, aw-right," she groused. "You heard her, Crawford."

Watching her carefully, he lowered his pistol.

"Now, git up here." Chicago Joe used her gun to motion toward the wooden steps fashioned onto the side of the building and leading up to her quarters. Drawing in a deep breath, Annetta lifted her hems and began the ascent.

As Bethany walked beside Luke to the door of Ralph Jonas's sorry excuse for a home, she prayed for wisdom in dealing with his six children. Lacey, Jesse, Nathan, Lorna, Jeb, and Michael ranged in age from thirteen to three months old. The three older ones Bethany knew from their attendance at school.

The door swung open before they reached it, and Lacey smiled a greeting. She held the baby in her arms, and a look of relief fell across her features. "Miss Stafford! Reverend Luke! Please come in."

Luke removed his hat and indicated Bethany should precede him.

She stepped into the cabin, which resembled more of a hut with walls constructed of sticks and mud. The ceiling was high to allow the heat to rise, but no platform had been built over the ground, resulting in a dirt floor. And yet Ralph Jonas's barn was the envy of Silverstone. The animals lived better than the people on this farm. Bethany hoped the man would soon build an equally adequate home for his family.

The baby began to cry. Bethany had noticed more than once that Lacey had become the mother figure now that her mama was dead. The young girl bore a great responsibility on her slender shoulders.

Bethany knew the feeling well.

"This baby's been cryin' on and off for hours, Miss Stafford." Lacey looked as though she might burst into tears herself. "I haven't slept all night."

"When did he last feed?" Bethany removed her bonnet and placed it over a wooden chair.

"Well, that's just it. He won't feed at all."

"Hmm…"

"And Pa…well, he's been hollerin' an awful lot because the baby won't quit cryin', but he's cryin' on account of Pa's hollerin'!"

"Where's your father now?"

"In the barn. Jesse and Nathan went with him." Lacey paused and looked down at the crying baby. "Pa's proud of the boys. They killed a couple of rattlers this morning."

"Snakes?" Despite the heat a cold terror made its way down her spine, spreading to her limbs. "In here?"

"Yep. They must've got under the wall or something. Nathan started hollering when he got up to milk the cows. For a while, everyone was hollerin' or screaming." She glanced at her baby brother. "Or cryin'."

Bethany turned on her heel to run but slammed right into Luke.

"Now, Beth, calm down." His hands rested on her shoulders. "Lacey said the snakes are gone."

The girl came up behind her. "Why, Miss Stafford…you ain't scared of rattlers, are you?"

"Of course she's not." Luke smiled at the girl before giving Bethany a pointed look.

She thought she understood. Revealing her fear of those venomous creatures would only burden Lacey all the more—either that or give her brothers ideas for tormenting their schoolteacher should they happen to learn the information.

Regaining her composure, Bethany faced Lacey. "I believe in maintaining a healthy respect for poisonous snakes." She took the bawling baby into her arms and tried shushing him.

Luke cleared his throat. "I reckon I'll go find Ralph and leave you and your, um, *healthy respect* to quieting that baby."

"Very funny."

Luke apparently thought so. He left the high-walled hut chuckling.

FIFTEEN

I THINK YOU'VE GOT A GOOD CASE OF GOUT."

"Gout?"

"That's right."

Annetta sat back on her haunches and peered up at Chicago Joe. Having considered the woman's pasty pallor and her notable size, Annetta determined she didn't properly care for herself. The empty whiskey flask on the table was another telltale sign. "You must stop drinking at once and begin taking walks every day—after your foot heals, of course. In the meantime I suggest a diet that includes dried cherries, apple cider vinegar, and black bean broth."

Chicago Joe's doughy face contorted. "Black bean broth?"

Annetta stood to her feet. "And soak that foot in Epsom salts. I have some at the clinic. I'll bring them to you."

"Apple cider vinegar?" An incredulous shadow crept over Chicago Joe's bland features.

"The mercantile carries it." Annetta strode to the window and peered outside. The curious spectators on the street had grown in size, both men and ladies alike. To avoid giving them the bloody scene they expected, Annetta knew she'd best leave. Fifteen minutes had nearly expired. "If that's all, I'll be on my way." She turned and regarded her patient, garbed in a revealing black and white checked housecoat. Her inflamed foot rested on a footstool.

"I trust that you will keep my ailment to yourself." Chicago Joe's dark eyes slanted in warning. "Or it'll be the last secret you share."

It took every ounce of Annetta's courage, but she refused to be cowed. "I hold my patients' conditions confidential. You have my word on it."

"Good. Because if the Winters find out I'm sick, they'll think they won. Old goats."

Folding her arms, Annetta tipped her head. "Won what?"

"The town!"

"Hmm…" So Jake had been right, not that Annetta doubted him.

"I laid claim to this land before the war and hired men to build and run my saloon. I'm in charge of the, um, *entertainment* part of business. Let's say it's my way of supporting the soldiers coming and going out of Fort Yuma. But then those church-going busybodies, Ed and Doris Winters, showed up with their people and built across the road. They had government papers and I didn't. So now they and those Bible-totin' preachers have plans to run me out of business." Chicago Joe smirked. "They sure try…except my business is booming and I've managed to pay off every Territory official that comes to close my doors." She tried to stand, winced, and sat back down. "So now you know."

"Nothing personal," Annetta retorted, "but your business sickens me."

"Good thing you're a doctor then. Heal thyself." The woman snorted.

Ignoring the blasphemous retort, Annetta surveyed the room more closely now. Chicago Joe's furnishings were, by far, the nicest she'd seen in a long while. A plush red velvet settee, matching armchair, and footstool were positioned closest to the window, and beyond them a wide bed with a thick mattress stretched out along the entire length of one wall. A silky red quilt had been heaped upon it.

She brought her gaze back to Chicago Joe. She had to muster every drop of professionalism in order to see the woman as her patient and not a harlot. "I don't care about town politics when it comes to caring for a person with a medical need."

"I'll keep that in mind."

"Please do." Annetta arched a brow. "Which is the reason I crossed the street in the first place. I wanted your...*employees* to know that if they take ill, I'm the new physician in Silverstone."

Chicago Joe sat forward. "Just watch yourself, Missy." She gave a toss of her head, and several fat curls fell from their pins. "You mind your own business, and I'll summon you if you're needed."

"I will come and go as I deem necessary. I'm a doctor."

Chicago Joe sighed. "I'll say this much for you. You've got a lot of guts."

"Take care of that foot." Annetta turned and strode from Chicago Joe's quarters. As she descended the outer stairwell, she spied Jake and Sheriff Montaño waiting at the end.

"You all right?" Concern lit Jake's brown-eyed gaze.

"I'm fine." Annetta had to admit that it felt good to have someone fret over her well-being. That hadn't happened in a long time.

"*Muy bueno.*" Sheriff Montaño removed his hat and wiped his forehead. "But you should not have gone up there on your own. Chicago Joe has a mean streak."

"I handled myself perfectly well." Annetta squared her shoulders and hoped neither man would sense how weak her knees felt.

"What did Miss Josephine want?" Jake helped her off the last step, which wasn't necessary, but she took his arm anyway.

"She had a medical question and I answered it. That's all I will say."

"Fair enough." Jake inclined his head in a way that made Annetta know he understood. After all, he kept many confidences in his job as a reverend.

His job...

Annetta felt her heart cooling. Was Jacob McCabe's concern just now how his ministry manifested? How had she started to believe his actions were personal?

The sheriff ordered the crowd to disperse, although Ed and Doris Winters sought Annetta out instead of returning to the boardinghouse.

"What happened up there?" Mr. Winters asked.

"I heard her place is a velvet den of iniquity." Mrs. Winters shaded her eyes with one hand. "Is it? What's it look like?"

Annetta shook her head. "I answered some questions. That's it. There's nothing more you need to know."

"Now, wait just a minute here. We have a right to know. Our town board brung you here from out East." Mr. Winters swung his gaze to Jake. "Ain't that right?"

Jake crossed his arms and leaned against the nearby door-frame. "It doesn't matter if the town board sponsored her or not. What goes on between Netta and her patients is nobody else's business."

Netta...he called me Netta. She'd forgotten that Gregory used that nickname also. Her gaze traveled up Jake's arm until she saw the strong set to his jaw.

"On the other hand, I know you both mean well. Your concern isn't in vain." Jake glanced at Annetta. "Ain't that right?"

"Yes." The word tumbled from her lips before she could think about it. In fact, Jake's nearness was having an all-around strange effect on her.

Jake crossed the road, tugging Annetta along with him as her hand was still hooked around his elbow. He steered her toward the clinic. When they arrived, Annetta pulled the keys from one of her skirt's deep pockets and unlocked the door. She stepped into the small reception area, feeling suddenly emotionally drained.

Jake entered and closed the door behind him. "You all right, Netta?"

She hadn't realized he'd followed her in. She considered him, tall and ruggedly handsome, standing by the doorway. "I'll be fine. Thank you for defending me. I realize it could have cost you your life."

Jake removed his hat and ran his fingers through his thick brown hair. "Praise God that Crawford wasn't trigger-happy this mornin' or else things might have gotten ugly." He moved forward, wearing a curious expression. "What possessed you to cross the street in the first place?"

"You did."

"Me?"

Annetta tipped her head and smiled. "Would you care for a cool glass of tea?"

"Sure would. Thank you." Jake moved to an armchair in the waiting area.

With her smile lingering on her lips for no good reason that she could think of, Annetta walked to the back of the clinic and stepped outside to the building's seldom-used kitchen. She'd brewed a large jar of tea yesterday in the sun. Then last night she'd allowed it to cool when the temperatures dipped, and this morning she had stuck the jar into the ground beneath the back porch, in hopes it would stay somewhat cool. Retrieving it, she decided her efforts had not been in vain.

She poured the sienna-colored liquid into two tall glasses and couldn't help thinking it matched the color of Jake McCabe's eyes. Shaking off the notion, she returned to the waiting room. She handed Jake his tea and watched as he drank most of it at one time.

"Mmm," he said, eyeing the glass. "Good tea." His gaze came to rest on her. "Now how did I influence you to cross the street this morning?"

Annetta took a long drink and then moved toward the splintery bench opposite Jake. "You said you preached to those women, and I wanted to let them know about my vocation as well. They might need me."

Jake sat forward. "Netta, promise me you won't venture over there alone in the future."

"What do you care what I do?" The ironclad wall around her heart went up.

Jake rolled his broad shoulders. "I can't give you a good reason. I just care."

"Like you care about the *soiled doves* across the street?" Annetta stood and strode to the front windows. Business up and down the street seemed back to normal.

"No, I think my caring for you is different in that you don't have family or a man looking after you."

She laughed, a bitter sound to her own ears, and whirled around to face him. "Oh, and you've appointed yourself that man?"

A look of chagrin and something else…hurt, perhaps…fell over his features. He set his glass down on a nearby table.

"I reckon I'll be on my way." Sweeping up his hat, he placed it on his head and walked to the door.

"Jake, wait." Annetta suddenly felt remorse over her harsh words. This man had not only befriended her but also saved her life.

He paused but stared at the doorknob.

"Please forgive me for being so rude. You've been more than kind, and I do appreciate it."

He sent her a weak smile. "All's forgiven." His hand turned the knob, but Annetta quickly put her body between him and the door.

"If anyone asked me who my friends are in Silverstone, I'd name you as one of them."

Jake stepped back, pursed his lips, and gave her a single nod. "That's real nice."

But there was more on Annetta's mind. "Did you mean what you said about those women across the street?"

"Remind me." Jake pulled his brows together. "What in particular did I say?"

"About them being able to go to heaven even if they're... impure?"

"Anyone can go to heaven, and we're all sinners. There's none righteous, no, not one."

"But why didn't God stop it?"

"Stop what, Netta?" He placed his hands on his hips.

For whatever crazy reason she wanted to tell him what happened to her the night Gregory was murdered, but the words wouldn't come. She'd never told anyone, not even her parents or her best friend in Parkersburg. Instead, she'd closed off her world and focused on becoming a doctor. Then she came here to escape the memories. Except they'd been haunting her of late.

"The bad things that happen to people. Why doesn't God stop them?"

"I don't know if I have a pat answer for that, although I do know God has a plan and a purpose for all His children."

"What if you're not His child? Then what?"

"There's a lot of evil in this world." Jake backed up and leaned his shoulder against the wall. "Evil men commit evil crimes. Many of those ladies across the street suffered at the hands of diabolical men who not only stole their womanhood but also decimated their self-worth until they felt so low and useless that working in a brothel seemed like their only choice of vocation."

"Yes, you've said as much earlier... and I agree." She dropped her gaze to the plank floor.

"So what's really on your mind, Netta?"

She glanced up at him, sensing his sincerity.

"Should I tell you what I think?" he asked.

"All right."

"Well..." He seemed to choose his words with care. "I sense that you've been deeply hurt. Did a man—a soldier, perhaps—harm you?"

Blood drained from her face, and a sort of chill crept over her. How had he guessed? She squeezed her eyes closed. Oh, God, she couldn't speak it. She battled the memory and steeled herself for the self-loathing that followed. "One night a renegade Confederate broke into my fiancé's home and terrorized us. Gregory was killed and...and..." Her voice broke off. "Maybe God wanted to punish me."

"No." Jake stepped forward and took her by the shoulders. He gave her a gentle shake. "Ours is a loving God. He wept with you after your fiancé died. He's been walking alongside you ever since, guiding and directing you."

"For what?" Annetta pushed out a harsh laugh. "This town?"

"For, maybe, this exact moment." Jake let his hands fall away. "How else would the Lord have gotten you to Silverstone? How else would He have caused our paths to cross?"

"Our paths?" What was the good reverend implying?

Jake straightened. "Why don't we sit down? There's something I'd like to share with you."

Annetta supposed that would be all right. She walked back to the bench, gathered her skirts, and sat. Jake claimed the armchair once more.

"I mentioned that none of us is righteous in and of ourselves. In order to spend our eternity with God we have to present ourselves as perfect to Him. But since that ain't going to happen, seeing as we're all dirt-stained from the sin of this world, God made a supernatural way for us to get washed clean, and He sacrificed His only begotten Son in order to do it.

"So Christ was born of a virgin, a miraculous birth that we

celebrate each year at Christmastime. Christ grew to become a man, and yet He was God too. Finally, He went willingly to the cross, allowed the Roman soldiers to nail His hands and feet to the wooden posts. As He hung there, God put the sin of the world on His Son's shoulders, and He bore the punishment we deserve. Christ wrestled with the devil himself for the souls of men. Then, hallelujah, He rose from the grave three days later. We celebrate that day as Easter Sunday." Jake paused. "I assume you're already familiar with much of what I've said.

Annetta rolled a shoulder. "It's not unfamiliar. When I was a child, our family attended church on a regular basis."

"Then do you know what you must do in order to be saved?"

"Live a good life. Be willing to sacrifice for others." Annetta thought she did that every day. Certainly this morning.

"Well, that's fine, but I'm afraid there's a little more to it than that." Jake scooted to the edge of his chair and folded his hands over his knees. "What I tell everyone is, you've got to confess the Lord Jesus with your mouth and believe in your heart that God raised Him from the dead."

"Believe?" She shook her head. "It's medically impossible to bring a dead man back to life."

"Ah, but it's God the Father who did the raising and God the Son who came back to life. All things are possible with God."

"I suppose…"

Annetta could concede to at least that much. She'd witnessed a few unexplainable events in medical school that had left her pondering. But she'd been stained by an evil man, and somehow she'd always felt the crime had been her fault. She should have fought harder, screamed louder.

"Oh, God…" She put her hands over her face.

Jake came to sit beside her. "He loves you so much, Netta."

The deep timbre of his voice sent a shiver down her spine. "But how—"

"Only believe it. God will do the rest, you'll see."

Moments passed in which Annetta managed to collect her wits. She could feel Jake's comforting presence beside her, but he didn't touch her—and her respect for him grew.

"And believe this too," Jake began, his voice just above a whisper. "Whatever happened that night makes no difference in your coming to Christ. You still can. In fact, that's been the plan all along. He's waiting for you to get on your knees and call out to Him. He is faithful. He'll hear you."

"But He didn't hear me that night." Her body trembled, and, oddly enough, she could hear God beckon to her. Nothing like this had ever happened to her. The pastor of her family's church would have been appalled if he understood, as Jake obviously did, what occurred the night Gregory was killed. She would have been shunned by friends and family alike.

"Netta?"

She enjoyed how the nickname rolled off Jake's tongue. She brought her gaze to his and saw earnestness in his eyes.

"It makes no difference to me either."

Her breath caught. Had she heard correctly? "What do you want from me?" Had she misjudged him?

But once again he refrained from touching her, not her hair, cheek, or hand. The nervous flutters inside Annetta's stomach quelled.

Jake pulled his gaze away and stood. "It's not what *I* want, Netta."

She supposed he'd proved that just now.

"But what the Lord wants."

"And that is?" She arched a brow.

"Your soul."

"My soul…" It seemed to have departed when bullets riddled the parlor in which she and Gregory had been sitting. Tears sprung into her eyes.

"There's still time to wrestle it back from that wily ol' devil. He's deceived you."

"What?" Suddenly Annetta recalled what she'd told Jake earlier in the week. That she'd lost her soul.

"God loves you, Dr. Cavanaugh."

She looked at Jake in time to see a very appealing grin spreading across his face.

Once more, he donned his hat before ambling to the door. "If I can be of any help where this subject is concerned, you know where to find me."

"Yes, I do."

He dipped the rim of his hat and left the clinic. After he'd closed the door, Annetta listened to the heels of his boots grow distant as he limped down the boardwalk.

It was then she finally broke down. *God, help me!* All the guilt she'd carried inside of her. All the pain. The memories, the nightmares. *God, take this away from me. Make me whole again. I believe. I believe…*

Drawing in several deep breaths, she regained her composure. It wouldn't do to have a patient enter and find her an emotional wreck, there in the reception area. She rose from the hard bench and strode to her office where she seated herself at her desk. She kept records of all the patients she saw, and Chicago Joe would be no exception.

However, concentration eluded her. Questions swirled around in her mind. Did God really have a purpose and a plan for her life? Had he really directed her journey here to Silverstone…and to a reverend named Jacob McCabe?

Then one question in particular piqued her curiosity. Why hadn't another female snatched up the handsome reverend and made a husband out of him?

Sixteen

It took Bethany nearly an hour to calm little Michael, after which he fell into a sound sleep. She hushed the other children each time they came bursting into the one-room home.

"Why do we gotta use quiet voices?" Lorna asked, doing her best to whisper.

Bethany smiled at the adorable child with strawberry blonde curls. "Your baby brother is finally fed and sleeping." Sitting at the kitchen table, Bethany cut up a freshly butchered and plucked chicken for their midday dinner.

"Can I see him?"

"No. Let him be." Bethany had placed the child in the wooden cradle near the only bed in the house. She imagined the girls shared it and the boys and their father slept in the barn. Not a safe setup for the girls and baby as far as Bethany was concerned.

"Can I hold 'im when he wakes up, Miss Stafford?"

"Shh!" Nathan commanded his little sister.

In reply, Lorna stuck out her tongue at him then buried her face in Bethany's skirt.

"Would you like to help me make dinner, sweetie?" Back home in Milwaukee, her younger sisters often enjoyed assisting Bethany in the kitchen.

Lorna shook her head and clung to Bethany, sucking her thumb. The notion that the little darling needed a mama to rock her and read to her entered Bethany's head. However, she felt confident that the role wasn't hers to accept.

Seconds later Bethany recalled Mr. Jonas's proposal. As much as she'd enjoy mothering his children, she certainly didn't relish the idea of becoming his wife. She remembered how she felt whenever Luke was near, and a dreamlike happiness made her smile right there as she cut up the chicken. But a pleasant memory soon resulted in a distasteful shudder as she imagined Mr. Jonas in a husbandly role. She was only too glad that Luke had promised to stay around all day, so Mr. Jonas wouldn't try to coerce her into marrying him again.

"Pa sure looks mad," Jesse said, staring outside. None of the windows had panes of glass, just wooden shutters that could be closed against the hot sunshine, driving rain, and dreadful dust devils. "And just listen to him layin' into Pastor Luke!"

"What's he sayin'?" Nathan came up beside his brother.

"I can't quite hear."

With Lorna still clutching her skirts, Bethany stepped to the window and looked out. Mr. Jonas seemed to be shouting about something, all right, and Luke indeed appeared to be the recipient.

"Come away from the window, children." Bethany didn't want to encourage eavesdropping. "You all can help me peel the bushel of potatoes that Luke and I brought with us today. Mr. Winters purchased an entire wagonload, and these particular potatoes are his gift to your family." She smiled. "Later I will help you all write a nice thank-you letter to Mr. Winters."

Jesse groaned but complied.

"Do you think they'll have a fist fight?" Nathan wanted to know. His gaze kept straying to the opened window.

"Of course not!" Bethany had to admit she wondered what was going on out there. Still she believed Luke wasn't a man to pull any punches. However, she didn't trust Mr. Jonas. But for the children's sakes, she added, "Christian men don't have to use their fists to solve problems. They have God."

"Yeah, you lead-head," Jesse told Nathan.

"Well, you're a—"

"Boys, I'll have none of that bickering and name-calling. Now apologize to each other and start peeling potatoes like I've asked."

"Pa calls me and Nathan lead-heads all the time. Ain't a bad thing if Pa does it. So why can't we?"

Bethany nibbled her lower lip as dismay settled around her. Hollering and name-calling from the man of the house? Mrs. Navis used to say such manners were despicable. Unfortunately they reminded Bethany of her own father. Worse, Lacey's perpetual frown only made her surer she'd done the right thing by leaving Milwaukee when the opportunity presented itself.

Nevertheless, something had to be done about Mr. Jonas's behavior.

With the chicken cut and placed in a black iron pan and the potatoes peeled, Bethany left the house for the outdoor kitchen. She instructed Nathan to look for any more rattlesnakes, and when none were discovered, she felt some of the tension leave her muscles. She fried the chicken to a golden brown perfection. Within a relatively short time, Bethany had dinner ready.

Luke and Mr. Jonas came in from outside and everyone gathered around the sturdy, rectangular table. Mr. Jonas asked Luke to say grace, and after he'd prayed over the food, the children lunged to grab their share. Bethany went around the table and served everyone a healthy portion of potatoes. As she placed a goodly dollop on Mr. Jonas's plate, she noticed the angry set to his mouth and the dark stares he sent Luke's way. He gulped down his food. He hadn't shaved in weeks, and both his scraggy beard and his hair looked filthy. Mr. Jonas's clothes were sweat-stained, and Bethany got the distinct impression he didn't like to bathe and change his clothes often.

Luke, on the other hand, seemed his light-hearted self,

obviously unaffected by whatever Mr. Jonas had been shouting at him about earlier.

"Beth, this is a mighty tasty meal."

"Thank you, Luke." The compliment pleased her, and she couldn't wait to cook for Luke after they were married.

But would they be able to settle their differences so they could wed?

The baby cried, and Mr. Jonas slammed his fist on the table. "A man can't even eat his supper..."

"I'll take care of him." Setting down the bowl of cooked potatoes, Bethany strode to the cradle and lifted the infant. Then she made her way to the rocking chair, and in only minutes Michael lay contently in her arms.

"I hope you plan on eating." Luke took a long drink of the cider they'd brought as a treat.

"I'll finish my dinner after Lacey is done. We'll take turns holding the baby."

Smiling, Luke turned to the kids. "Did you know Miss Stafford once made the most interesting baking-powder biscuits I ever did see?"

"Oh, Luke, don't tell them that story."

"Please, darlin'? It's funny."

The endearment hadn't been lost on Bethany. "All right." She smiled. It was rather amusing. "Go ahead."

"Yeah, tell us about Teacher's biscuits." Nathan clapped his hands.

"We like stories," five-year-old Lorna declared.

By contrast, Mr. Jonas threw his fork down onto his now-empty plate and slid back the chair. The children cowered while Bethany and Luke exchanged troubled glances.

"Now, Ralph, don't go stormin' out of here. Aren't you going to stay and listen to this funny tale?" Luke grinned. "I believe it'll even have you smiling."

"No, Preacher, I don't want to hear nothing you have to say." With that, he left the cabin, slamming the ramshackle door behind him.

Baby Michael began to cry again.

"There, there, sweetheart," Bethany crooned until he hushed. She noticed too that with their father gone, the other children relaxed.

"Tell us the funny story, Reverend Luke," Lacey insisted.

"All right." His smile widened and he rubbed his palms together. "Well, in order to get here, to Arizona, we joined up with a big wagon train that started off way back in Missouri. While Miss Stafford and I were traveling, she and a nice German lady named Mrs. Schlyterhaus shared the cooking responsibilities.

"So one evening," he said, his blue eyes twinkling, "I had my mouth all set for some good ol' hot biscuits...you know, the kind that melt in your mouth?"

Already the children bobbed their heads with eyes wide and curious.

"But what do you suppose happens when I bite into one of Miss Stafford's creations?"

"What?" several of them cried in unison.

Bethany laughed to herself.

"It don't let go!" Luke replied dramatically. "My biscuit stretched like gum, longer and longer, then it snapped right back in my face."

Lacey put her hand over her mouth and giggled.

"Did you finally eat it?" Nathan asked as a lock of his mud-brown hair fell over his forehead.

"No, sir. It didn't want to get ate. But it wasn't long till I discovered those biscuits had some bounce, and pretty soon me and some other fellas were tossing them at each other."

"A ball game? With biscuits?" Jesse laughed, and the other children hooted, adding their own silly remarks.

"Well, here's the best part. I got friendly with those boys and told them about Jesus. Three of them prayed and asked the Lord into their hearts that very night."

"Did you hear the angels rejoicing in heaven?" Nathan sat up straighter in his chair.

Bethany was impressed. The boy must be paying attention in school. When Bethany taught reading and writing, she often used the Bible. They followed along while she read Old Testament stories such as David and Goliath or the New Testament Gospels, and then they practiced penmanship by copying verses from God's Word. In addition, every Wednesday Luke taught them for an hour and emphasized morals and principles. It warmed Bethany's heart to see at least one of her pupils responding.

"Angels?" Luke made like he had to think it over. "You know, I believe I did hear their heavenly chorus. What about you, Miss Stafford?" He looked her way. "Did you hear the angels after the boys got saved?"

"No." She shook her head. "All I heard was Mrs. Schlyterhaus muttering about my ruining a batch of perfectly good biscuits. I never did figure out what happened."

"I know." Jesse pushed his shoulders back. "The angels got into your recipe when you weren't looking so Pastor Luke could have a ball game and tell those boys about Jesus."

Bethany stood in a moment's stunned silence. Jesse Jonas paid attention too! *Thank You, Lord. My teaching is making a difference!*

"You know, Jesse," Luke said, "you make a good point. One never knows how God might use His angels."

By now the baby had fallen asleep, so Bethany carefully set him into his cradle. Next she dished up a plate of food for herself and ate while the jovial table conversation continued. Once supper ended, Bethany cleared the wooden plates and utensils, enlisting the girls' help with their washing. Luke lifted little Jeb onto his shoulders as he, Nathan, and Jesse ambled outside to find some work to finish before he and Bethany took their leave.

"I like Pastor Luke," Lorna said as they washed the dishes.

"Yes, I like him quite well myself." In fact she loved him. But in spite of the enjoyable dinner with the children, Bethany still smarted over Luke's ultimatum.

But wasn't that the same thing she'd offered him? Marriage based on a contingency?

She thought on it until the dishes were done. After that Bethany and the girls began gathering soiled laundry. With Lorna attached to Bethany's skirt, she marched into the yard with the dirty clothes. Bethany and Lacey scrubbed the clothes thoroughly in the washtub, and with the help of a stool Lorna hung them out to dry. As the last of it was fastened to the line, baby Michael's cries could be heard from inside the cabin.

"Good timing, girls." Bethany dried her hands on her skirt, since she couldn't find a clean apron. "Michael is due for his feeding."

Turning, she took several steps forward, but halted when she saw the figure of a man in a deerskin tunic, pants, and moccasins standing in the shadows under a tree. His face was coppery, and his long black hair hung past his shoulders. In one of his hands, a knife's blade glinted dangerously against a slim ray of sunshine, streaming through the treetop.

"Luke!" Bethany screamed, shoving the girls behind her. "Luke, come quick!"

Luke heard Bethany scream, and his heart fell to his toes. He dropped the harness he'd been trying to repair and sprinted from the barn. Jonas trailed him, rifle in hand. As he came around the house, he spied an Indian brave who wielded a knife in his hand.

"Aw, it's just you, Warring Spirit," Jonas muttered irritably.

Luke grinned. "Warring Spirit?" He squinted. Sure enough.

A flash of recognition entered the brave's dark eyes. "Preacher Luke McCabe." He nodded, albeit warily.

"You know him, Luke?" Beth stood close to him, her gray eyes wide with a mix of fear and surprise.

"I met Warring Spirit last week over at Harlan's place."

"Oh…yes, now I remember you telling me about it in the schoolhouse."

Jonas spoke with the Indian in a language Luke wasn't familiar with. He watched with interest. What Jonas couldn't communicate in the brave's native tongue, he signed by using demonstrative gestures.

At last, the Indian chuckled.

"What did you tell him?" Luke set his hand on Beth's shoulder. He couldn't help enjoying the way she ran to him for protection. And he was more than happy to oblige her.

"I done told him to quit scaring the churchwomen who come out here to cook and care for my children. Warring Spirit thinks it's funny."

Beth clucked her tongue in annoyance as Michael's cries grew more demanding. "The baby…"

"Go on, take care of him," Jonas barked while he disarmed his weapon.

Beth glanced at Luke. "I'll thank you to watch your tone, Ralph." He and Jonas had shared words earlier, and Luke wasn't above taking Beth home right now, leaving the man to care for his own family—as he should. Still, he understood why Jonas felt overwhelmed. Luke squeezed Beth's shoulder. She turned and strode to the ill-constructed cabin where the baby boy's wails seemed to fill the space around them. Then came the collective sigh when the infant quieted.

"Your woman, Preacher Luke McCabe?" Warring Spirit walked toward him.

"She sure is." When the brave reached him, Luke held out his right hand.

Warring Spirit took it. "Peace."

Luke nodded. "Peace."

Bethany quelled her racing heart. She'd never seen an Indian brave up close. He'd scared the daylights out of her. She thanked God that Warring Spirit had come alone and that he meant no harm.

She fetched Michael and held him in her arms. The baby's face was red and blotchy from weeping. Walking back to the doorway, Bethany called for Lacey to fetch some milk.

"There, there, now." Bethany rocked him. "You'll get fed. I promise."

Standing near the doorway, she watched the men converse. She admired Luke's intent expression and his easy stance. He never seemed afraid of confrontation or meeting someone new, and snakes were simply a mild concern for him. But to Bethany this rugged world of poisonous creatures and painted braves was a far cry from the simple farm life she'd known in Wisconsin. Why couldn't Luke understand? And if he truly loved her, wouldn't he agree to make their home in Jericho Junction?

Lacey returned with a pail of milk. "I'm going back to the yard. I like it when Warring Spirit comes. He brings us gifts sometimes. Once he gave Jesse a whistle, and he showed me how to make a piece of jewelry with colored beads."

"Is that so?" Bethany was amazed that the fierce-looking man acted kindly to the children. On the trail she'd heard horror stories about Indian attacks. "All right. Let me make up some food for Michael, and then you can go and enjoy some free time."

"Thank you, Miss Stafford."

Handing off the baby to Lacey, Bethany stepped from the cabin to the outdoor kitchen. She lit the stove and then made up a fresh batch of infant pap, adding fresh milk to a tiny bit of flour along with a pinch of sugar. When the formula bubbled, Bethany removed it from the flame and allowed it to cool enough so she could pour a portion into a small glass bottle. A tin pap feeder fit inside the bottle. Then she reentered the hut and collected Michael from Lacey's arms.

"All right, you're free to go. This might be your last chance to have time for yourself for a while since Luke and I will be heading back to town soon."

"I wish you didn't have to go."

"But I must."

Lacey's smile waned slightly as she left the cabin, and Bethany's heart went out to the girl. Would it help if she told Lacey that she sympathized? And yet, Bethany's home in Milwaukee had been luxurious compared to this hovel.

Sitting in a rickety armchair, Bethany began to feed Michael. The sound of children's excited voices wafted in from outdoors, and she allowed herself to enjoy the feel of a baby in her arms. Soon, however, she started missing her siblings and hoped her father refrained from mistreating them. Her reminiscing then unfolded into thoughts of bearing her own children—Luke's children—and the idea was not at all unpleasant. But how could she think of children when she and Luke couldn't agree on marital basics, like where to live?

Bethany gazed at Michael, now sleeping angelically. Standing, she carefully made her way toward the baby's cradle when Ralph burst into the cabin with as much tact as a freight train.

She silenced him with a wide-eyed look filled with warning.

"Beg yer pardon." He spoke in hushed tones. "I know women get waspish when us men wake the babies. I'll keep quiet."

Quite the turnabout. "You're very wise, Mr. Jonas."

The baby whimpered.

Bethany sighed. "Only you're too late."

"Huh? Oh…"

He crossed the cabin and peered at his son. Bethany watched him, wondering if Mr. Jonas blamed the infant for his wife's death. Or perhaps he blamed himself. Regardless, the bland expression on the man's face masked whatever he felt inside.

"He's got blue eyes," he finally muttered.

"Excuse me?"

"That boy… he's the only one of my brood that's got blue eyes. Lacey told me that. Rest of them's got brown eyes like me."

Bethany looked down at the baby, resting contentedly in her arms. His eyes were definitely blue. Back to Mr. Jonas, she asked, "Were your wife's eyes this color?"

"Must've been."

"You mean you're not sure?"

"Aw, now, Miss Stafford, don't use that sharp tone on me. It's been a long time since I stared into a woman's eyes, even if she was my wife. A man gets busy, you know?"

Bethany swallowed a retort, feeling appalled, but too flustered by the topic to call the man on it. However, it seemed to her that if he'd taken time to marry his wife and beget children, he ought to at least know the color of their mama's eyes.

Turning her attention to the baby once more, she smiled at him lovingly. Such a dear little thing. He gurgled softly as if trying to communicate, and then the most amazing thing happened. Michael's gaze seemed to penetrate her own. She'd never had an infant look at her quite so intensely, and in that very moment, something stirred deeply within Bethany's soul. It was as if her spirit reached out and touched the child's as only a mother's can do.

This is my baby.

She shook off the notion just as it took form. Of course Michael was not hers—he belonged to Ralph Jonas. Yet, an inner prompting, subtle and undefined, seemed to be telling her the contrary.

My baby. My baby.

No, he's not!

"That boy sure is fond of you," Mr. Jonas observed. He stood close to her ear, and his warm breath caused her to shudder in mild revulsion. "Fact is, my children like you best out of all the other churchwomen who come." He lowered his voice, adding, "So do I."

Unnerved, Bethany quickly placed Michael in his cradle. "Luke will want to leave soon..."

She hurried out of the cabin, praying Ralph Jonas wouldn't follow her.

Several hours later, Bethany felt more than glad when Luke assisted her into the wagon and drove off the Jonas's property. Almost immediately, she recounted the experience involving Michael.

"I've never had anything happen to me quite like it," she told Luke, who listened quietly beside her. "It seemed like a premonition, a whisper from heaven, telling me Michael is going to be my baby—I would be his mother. But if that's true..."

"Now, Beth, don't go reading so much into the feeling. I remember Valerie saying something similar whenever she held Leah's kids." Reins in hand, he gazed off in the distance, looking pensive. The evening sun began its descent in the western sky. Hues of pink, violet, red, and orange were painted across the horizon. "Women are supposed to have that certain longing concerning children. If they didn't, the human race would be in a heap of trouble."

Bethany laughed softly at his response. "I guess you're right." She felt her smile shrink. "It just...well, I felt confused." She couldn't even speak her fear that perhaps the Lord willed for her to marry Ralph Jonas for the sake of his children. "Luke, how does a woman discern what is the will of God?"

"Through prayer, Bible reading, and the prompting of the Holy Spirit."

Her conscience pricked. She hadn't been very faithful in communing with the Lord. "Maybe I won't make such a good pastor's wife."

"I tell you a secret." Luke leaned toward her and gave her shoulder a playful bump. "Most times I don't think I make such a good pastor."

"But that's not true. You preach with conviction. You try to live out what you believe."

"All right." He chuckled. "I reckon I could say the same about you."

Bethany sighed.

"Beth, don't doubt yourself, especially when you're tired. You worked hard today."

"You're saying my mind is playing tricks on me?"

"I'm saying don't rush headlong into any decision based on some kind of feeling you got while holding a baby."

His words made sense. "But it seemed so real, Luke."

"I'm sure it did."

Bethany chewed her lower lip in consternation. "Have you ever experienced anything similar to what I described?"

"All the time."

She brightened. "Really?"

"Mmm-hmm. God's Holy Spirit prompts every Christian, but we've got to make sure we're not adding human sensibilities to the Lord's direction for our lives."

"And you think I am?"

"We-ell," he drawled with a smile in his voice, "it's been my experience that women plus babies equals a whole lot of emotion."

He chuckled. "I remember when Leah had her youngest. She, Ma, Sarah, and Valerie were gigglin' and cryin'." Another laugh. "Us boys just stayed out of their way."

Bethany grinned and imagined the scene in detail. Inwardly, she admitted there was a good amount of truth to Luke's babies-and-women-equaled-emotion statement.

"And don't forget," Luke added. "God is not the author of confusion but of peace."

She recognized the scriptural paraphrase. "That's true." Bethany didn't add that she had no peace about remaining here in Silverstone—which made her earlier prompting even more bizarre. Marrying Ralph Jonas was a life sentence to hard labor in poor living conditions here in the Territory. And marrying Luke…

The very thought sent liquid warmth through her veins. A longing she'd never experienced before caused her to touch his hand.

Luke gave her a sideways glance. "If you're tired, you can put your head on my shoulder."

"I'd like that."

He replied with a smile.

Slipping her arm around his, she leaned her temple against his muscled arm. She didn't sit tall enough to reach his shoulder.

As the wagon bumped along, Bethany reveled in these few quiet moments with Luke. She wanted to marry him and be his wife. A good wife.

She gazed upward and surreptitiously admired his rugged features against the backdrop of the setting sun. In an instant, she knew Luke belonged here in this wild Territory. She had, of course, suspected that truth all along. Now she felt certain of it.

Her heart sank. Luke belonged, but she didn't. And yet she loved Luke. How could such a great divide ever be bridged?

Seventeen

Dusk had settled over the town when Luke pulled the wagon to a halt near the cabin he shared with Jake. He'd already let Bethany off in front of the boardinghouse.

He smiled as he jumped from the wagon, remembering how she'd snuggled up against him on the road home. He enjoyed the feeling of her close beside him and hoped their wedding day would come sooner rather than later. There was no doubt in his mind that Beth loved him. They'd be happy together…here in Silverstone.

Jake appeared at the doorway.

"Got that cabin of yours built yet?" Luke grinned.

Hanging his head back, Jake chuckled. "Are you kidding? I barely had a few hours to work on it today."

Disappointment enveloped Luke. "How come?"

"Let me help you with the horses and we'll talk."

That was Luke's first clue that something significant took place.

"How's the Jonas family?"

"'Bout the same." Luke peered at his brother over the neck of the tall, black gelding. "Except Ralph threatened me."

"How so?"

"He said he's going to do his best to win Beth over. Said he prayed about it, and he's certain she's supposed to be his children's new ma."

"Well, then, one of you ain't hearin' God's voice," Jake quipped. "You can't both marry Beth."

"Go on." Waving off Jake's remark, Luke led his horse to the public stables behind their cabin. For the most part Ed Winters had built the large barn, but Jake had lent a hand, which was likely why the roof hadn't blown off yet.

"What are you worried about, Luke? Beth accepted your marriage proposal now, didn't she?"

"I don't like the way Jonas plays with her mind. All her life, Beth took care of her brothers and sisters. Jonas likes to wield the guilt and make her feel like she ought to be caring for his young'uns in the same fashion."

"Well, it might work for, say…a half hour. But the fact is Beth loves you."

"Yeah?" Luke couldn't help but smile.

Jake's laugh wafted over from the next stall. "I'm sure you'll hear from her pa anytime now. I believe he'll give his blessing."

"No doubt."

Luke met Beth's father over a year ago, and they'd been friendly enough. After all, the older man had entrusted Beth's care to him and Jake. But Luke did wonder why she didn't mention her family too often. Never even wrote to them as far as he knew. On the other hand, she enjoyed conversing about the McCabes back in Jericho Junction.

Which brought up another set of issues.

"I told Beth that I planned to stay here in Silverstone—we can get married in Jericho Junction, but I'm aiming to turn around and come right back here. So I told her that if she's going to be my wife, Silverstone will be our home."

"What'd she say to that?" Jake peered at him over the top plank of the stall.

"Beth wants to stay in Jericho Junction."

"Uh-oh."

"I'm inclined to agree with your reaction, brother. We've got ourselves a situation."

"Well…" Jake moved around the second horse and stretched. "Unless Jonas promised Beth the moon, I'd say you've still got the upper hand."

Luke reckoned he was right.

"Of course, she could always stay engaged to you until spring-time in order to quell the gossips and then break things off with you once she's safely back in Jericho Junction."

That's the very thing Luke worried about. "Think she'd really do that?"

"You didn't give her much choice."

Jake walked out of the barn, and Luke trailed him. Maybe he'd backed Beth into a corner. Regrettable, seeing as he'd just meant to be honest.

"If I heard right, Beth wants to get married in Jericho Junction."

"Yep. But I'm afraid if that happens, she'll never leave there. And, Jake, this is where my home is."

They continued up the path to their cabin.

"Let's face it, Luke; you could settle anywhere and be happy. I don't know why you're being so stubborn about this."

"So you're taking Beth's side."

"Yep."

Luke's jaw tensed while Jake lit a lantern. He set it down in the middle of the table. The wooden shutters on every window had been pulled back, allowing cool evening breezes to drift on in.

"Look, you refuse to carry a weapon, and that concerns most everyone around here," Jake said. "It's only a matter of time before you'll have to face a barrel of a gun."

"And how's wearing one on my hip gonna save me?" he retorted. He thought of Warring Spirit and how the brave had lowered his weapon when he learned Luke was unarmed. "God is the owner of life and death."

"I agree. And I gotta admit my gun didn't do me any favors today."

"What?" The comment got Luke's attention.

"Oh, yeah." Pulling out a chair, Jake sat down at the table. He gave a habitual wince until he straightened out his bad leg. "I had a run-in with Miss Josephine and her hired man, Dirk Crawford."

Luke raised his brows, surprised.

"Both threatened to kill me on account of one Dr. Annetta Cavanaugh."

"You don't say?"

"Say." A hint of a grin split Jake's shadowed jaw. "Have a seat, and I'll tell you all about it."

Luke drank down his second cup of coffee as Jake recounted the last of his tale. "So what did Chicago Joe want with Annetta?"

"Netta wouldn't give any details."

"I reckon it's a private matter between a doctor and her patient."

"You got it."

Luke nodded. More than an hour had passed, in which time Jake had made a fire in the hearth for some warmth. It seemed an irony, given the heat of the day. But at this time of year temperatures plummeted once the sun set. "So then what happened?"

"I saw her safely back to her office."

Luke frowned. "But that all took maybe half a day. Where'd your afternoon go?"

"It went to giving explanations to passersby—and I'm talking most of Silverstone."

"Ooh." Luke winced.

Jake deciphered his expression. "Right. Tongues were waggin' to be sure!" He sighed. "I took it upon myself to set the record straight."

"Good for you."

"So I didn't get much work done."

"Bad for me."

Jake sent him a quick glare.

"Look, I want to marry Beth. Once she starts measuring the windows for curtains, she'll be happy. Trust me."

"You know what your problem is? You're too self-confident, Luke."

A retort formed, but before he could speak it, a knock sounded at the front door.

"More curious townsfolk," Jake muttered as he strode across the cabin. Lifting the latch, he pulled the door open. Then he pulled back slightly. "Annetta."

Luke stood, stepped into the shadows, and tucked his shirt back in.

"What brings you out this time of night?"

She stepped inside, and Luke spied the heavy basket she carried. Gentleman that he was, Jake quickly took it from her.

"One kind act deserves another," she said rather crisply. "When you didn't show up at the boardinghouse for supper—"

"Aw, I forgot." Jake rubbed the back of his neck with his free hand.

"I asked Rosalinda to pack some food for you."

"Mighty kind of you, Netta. Please come in."

"No, I can't stay."

"Just for a few minutes."

"Well…"

Luke observed the way Annetta gazed up at Jake, all starry-eyed. It could only mean one thing. Luke grinned. She was sweet on him.

Just as quickly, Luke wiped the smile off his face, although it was kind of funny how she hadn't even noticed him yet.

"Annetta, I'm sorry." Jake made quick strides to the table and set down the basket. "I lost track of the time."

She jerked her chin.

"Forgive me."

Luke lowered his head and swallowed a chuckle. It wasn't every day he got to watch his older brother eat some humble pie.

"I'm glad you came by." Jake took her elbow and urged her farther into the cabin.

And that's when Annetta saw him. "Luke." Her cheeks turned a pretty pink. "I–I didn't see you standing there."

"Good evening, Annetta."

She gave him a smile before looking back at Jake.

"He's the reason I didn't meet you at the boardinghouse tonight." He glanced at Luke with a glint of amusement in his eyes.

Luke wasn't about to let Jake's blunder go. "Oh, no, don't you go blaming me for your forgetfulness." He leaned toward Annetta. "I think he needs some sort of mental testing, Doctor."

"Hmm, perhaps so." Annetta folded her arms.

Chuckling, Jake poked around in the basket. "Smells good."

"See how he flits from subject to subject?" Luke persisted with a laugh.

"Well, now, I do indeed." Tipping her head, Annetta studied him like a specimen.

"All right, you two. I surrender." Jake turned to Annetta. "On a serious note, please accept my apology for not meeting you at the boardinghouse this evening."

"But note that it will happen again," Luke interjected. "On account of his mental status."

"Will you keep quiet?"

Luke swallowed a chuckle.

Jake narrowed his gaze. "Don't you have something to do?"

"Not particularly."

Annetta seemed to ignore the banter. "I told you I had something to give you, Jake." She lifted a flask from the basket. "Just a few drops of this in a glass of water might ease the pain you have in your leg, assuming it keeps you up at night from time to time."

"He'd never admit it," Luke said in all honesty, "but that leg keeps him awake plenty of nights."

Jake sent him a sharp glance.

"Then this should help." She held the brown glass bottle out to him.

"I'm not a drinking man, Netta, but thanks all the same."

"Oh, it's not whiskey or anything of the sort." Annetta smiled patiently. "It's quinine."

"Quinine?" Surprise lifted Jake's features. "Isn't that for malaria?"

"Yes, but some people find it's an effective pain reliever. Try it." Annetta dug into the basket and retrieved a jar of tea. "Here, we'll mix it in with tea." She opened the flask and expertly poured out only a few drops into the jar, before lifting it and swirling the liquid around. "All right." She handed it to Jake. "Drink up."

He hesitated, and Luke grinned. "You scared?"

"Scared of what?" After a quelling look in Luke's direction, Jake opened the jar and swigged the tea down in about five gulps. Then he wiped the corners of his mouth with the cuff of his sleeve. "Reckon I was thirsty." He suddenly winced. "Ugh, that was some of the bitterest tea I ever tasted."

Luke stomped his booted foot and laughed at his brother's expression.

Annetta smiled. "I'm afraid the quinine tastes terrible. But you did the right thing by swallowing it all at once."

He shrugged, still wincing. "I was more thirsty than I realized."

Annetta gazed at him. "Now we'll just have to see if the quinine helps your leg."

Jake pursed his mouth, looking none too impressed.

"Well, enjoy your meal." Annetta pulled her shawl more tightly around her shoulders.

"You're welcome to join us."

"I can't really, although..." Her gaze searched Jake's. "I have a favor to ask of you."

"Name it." Jake set his hands on his hips.

"I need to ride out to the Jenkins' place tomorrow. Calvin Jenkins was in town, buying supplies earlier, and left a message for me with the Winters, requesting that I come out to the ranch and bring some medicine for a persistent fever that his father's had for more than a week. It's nothing urgent. Tomorrow will be soon enough. But I can't ride out there alone. I need a guide. Can you accompany me?"

"I'd like to, Netta, but I ride a circuit every Sunday while Luke does the preaching at our church here in Silverstone."

"May I ride with you?"

Stunned, Luke's hand paused in midair near the basket of food.

"You want to accompany me on the circuit?"

"Well, only if we can fit in a visit to the Jenkins' place."

"I imagine we could, although..." Jake grinned and shook his head. "I don't think you'd find riding my circuit very exciting. Two church services and a hard ride in between 'em. Besides, you'd have to suffer through my preaching twice—same message too."

"I suppose that won't kill me." A glimmer of amusement lit her gaze. "And I can assure you I'll keep up. I'm not a bad horsewoman."

Luke rubbed the side of jaw, hiding his amusement and trying to guess how Jake would respond next.

Jake took several moments to think it over. "Well, it's fine by me. But I leave at dawn."

"I'll be ready." Annetta smiled and gave Jake another of those starry-eyed looks.

Mmm-hmm, she's sweet on him, all right. Luke chuckled under his breath.

"I'll bring the horses around and meet you in front of your clinic."

Luke glanced at his brother. And the way Jake looked back at her made him think Jake might be sweet on her too.

Annetta left and Jake watched her go for several long minutes. Then he closed the front door of the cabin, latching it securely.

"You know what you just did?" Luke sent him a look as he unpacked the basket. His stomach rumbled in hunger at the smell of enchiladas and salad. "You just agreed to let a woman ride the circuit with you tomorrow."

"I reckon I did—but for a good cause. Ol' Mr. Jenkins is ill again." He sauntered over to the table and lifted the jar from which he'd drunk the tea.

"Annetta could find another respectable man to accompany her to the Jenkins' ranch."

"I know." A speculative light entered his gaze "Must've been that potion she gave me."

Luke replied with a hearty laugh. "Must've been." However, he knew better.

EIGHTEEN

THE AIR WAS STILL, THE STREET QUIET. ONLY BETHANY'S booted heels thumped along the boardwalk. Very typical for a Sunday morning in Silverstone. The south side of the street hadn't yet awakened from all their carrying-on last night. Bethany sent a glance that way and hoped Angie was all right. She felt burdened for her and prayed that soon Angie would somehow escape from a lifestyle of prostitution and abuse.

Gravel crunched as a carriage rolled up the street. Bethany looked to see the Phillips family. They waved as they passed. Bethany quickened her steps so she wouldn't be late.

Self-consciousness gave her stomach a tweak with each step she took. Last night Mrs. Winters had caught sight of how long Bethany's hair had grown, and for whatever reason, Bethany allowed her to trim several inches off the bottom. But the trim turned into a noticeable cut!

At first Bethany felt ill when she glimpsed her hair, now only as long as her shoulder blades. While still in shock, she allowed Mrs. Winters to roll her hair, and this morning Trudy persuaded her to wear curled tendrils around her face. The back was pinned up in a loose chignon.

"You're beautiful!" Trudy had exclaimed with a gasp.

Was that surprise?

But it was true. The looking glass didn't lie. Bethany actually looked...*pretty.*

She fingered a curl hanging loosely below her bonnet. What would Luke think? Papa hadn't liked it when she tried to wear her hair like other young ladies, curled and hanging freely. Perhaps if she had, she wouldn't fit his description of her. *Plain as a field mouse.*

She pressed her lips together in an angry frown. If he hadn't worked her like a farmhand, and if she'd been allowed to eat a supper without one of her younger siblings interrupting with a demand that needed attention…and if he'd given permission for her to wear her hair down, then maybe…

Bethany shook herself and drew in a deep, cleansing breath. She'd do better not to think about Papa as she walked into church.

She climbed the few stairs that led into a narrow vestibule. Wooden pegs lined one wall for coats. Bethany wondered if people in Silverstone ever used wraps enough to have to hang them up. It was shaping up to be another hot, sunny day.

As she walked up the aisle she greeted the Thomas family then Mr. and Mrs. Stack before claiming a place on the front row bench. The Mendez family sat beside her, and little Augustina leaned forward and gave her a vigorous wave. The seven-year-old attended school, and Bethany couldn't help but feel fond of her. Intelligence pooled in those deep brown eyes; Augustina loved to learn new things. Smiling at her now, Bethany lifted a gloved hand in greeting.

Mr. Winters soon made his way to the altar and led the congregation in singing "When I Survey the Wondrous Cross." Several attendees didn't know the Isaac Watts hymn, but Bethany could hear Augustina singing it out loudly. Bethany had taught it to the children in school.

Luke had been sitting off to the side and now strode to the podium, which Jake had built. It wasn't fancy, but Bethany had always admired its solid craftsmanship.

Then suddenly Luke's gaze met Bethany's. She held her breath. Would he notice the curls framing her face?

He gave her what appeared to be an affectionate smile before flipping open his Bible.

Bethany exhaled in relief. But then again, she may not look so different with her bonnet still covering her head.

"I'd like to begin by reading the Scriptures."

Bethany stood, as did the rest of the congregation.

"St. Matthew chapter twenty-two, verses thirty-seven through thirty-nine." Luke cleared his throat. "Jesus said unto him, Thou shalt love the Lord thy God with all thy heart, and with all thy soul, and with all thy mind. This is the first and great commandment. And the second is like unto it, Thou shalt love thy neighbour as thyself." He paused. "Let me ask y'all. Do you love yourselves?" He grinned. "Oh, now, I don't mean love yourself like someone vain, who thinks he's the handsomest thing that ever walked the earth. And not like a one who believes he's above reproach. I mean love…as in respect of ourselves. All humans are created in the image of God. What's not to respect?"

Bethany dropped her gaze and stared at her folded hands. She continued to listen intently.

"And if we respect ourselves, we're going to respect our neighbors, aren't we? Our neighbors include folks of all skin colors. That means we're not liable to draw on a man if he ain't armed," Luke drawled. "We're not liable to stir up trouble just because we can, and we're not about to shred someone's character just for the sake of spreading a little gossip."

In her peripheral view, Bethany glimpsed a heavy-set woman shifting uncomfortably.

Then Luke went on to say that if men and women loved themselves as God loved them, there'd be less hatred in the world.

"So let's leave here this morning with a little more love for ourselves and for one another, shall we?" Luke smiled. "Let's pray…Mr. Watson? Please stand and close our service."

As the gentleman prayed, Bethany glimpsed Luke making his

way down the aisle to personally greet his small congregation as they left the church. At the final "Amen," people filed out into the center aisle. Since Bethany sat in the front bench, she was one of the last to go.

"Will you look at that?" Mrs. Mendez took hold of Bethany's arm. "Why, that family…up against the back wall. How rude!"

Bethany followed the rotund, dark-haired woman's gaze and saw the Jonas family fast asleep. She inched forward, getting a closer look, and noticed that Mr. Jonas had shaved his beard. His shaggy light brown hair looked washed, his clothes were clean, and his children looked sufficiently bathed as well.

Then she saw little Michael, slipping ever so slowly out of Lacey's grasp. She apologetically brushed passed Mrs. Mendez and gently lifted the baby from out of his sister's tentative hold. Lacey opened her eyes, smiled at Bethany, and closed them again.

"That baby kept us up all night," she murmured drowsily.

"Well, it's all right. I've got him now." Bethany gazed at the child, sleeping in her arms, and again that strange feeling came over her. She found herself actually wishing Michael belonged to her.

In fact, she wished all these children were hers.

She peeked at Mr. Jonas from beneath lowered lashes. But that would mean marrying their father.

No! No! No!

Same as yesterday, the thought of becoming Mrs. Ralph Jonas left an indescribable hollowness inside of Bethany. But when she gazed at Luke, standing so tall and confident near the doorway now, a multitude of different emotions assailed her…

Like love.

"Sorry, baby," she whispered, kissing Michael's cheek, "I can't be your mama." She gazed at him, noting the soft lashes fluttering against pale cheeks, the perfectly tiny nose, and the wet rosebud lips. She decided Luke had been right. She was being overly emotional, although this boy had certainly captured a part of her heart.

Bethany held him until the last of the church members had exited. Once they'd gone, Luke made his way back up the aisle to her, and she handed off the baby to Lacey.

Luke reached her and smiled.

She smiled back.

"You look right pretty today, Beth."

Bethany felt her cheeks warm. "Not now, Luke." Her gaze flitted to Lacey before she looked back at him.

Donning a more serious expression, he turned his attention to the dozing Jonas clan. He shook his head. "It's a sad thing to see what my preaching does to some folks."

Bethany smiled. "Yes, well, you'll be pleased to know your message didn't put me to sleep."

"Why, thank you, Beth." His gaze met hers, and tenderness pooled in his eyes. "We've been invited to the Raddisons' for noon dinner. What do you suppose we ought to do with Ralph and his kids?"

Before Bethany could reply, little Jeb opened an eye. "Dinner? I'm sure hungry." He stretched like a cub.

Jesse was the next to awaken. "Is service over? Oh...hello, Reverend Luke."

Luke nodded a greeting, and Bethany could tell he was trying to hide his amusement.

"Pa, wake up. Church meetin' is over."

At Jesse's prompting, Mr. Jonas roused and muttered a series of apologies. Then he awakened the rest of his children. Standing, he turned his attention to Bethany. She averted her eyes, not wanting to meet his probing gaze.

"All's forgiven, Jonas," Luke said. "Why don't you take your family to the boardinghouse for a noon dinner?"

"I ain't got money for that."

"Jake and I will take care of the tab." Luke held up a hand to forestall an argument. "Meanwhile, there are plenty of women at the Winterses' place to help with the little ones. You and your family could obviously use the respite."

"Reckon that's all right." Mr. Jonas grumbled the reply. "Will you be comin' too, Miss Stafford?"

"No, I'm afraid not." She glanced at Luke. The muscle in his jaw worked as he set his hands on his hips.

"That's a shame. I know my young'uns will be sorry you're not at the table with them."

Luke began to reply, but Mr. Jonas cut him off.

"And that baby...well, he sure has taken to you."

The remark gave Bethany's heartstrings a good tug.

"That's enough, Jonas."

"Oh, now, Preacher, I don't mean nothin' by it." His voice took on an unnatural, sugary tone. "But I did wonder, Miss Stafford"—his gaze fixed on Bethany again—"if you'd mind takin' the baby with you this afternoon. That'll be a huge burden lifted."

"Yes, I suppose I can do that." Beside her, she heard Luke draw in a deep breath. She glanced at him. "That's all right, isn't it, Luke? The Raddisons are a young couple. I'm sure they're fond of babies."

Luke folded his arms. After giving Mr. Jonas a hard stare, he looked at Bethany and his features softened. "I'm sure it's fine, Beth."

"Well, much obliged." Mr. Jonas started making his way out of the church. His children following like eager ducklings. Lacey paused only long enough to give Michael back to Bethany.

Bethany watched the clan leave. But then Mr. Jonas stopped short and came back, standing in front of Luke.

"Preacher, I reckon I owe you an apology for my rude behavior yesterday. Truth is, I've been an ill-tempered man on account of my wife's untimely passing. I know that ain't much excuse for bad manners." He paused and wetted his lips. "You've been nothing but kind to me and my young'uns, and I'm grateful to you in that regard."

"Well…" Luke seemed taken by surprise. "Apology accepted."

"Good." Mr. Jonas nodded, but then he eyed Luke like a man picking a fight. "But I've got to add this. I meant what I told you. It ain't no idle threat."

Luke pursed his lips in casual reply. Bethany watched in a mixture of curiosity and fear as the two men stared long and hard at each other. Contention crackled in the air between them. However, where Mr. Jonas glowered, Luke's expression remained calm.

Bethany's protective hold on Michael tightened.

Mr. Jonas's focus suddenly swung to Bethany. He produced a quick smile. "Have a nice afternoon, Miss Stafford."

"I will," she breathed in relief. "Thank you."

Once he'd left, his children with him, all except Michael, Bethany turned to Luke. "What was that all about?"

"Aw, nothin'."

"Luke?"

He tore his gaze away from Ralph Jonas's retreating form and smiled into her eyes. "Nothing you need to worry your pretty head over. Now let's get on over to the Raddison place. I'm starving!"

Nineteen

ANNETTA REINED HER HORSE INTO AN EASY WALK. JAKE had been right. It had been difficult to keep up with him. It didn't help matters that she'd had to look in on Mr. Jenkins in between Jake's services. The visit pressed them for time, so they'd had to ride hard to the second location to make up for it. The good news, however, was that Mr. Jenkins would be fine in a few days. She'd treated his fever with nitrate of potash. And now that he'd preached his second church service of the day, Jake had slowed their pace a bit.

Thinking back on the day, Annetta felt impressed by what she'd heard from Jacob McCabe. He'd preached his first sermon beneath a canvas drape in the desert, somewhere between Silverstone and Arizona City. Four families and a few lone ranchers came to hear God's Word. Jake read from the book of St. Matthew and called them the "saddest words in all the Bible." Annetta had to admit they struck a chord of unease within her soul, especially since she had to hear them again at the second church service, which was held at a rancher's home. *Depart from me, ye cursed, into everlasting fire, prepared for the devil and his angels.*

How could Jesus say such a thing?

"I'm mighty impressed." Jake's voice brought Annetta back to the present. He twisted slightly in his saddle. "You've kept up with me every mile."

Annetta smiled, pleased by the compliment. "Well, it hasn't been easy—and I know," she quickly added, "you warned me."

"That I did."

He chuckled and turned back around, facing the dusty trail leading back to Silverstone. Minutes later, he pointed off to his left.

"There's a good rest spot over yonder. We can water the horses and cool down awhile."

She nodded and followed his lead down a natural incline to a small stream. Jake dismounted and stretched in a way that made Annetta wonder if his leg was sore. She swung her right leg over the saddle, and Jake helped her off her mount, whose name was Buckshot. Jake's horse was Cannonball.

Her feet touched the ground. "Thank you."

"Welcome."

She handed Jake the reins then straightened her full, split skirt.

Beyond them the stream looked inviting. Fetching her canteen, she walked the rest of the way down the gravelly bank and filled the container. She drank her fill, and soon Jake hunkered close by, doing the same. After the last church service he'd removed his black dress jacket and rolled the sleeves of his white shirt up to his elbows. As he leaned forward, Annetta saw his shoulder muscles move beneath the light fabric. She conceded again her attraction to Jake McCabe, the Confederate preacher.

She shook her head at herself. What irony. What would Gregory think? Could he think out there in eternity? Was he looking down at her now, ashamed of the woman he once loved?

Jake suddenly grabbed her attention when he poured a canteen of water over his head. He gave his dark head a good shake.

"*Whoo-whee!* That feels good."

Annetta laughed at his antics. He made quite the handsome figure, standing near the stream with the wide Arizona sky as a backdrop.

"If you'd like, we can sit under that over there." He nodded toward a large blue palo verde. "It'd be good for the horses to get some shade too."

"Yes." Lifting her hems, Annetta climbed the stony incline. Jake was soon beside her and took her elbow in assistance. In his other hand, he held the horses' reins. When they reached their destination, Jake tossed the reins over a low-growing branch and then walked the circumference of the tree, kicking at the brush with his black boots.

"What are you doing?"

"Making sure we don't have any unwanted company."

"Like rattlesnakes?"

"Among other creatures."

With a grimace Annetta reminded herself to take greater care in where she walked and sat. It had to become second nature to her now that the desert was her home.

Having made his way around the tree, Jake reached the horses again. He pulled a gray, wool blanket from his saddle roll and shook it out. Motioning with one hand, he offered half to Annetta before he sat down.

Stepping forward, she lowered herself onto the spread and sighed.

"Nice day."

"Nice and hot." There didn't seem to be a single cloud in the sky.

"I reckon it's only about eighty degrees." He grinned. "Almost feels cool after the triple-digit temperatures we had back a couple of weeks ago."

"True." Annetta recalled how exhausted she'd felt on those days. "The heat was almost unbearable then."

"You'll grow accustomed to it. Just takes a little while." Jake stretched out on the blanket. Knees bent, he put his hands beneath his head and closed his eyes. "So what did you think of my message today?"

She grinned. "I think it was better the second time."

"Oh?" He opened one eye and peered at her. "Why's that?"

Annetta shrugged. "Probably because you'd delivered it once so you felt more confident the second time."

"Hmm, reckon you're right."

"As for the message itself…" Annetta wasn't sure how to explain the feelings his sermon conjured up. "I started thinking about my deceased fiancé, Gregory."

"What about him?"

"Well…" Surprisingly the sorrow, regret, and anger she usually felt when talking about Gregory didn't fill her heart today. "I began wondering where he is now and if he's watching over me."

"God is watching over you, Annetta."

"But…"

"Was your fiancé a believer?"

"I think so. We were both faithful in attending church and doing charity work."

"Hmm…" Jake hiked himself up on one elbow. "Well, rest assured that he is with the Lord. Believers meet him as their Savior while the rest meet him as their Judge."

Again a restless feeling crept over her. She picked at the imaginary lint on her skirt. "Perhaps God has already judged me." She hurled a glance at Jake. "Maybe He's already said, 'Depart from me…'"

"I doubt it." A hint of a smile curved his lips. Then he narrowed his gaze. "I s'pect we wouldn't be having this conversation if that were the case."

Something about Jake's reply calmed Annetta's jangled nerves.

"I believe," she said, "and years ago I wouldn't have dreamed of doubting God's love for me. Except He didn't save me from—" Raw emotion choked off the rest of the sentence.

"Netta, I can't tell you why God allows evil men to roam this planet and why bad things happen to perfectly innocent people. But I can promise you that God saw what occurred that night, and the man who hurt you and killed your fiancé will be judged."

"He was caught and hanged…for murder." She'd never told anyone about the rape. How could she? Her parents would have been mortified. She would have lost her friends, and she so desperately needed their support.

"Listen, he faces a second judgment that'll make his hanging look like a child's birthday party."

The thought gave Annetta a twinge of vindication.

"And if you give your heart to Christ, Netta, I can promise you that He'll save your soul and heal your shattered heart."

Looking away, she pushed to her feet. It was almost excruciating to hear the tender way in which Jake spoke to her. She didn't know why. But maybe because it stirred the womanly part of her, softening her. But staying angry and hateful was easier than accepting forgiveness and…forgiving those who'd robbed her of everything!

Annetta folded her arms tightly and walked along the bank. She wanted desperately to be loved again, and it seemed apparent that Jake knew and understood the extent to which she'd been violated. As for the Almighty God of whom he preached today, Annetta wasn't sure she could wholly trust Him. He'd let her suffer the unimaginable. How was that love?

Moments later she recalled something Jake had told her earlier this week. Something about God being there and weeping right along with her that night…

But if that's true, then why didn't You stop it, God?

In the next second, the strangest thing happened. She heard the answer to her question, not in an audible voice, but like a thundering in her soul. *You wouldn't be here if I had stopped it, beloved.*

Annetta spun around on her heel and stared at Jake. He'd stretched out again on the blanket. "Jake, did you just say something?"

He half sat, supported by his elbows. "What?"

Annetta swallowed hard. "Did you just say something?"

"Nope." He looked somewhat abashed. "I was praying, and I think I fell asleep in the middle of it."

She gave him a weak smile, wondering if she was losing her mind. "Maybe we should be on our way." She strode toward him. "We're both obviously exhausted. I think it's best we get back to Silverstone."

Jake stood, a frown creasing his brow. "Something wrong?"

Annetta shook her head and lifted the blanket. After giving it a hard shake she folded it and handed it to Jake.

"Was it something I said?"

"No." *Something Someone else said.* But she didn't dare describe her experience. "Maybe it's…well, the hard ride and the sun seem to be affecting me."

"You only shaded yourself a whole three minutes. Let's set back down. We have time."

"No, thank you. I'd appreciate it if we could get back."

"All right."

Annetta caught his curious expression, and remorse swelled like a knot in her chest. She'd like nothing better than to sit lazily in the shade with Jake McCabe. But he and his God spooked her. There seemed no other way to describe it.

They repacked and mounted, getting back on the dusty trail. Jake urged his mount into a canter, and Annetta followed suit. After about fifteen minutes, he slowed to a walk again and then pulled to a halt on a hill.

"Are we close to home?" She felt a little breathless.

"Sort of." His gaze was fixed on something off in the distance.

Annetta followed his line of vision and saw a brown cloud towering into the sky. "Smoke?"

"No."

"What is it?" The idea of encountering Indians entered Annetta's mind.

Jake squinted, and his gaze roamed across the cacti-dotted plain. "Dust storm. And it's heading our way. We need to find shelter. *Fast.*"

"But…" Annetta didn't feel any imminent danger. "Can't we make it to Silverstone?"

"No, 'cause that would mean riding into the storm and risking our lives." Jake turned his black gelding around. "Old Man Potter's ranch is about a mile east. We'll seek shelter there. But the storm's coming up quick."

Annetta saw that the brown wall grew wider and higher with each passing second.

"We'll have to ride hard to beat it." Jake took his eyes off the horizon to look at her. "Ready?"

"Ready."

Annetta jerked the reins to the right and spurred her horse on after Jake. She wasn't exactly sure what they were running away from. How harmful could a dust storm be? Ahead of her the sky was azure and nothing seemed amiss. But then the next thing she knew a swoop of wind slapped her backside.

"C'mon, Annetta!"

She saw Jake's hat fly off his head. It hit her foot before being carried away on the haze beginning to envelop them. Up ahead a weathered barn came into view. But her eyes stung, and she tasted sand on her lips. The haze started irritating the back of her throat, as if she'd been in a room filled with cigar smoke all afternoon.

"C'mon, Annetta!" Jake's voice sounded far away. "Just a little ways more."

Suddenly she could barely make him out.

He let out a shrill whistle that Buckshot seemed to understand. Without her lead, he turned off the road and galloped across the plain. A feeling of utter helplessness came over Annetta. She hung on to both the reins and the horse's mane with all her might.

Not a minute later, the barn loomed in front of her. Buckshot slowed and followed Jake's horse around to the side, and they rode right into the doorless entrance. Thankfully the opening faced away from the leading edge of the storm.

Jake jumped down from his saddle to help Annetta dismount. She coughed and couldn't seem to catch her breath, between the ride and the blowing dust. Pulling out his canteen, he opened the top while taking Annetta's hand. "Splash a little on your face. That's right. Good. Now take a drink. It'll help you stop coughing."

She sipped from the canteen, and her hacking abated. Next she glanced up at Jake and saw that his hair looked hoary, thick with sand and dust. Around them the barn walls shook as the wind screamed through the cracks.

"Shouldn't we be in a cellar?" She'd never experienced anything like this before.

"Naw. It's only a dust storm. We must have rain on the way." He unstrapped his saddlebags. "I wondered why my leg's been bothering me more lately. God willing, there'll be a break in the storm long enough for us to ride back to Silverstone. For now, this barn'll be adequate shelter."

Sand and dust blew through the crevices in the walls. The rafters creaked from the force of the wind. Its shrill screech unnerved Annetta. She stepped closer to Jake and clutched the fabric of his shirt at his waist. Her gaze darted around the empty structure. "It's not going to fall on us, is it?"

"Not likely." The strong timbre of his voice reverberated in his chest. "Let's go sit against that far wall."

He pulled out his rifle and led her away from the horses. He dropped his saddlebags and poked around the straw-strewn area with the nose of his rifle. A mouse scampered away, and Annetta screamed.

Jake laughed. "C'mon, Netta. You ain't afraid of a little

mouse. You faced Chicago Joe. I didn't think you were afraid of anything."

She sent him a sharp glance. "Very funny."

He chuckled again while spreading out the blanket. "Go ahead and make yourself comfortable."

Removing her windblown bonnet, Annetta sat down and leaned against the barn's wall. She could feel the wind gusts pushing against the planks. Jake lowered himself down beside her. It seemed to grow darker inside the deserted barn. Anxious flutters filled Annetta's gut, and before she realized what she was doing, she'd wound her arm around Jake's. She felt the warmth from his body radiating through the sleeve of her blue and green checked blouse.

She slowly lifted her gaze. His brown eyes stared back at her just as the wind hurled something heavy into the side of the barn. The impact was inches above Annetta's head.

A scream formed in her throat as she sprang into Jake's arms. "Won't this be over soon?"

"Pretty soon." He held her.

The wind's howls sounded ominous as sand, twigs, and small stones blew through the gaping entryway.

Annetta laid her head against him. A sense of security enveloped her. "Back home we had tornadoes, but I always managed to get into the cellar. I never saw one, personally. I've only seen drawings."

"You're fortunate, then. I saw plenty of twisters in Missouri, mostly on the outskirts of our town."

"Do you have a lot of family there?"

"My folks, a brother, sister, and their families. Cousins."

"A big family?" She straightened so she could look at him as they talked.

"Average, I'd say." His gaze swept over her face. "What about you?"

"Parents. A sister whose husband is in politics."

"Is that right? I dabble in a bit of politics myself."

"The town board?"

He nodded.

"The same one that wanted a male doctor."

"Now, don't hold that against us. You're doing as fine a job as any man."

She smiled and brushed the dirt from Jake's hair.

"I got a head full of it after my hat flew off." He sounded apologetic.

"I don't mind…" His hair felt thick and soft between her fingers, and she took her time ridding it of debris. Then she dusted off his shoulder, and her knuckles grazed his stubbly jaw. He turned slightly and Annetta gazed into his eyes. Would he kiss her?

Yearning melted her insides. Yes. For the first time since Gregory died, she wanted a man to kiss her. She inched toward him, her lips poised and ready to greet his unabashed. Her hand slid along his neck. Yes. She wanted Jake McCabe…

Then suddenly he stood with an abruptness that sent her reeling backward. She landed hard on her backside, and a startled gasp escaped her.

"Pardon me, but I'd best check the horses."

Wide-eyed, Annetta didn't know what to think. He'd rejected her—except hadn't she glimpsed the longing in his eyes? Hadn't it matched hers?

Wrapping her arms around her knees, Annetta sat quietly and watched Jake unsaddle Cannonball and Buckshot. He took his sweet time removing their bridles and saddles. Tears stung, but Annetta refused to give into them. She'd never had a man reject her before. In fact, she was usually the one thwarting their advances. On the other hand, Gregory had always enjoyed stealing a kiss when heads were turned.

Annetta's gaze remained on Jake. He intrigued her. Could it be the good reverend actually practiced what he preached?

Shame gave her heart a yank. How could she have behaved so brazenly? And yet, she wished with all her soul that Jake had kissed her.

The wind silenced. Jake strode to the barn's doorway and leaned against the frame. Beyond him Annetta could see the dusk of evening and more dark clouds. Pushing to her feet, she walked over to where he stood. A flash of lightning suddenly split the sky, and Annetta jumped back.

Jake glanced over his shoulder and grinned. "God's fireworks on display." He hesitated then held out his hand. "Come and see."

Drawn to him in an instant, Annetta reached for his out-stretched fingers, and he pulled her up next to him. Another fork of lightning cracked down, and she tensed.

"Jake, I must apologize for my behavior…"

"No need."

"I've never been so forward with a man."

"I figured." He continued to gaze off in the distance. "And don't think for one second that I wasn't tempted."

"Which is why I'm all the more sorry."

"Well," he drawled, "you were frightened, and I have to admit I enjoyed comforting you." He faced her. "Annetta, you're a beautiful woman."

Pleasure warmed her face. "But…?" She sensed the word was forthcoming.

And then it hit her.

Pulling her hand from his, she jutted out her chin. "But I'm not good enough for a reverend such as yourself." It was her worst fears realized. The man she loved knew of her past and deemed her unfit for his wife. And perhaps she didn't actually love Jake McCabe. Not yet. But she'd certainly fallen for him in an inexplicable way.

"Don't go putting words in my mouth, Annetta."

She folded her arms and glared at him.

Jake grinned. "I was going to add that I felt a certain spark between us on the first day we met." He grunted out a chuckle. "I suppose you don't remember that day."

She searched her memory and came up blank. "I've kept to myself...up until a few days ago."

"Yes, I know."

"Do you?" She didn't think he had a clue. "Are you aware of the risk I took, opening myself up to you?"

"I think I'm very much aware. And God help me if I would ever shatter that fragile trust you've given me."

Her defenses crumbled. "Is that why you didn't kiss me?"

"That...and I have my own personal reason."

"Will you tell me?"

"Promise not to laugh?"

"I promise."

He inhaled deeply. "I vowed that the first time I ever kiss a woman would follow the words 'I do.'"

"You mean...?"

"That's right. I'm saving that first kiss for my bride."

She tried to conceal her grin, although it wasn't a result of amusement. "I think that's very noble and sweet." Annetta's respect for this man increased twofold.

Another searing white bolt shot across the darkening sky. Thunder rumbled in the distance.

Annetta took his arm. "Would it be all right if I just hold onto your elbow?" His nearness distracted her from the danger surrounding them.

"Reckon I'd enjoy it."

She smiled, and they stood there for quite some time. Darkness enveloped them until Jake found a lantern and lit it.

When the storm grew less violent, Annetta approached him again. "Should we saddle up and get back to town?"

"Not in this lightning. That's why we've been sitting here."

Annetta felt a blush heat her cheeks. "And all along I thought you just enjoyed my company."

Jake chuckled. "Well, that too."

Her blush intensified.

"Besides, right now we couldn't outride the driving rainstorm that's approaching. It's safer if we stay here till it's over."

"I trust your judgment." *And I trust you*, she added silently.

Several moments of silence went by, then Jake gently shook off her hold and strolled to the center of the barn. He stared straight up before looking her way. "I think we should try to build a fire before the temperatures drop. I don't think there's a risk of burning this place down. Place is empty. Rafters are high enough."

"Good idea. What should I do?"

"Want to scout around and see if there's anything worth burning? But don't venture outside because the wind has stirred up more than just sand."

Annetta understood. The threat of snakes, scorpions, and other deadly creatures was great, and she might not see them in the gathering darkness.

"I'll get the flint and matchsticks from my saddlebags," Jake said, "and—"

A sudden fluttering of feathers near Annetta's skirt gave her a start. She yelped and jumped sideways. To her relief it was nothing more than a rather confused-looking chicken.

"Well, lookie here." Jake grinned and set his hands on his hips. "The Lord not only kept us safe, he's provided us with supper too."

TWENTY

ETHANY ROCKED THE SLEEPING BABY IN HER ARMS.
Ralph Jonas hadn't made it back to the boardinghouse to pick up Michael, most likely because of the terrible dust storm this afternoon.

"Luke?" She turned to him. He sat beside her on the settee. "I hope the Jonas children are all right. It'll be a miracle if that hut of theirs survived the storm."

"Here's hoping they all took cover in the barn."

Bethany gave a nod. She prayed they had.

"Ralph is no stranger to this land. He's lived through his share of dust storms. He knows what to do to protect himself and his family."

"I hope so."

Luke smiled and stretched his arm out along the back of the settee, causing a pleasant burst of warmth to push into her cheeks. Still very respectable, but his action made Bethany feel special.

"I'm sure they're all fine, Beth."

She put a lot of stock in anything Luke said, so his reply eased her mind.

"It came on so fast." Bethany had never witnessed anything like it—like a wall of dirt and debris converging on the entire town. Then the wind had beat against the boardinghouse's exterior walls in the most frightful way.

"I'm glad we were safely back from the Raddisons' when it hit."

"Indeed."

With his free hand, Luke kneaded his jaw. "You know, Beth, your hair looks real pretty."

"Thank you." She looked at the sleeping baby in her arms as she replied, except she savored Luke's compliment. She'd wondered all day what he thought of her haircut.

"You look older...like a refined schoolteacher."

"Well, that's good." Bethany smiled. "Because that's the very reason you brought me to Silverstone—to be a refined schoolteacher." She chanced a glance at him.

"I reckon that's true enough." Luke sent her an affectionate wink.

Bethany's smile grew, but before she could reply, a flash of lightning lit the room. In fact, it seemed to blaze straight through the parlor.

"Luke?"

"Not to worry. Just a little lightning." He drew in a breath. "Usually means some rain is on the way."

"It seemed so close."

"Around here a man could catch a lightning bolt in his fist if he was fast enough."

Bethany rolled her eyes. "Do you really expect me to believe such a thing?"

"Might be in one of them dime novels you read."

"Oh, stop it, Luke." Unfortunately, Bethany couldn't conceal her laugh.

Then a second later another flash of lightning caused her to cringe.

"Whoo-whee! God's puttin' on a show tonight." Luke stood and ambled to the front windows.

"Be careful now, Reverend Luke. Don't stand too close."

Bethany looked toward the door in time to see Mrs. Winters enter. Trudy bounded in moments later.

"The lightning's a fright!" Trudy flounced into Luke's vacated seat.

"Shh, Trudy," Bethany whispered, "Michael's finally asleep."

"Would you like me to take him upstairs for you, dear?" Mrs. Winters came over and collected Michael before Bethany could reply.

"Certainly, that would be fine. I made a makeshift cradle from one of my dresser drawers. I hope you won't mind my using it that way. But Michael fits in it so nicely, and it seems safer than allowing him to sleep on my bed. He's just beginning to roll over by himself."

"I think that's just fine."

Carrying the infant in her arms, Mrs. Winters left the parlor and headed upstairs.

Bethany stood, smoothed down the skirt of her dress, then walked to where Luke still stood, gazing outside. Just as she reached him, a lightning bolt zigzagged across the sky accompanied by an explosive *boom*.

Bethany jumped backward. "Sounds like it struck a tree."

"Sounds like." Luke reached for her hand. "But no need to be afraid."

The warmth of his palm surrounding hers felt comforting, and Bethany marveled once more at Luke's ability to quell her fears.

Moments later the flicker of flames could be seen shooting up from behind the saloon and brothel across the street.

Luke spotted it just as Bethany did. He turned from the window and dropped her hand. "Trudy, is your father nearby?"

"He went out back to make sure the animals were in the stable." The girl came forward and then screamed when she spied the growing blaze across the street. "The saloon's on fire!"

"All right, now, stay calm, ladies." Luke headed for the parlor's doorway. "Stay inside. I'm going to see what I can do to help." He disappeared through the entryway.

"I don't know why Reverend Luke is even bothering." Trudy rolled a shoulder. "Let it burn to the ground."

Bethany had to admit she shared the sentiment. However, there were souls inside the building...

Angie's in there!

The thought of her new friend coming to any harm momentarily stunned Bethany. She turned back to the window. Already people had left the building and stood in the middle of Main Street. Bethany strained to see if Angie was one of them, but she couldn't find her.

Men were shouting and forming a bucket brigade. But it looked like a futile attempt.

Then Mr. Winters ran through the boardinghouse, calling to his wife and Trudy. "We need to get up on the roof and keep it wet so the fire won't spread to our building."

"Can I help?" Bethany caught Mrs. Winters by the elbow as she headed for the back.

"No, dear. I'd prefer you stay downstairs. I'll send Trudy for you if we need you."

"All right."

Feeling useless, Bethany ambled back to the parlor. Again, she gazed out the front windows. By now flames danced out the first-floor windows. The wood-framed saloon and its second-floor brothel were aflame like a tinderbox, and her thoughts turned to Luke and her friend Angie. Anxious flutters filled her insides. Small explosions caused her to start until she realized they most likely came from the alcohol the saloon served.

Lord, what about Angie? Is she safe? Is Luke safe?

Suddenly Bethany couldn't stay still a moment more. She needed answers—now.

Leaving the parlor, she ventured outside the boardinghouse. A throng of humanity filled the walk and street. Bethany pushed through them, searching for either Luke or Angie. Thunder rumbled.

Then suddenly Bethany glimpsed Angie's blonde head. She moved in her direction, squeezing between men and women who stared, almost fixedly, at the blaze.

"Angie!"

She turned, and Bethany saw her face was streaked with ash. Her faded coral-colored dress had been blackened down one arm.

"Are you all right?"

"I barely made it out alive." Angie choked on a sob.

Bethany embraced her.

"It's a miracle that I survived. I was trapped in my room. I had to run through flames, but I didn't suffer a single burn."

"God protected you through the fire."

Angie paused, her blue eyes wide. "He did. It had to be God."

With tears rimming her eyes, Bethany locked arms with Angie. The rain began to fall. Together they ran for the overhang in front of the boardinghouse and watched as the saloon burned.

Suddenly someone began hollering that Chicago Joe was trapped in her quarters. Murmurs spread through the crowd.

"It's her foot," Angie told Bethany. "Chicago Joe can't walk on it."

Bethany barely took in Angie's explanation when she saw Luke and Sheriff Montaño climbing the outer stairway, two by two.

"Why on earth would the reverend go in after a woman like Chicago Joe?" Mr. Winters asked the onlookers. Then he hollered to Luke and the sheriff, "Just leave her up there, men. Save yourselves!"

Another man concurred. "The woman ain't worth killing yerselves over!"

"No, Luke!" Bethany screamed. She moved to run after him, but Angie held her back.

"If God would protect a woman like me, he can take care of your man and the sheriff."

Bethany couldn't argue. In horror she watched as Luke kicked in the door. Then, getting down on his knees, he crawled into the burning building. The sheriff followed. Bethany held her breath. *Oh, Father God, please protect them!*

As if sensing her anguish, Angie gave her arm an affectionate squeeze.

Grumblings made their way through the crowd.

Bethany's heart crimped. *I love him, Lord. Please don't take Luke from me now.*

The prayer had just taken flight when suddenly Luke appeared. He and Sheriff Montaño pulled Chicago Joe through the door of her quarters. Coughing uncontrollably, they managed to stumble to their feet. Seconds later, each took one of Chicago Joe's arms and legs and carried her down the steps and into the street to safety. Bethany heaved a sigh of relief. Luke was all right. *Thank You, Lord.*

"I've only seen Chicago Joe's face in the window," Bethany remarked. "I didn't know she was such a large woman."

"She doesn't go out much because of that bad foot of hers." Angie nodded. "But, yes, that's her, all right."

Bethany moved forward and saw Luke on his knees, still coughing. "Go to your man," Angie said. "Go on."

With a nod, Bethany pushed her way through the throng and finally reached the other side of the street. She could feel the heat from the burning saloon. A safe distance away, men stood around Luke and the sheriff, offering them water and slapping them between the shoulder blades as they coughed the smoke from their lungs. She didn't know what she could do for Luke at the moment. To their right, women surrounded Chicago Joe. She choked and sputtered, but otherwise appeared unharmed.

And then it dawned on Bethany. With all the commotion, this might be the perfect time for Angie to slip away unnoticed.

In a heartbeat, she knew what she had to do. Luke didn't need her at the moment. Angie did.

Making her way back through the crowd, Bethany reached the overhang and took Angie's hand. "Come with me."

"Where are we going?"

"God's made a way for your escape. Come on!"

Bethany led Angie up the boardwalk and then around the gathering townsfolk who didn't seem to notice them between the excitement of the rescue and the fire. Then suddenly the remainder of the saloon and brothel crumbled beneath the flames in a loud *whoosh*. Men shouted. Women screamed, creating even more of a distraction.

And then it began to rain harder. A veritable deluge fell from the sky, and the temperature plummeted.

Bethany and Angie quickened their pace until they reached the back door of the boardinghouse. Once inside, Bethany turned the lock to deter anyone who might have followed them.

"My room's upstairs. This way."

Up the back stairwell, Bethany led Angie to her room. Reaching it, she unlocked the door and let herself and Angie inside. Hot, still air greeted her, but Bethany saw that Michael still slept soundly in his makeshift cradle. Meanwhile, she and Angie were soaked to the skin from the downpour.

"Perhaps one of my dresses will fit you." Bethany opened the front window to allow some air inside. Although damp, it felt cooler than the air in her room.

"I'm grateful for anything right now." Angie peeled off her torn and soiled dress. "I lost everything in the fire," she whispered. "Even your books."

"Books are replaceable. People are not."

"I think your books were more valuable than me."

Bethany collected some under-things then found a gown from her wardrobe and handed it all over to Angie. "You are most definitely more valuable than my books. God created you, and you are special. You are His prize. He loves you."

"How can that be?"

"It's hard to fathom, I know. I must admit I struggle myself at times." Bethany began to remove the soaking garments from her body. "I often wonder why God chose me, a plain little field mouse, to be His princess." Bethany smiled. "You see, God is the Lord of lords and King of kings. That makes His children *royalty.*"

"It sounds like a fairy tale." Cynicism laced Angie's voice, but Bethany couldn't blame her for her unbelief.

"Angie, if you would just keep your mind open to the truth, and read God's Word—"

"Oh!" Anguish filled her tone. "The Bible you gave me burned also."

"Luke and Jake have extra Bibles to give to those who truly want them. Meanwhile, you may use my Bible."

Despite the darkness, Bethany glimpsed Angie's nod.

"I think you'd best know that when Chicago Joe finds out I'm missing, she'll send her hired gun, Dirk Crawford, to find me. He's a ruthless man, Bethany. When he finds me, he'll beat me for sure." Angie's voice shook. "He may even kill me. And... well, he might kill you too."

"I doubt you're the only working girl that goes missing tonight." Bethany figured any one of those women would run for their lives.

"Perhaps others escaped too. But still..."

The sound of angry voices wafted up from the street.

"Don't come back here!" It sounded like Mr. Winters. "You and your ilk aren't welcome in Silverstone."

"Silverstone should be mine, the bank included!"

"It's Chicago Joe," Angie whispered. "And look…there's Dirk Crawford, driving the wagon."

Bethany peered out the window beside her friend and saw that, indeed, a wagon had been pulled around in front of the smoldering ruins. She couldn't make out the man's features as he wore a wide-brimmed hat, but she could see the reins in his large hands. Chicago Joe sat in the wagon bed, and women were climbing in beside her.

"This town never belonged to you," Mr. Winters bellowed. "It belongs to the decent folks who work hard to make this a respectable place to live. You and yours only brought danger and death to Silverstone. As for the bank, Les Beasley opened up and withdrew your money plus interest. You've got it now, so leave and never return!"

"This isn't the last you'll hear from me, Winters."

"It better be. I got the law on my side."

Angie whispered to Bethany, "Chicago Joe and Crawford never abide by the law."

Foreboding shimmied up her spine. Bethany moved away from the window and finished changing her clothes.

"Now Chicago Joe is talking to your man."

Bethany rushed forward and knelt beneath the window. She wondered why Luke would save such an evil woman's life. But he had, and now, just as Angie said, he stood in the middle of Main Street, speaking with her. While she couldn't hear what was being said between them, she figured Chicago Joe was thanking Luke for saving her.

"Most of the other girls wished your fella would forget his religion and pay them a call. Some even bet on whether he would or not. He wouldn't be the first preacher to fall from grace."

Bethany gasped. "No!"

"It's true. But don't worry. Reverend Luke never came calling. Neither did Reverend Jacob."

"I'm relieved to know it." Quickly Bethany brushed out her hair and repinned it at her nape.

"They're fine men, those McCabes."

"Yes, they are."

"Unlike that filthy Dirk Crawford." Angie stepped away from the window and sat down on the side of the bed.

"He scares me, that Crawford fellow."

"He ought to scare you." Angie paused before continuing. "I heard he's from somewhere out East. He fought with a militia during the war, then like many people, he came out West afterwards."

"Same with Jake. That's how he came to know Silverstone existed. It was during the time he served under McCulloch, before the war even began. His regiment built Confederate alliances with several Indian nations."

"Well, I wouldn't dare put Crawford in the same league as Reverend Jacob. No, sir. Crawford is the kind who prefers to only come out at night. He's the sort of reptile that stays in the shadows and kills anything or anyone that crosses him."

Bethany's mouth suddenly went dry. "I can only imagine how he got hooked up with Chicago Joe." Disgust filled her.

"Dirk Crawford is the most savage and soulless man I've ever known."

Again Bethany heard a frightened wavering in Angie's voice, and it sent a chill straight through her. She didn't regret hiding Angie. She even believed she'd done the right thing. However, she sensed that she was in well over her head now. But Luke would know how to handle the situation.

"Angie, I need to go find Luke and make sure he's all right."

"Go ahead. I'll stay here and mind the baby." There was a smile in her hushed voice. "It's been a long, long while since I held a baby, but I haven't entirely forgotten what to do."

"Pull the shutters if you want to light a lamp," Bethany warned.

"Don't worry. I'm not about to ruin this chance to escape. Did I tell you? I have a sister in San Francisco. She wants me to come and live with her—told me so in her last letter."

Bethany recalled the missive she'd taken to Angie.

"If there's some way I can get to San Francisco..."

"I'll talk to Luke. He'll know what to do." Bethany's hand turned the knob. "I'll be back shortly. In the meantime, try to get some rest."

Leaving the room, she closed the door behind her. The upstairs hallway was empty, and Bethany felt sure Angie and Michael were both safe. Downstairs the sounds of talking wafted up to the second floor. Bethany decided to use the back stairwell so she wouldn't arouse any suspicions.

And then she needed to find Luke, after which she'd have an awful lot of explaining to do.

TWENTY-ONE

"Miss Stafford!" Trudy hiked her hems and ran toward Bethany. "Where have you been?"

"I went back to check on the baby."

"Oh." A sober expression crept across her face. But then a second later her eyes sparked. "Miss Stafford, you would have been proud of me if you'd seen. I bandaged a man's arm this evening. The poor fellow got an awful burn, running from the saloon. I did so well that Mama said I should talk to Dr. Cavanaugh about learning doctoring skills."

"Why, Trudy, I am proud of you." Bethany hugged the girl and glanced over her head, hoping to catch sight of Luke. "Have you seen Reverend Luke recently?"

"Yes, ma'am. He went home to wash up and change. I heard him tell that to Papa."

"I see. Well, I need to take care of a matter, but later you can tell me all about your experience nursing."

"Yes, Miss Stafford." Although put off for the time being, the excitement still shone in Trudy's eyes. She flounced into the lobby.

With Trudy occupied, Bethany left the boardinghouse and stepped into a throng of people. The fire seemed to be the pressing topic, although some men lamented the loss of their favorite "waterin' hole."

Sheriff Montaño stood on a step and spoke to the gathering townsfolk.

"Chicago Joe will try to rebuild—unless the town board writes up an ordinance banning a saloon and…house of ill repute. Then I would have no choice but to enforce the new law."

"Good idea, Sheriff!" A pleased look shone from Mr. Winters's face.

Meanwhile shouts of "nay" as well as shouts of "yay" emanated from the crowd.

"I demand a vote!" one man hollered.

Mr. Winters shifted his stance. "All right, then." A frown furrowed his brow. "A vote it is. But not tonight. We'll have a regular town meetin' at the church next week."

"And speaking of church," the sheriff said, "we have a hero in our town. Reverend Luke risked his life to keep a woman from burning to death."

"But she ain't worth it!" some man yelled from the crowd.

Bethany clenched her fists at her side.

Montaño refuted the retort. "In spite of what she has done and what she is, Chicago Joe didn't deserve to die in such a horrifying way while we all stood in the street and watched. If you are Christians, you would have to agree, *sí*? Any human life is worth saving."

No one argued, and Bethany glanced down at the toes of her boots in effort to hide her smile. Her respect for Paden Montaño went up a few notches. As for Luke…

She glanced up the street but didn't see any sign of him. Was he all right? Had he been hurt after all?

The rain had stopped, and Bethany figured that at a quick jog she could reach the McCabes' cabin in minutes and with minimal danger, what with all the activity going on in front of the boardinghouse. Once there, she figured that she and Luke would be properly chaperoned. Surely Jake had arrived back from riding his circuit. Perhaps he would have some good input as to how to get Angie to San Francisco.

In any case, Bethany knew she wouldn't rest until she learned that Luke was all right.

Skirting around the crowd, she started off in a rapid pace. A swell of thick smoke still hung in the air. Thunder rumbled off in the distance. She quickened her steps and then, as she neared the schoolhouse, she heard a rustling at the end of the boardwalk. She slowed, thinking she saw a figure of a man standing in the darkness. And she would have screamed for Luke, but with the next flash of lightning, she realized the man's identity.

"Warring Spirit?"

He stayed in the shadows, but Bethany could see he wore a long tunic, pants, and moccasins. "I come to see what makes great smoke in the sky."

"The saloon and brothel burned down." Bethany had to say she was glad about it. Maybe now this town would begin drawing good, decent people instead of lawless men who had gunfights in the middle of the road and in front of innocent children.

"Preacher Luke McCabe walked through fire."

"You saw that?" Bethany brightened. "Luke saved Chicago Joe."

"His God is very powerful."

"Yes, He is." Bethany felt humbled at the admission. *Thank You, Lord, for sparing Luke's life.*

"You go to see Preacher Luke McCabe now?" Warring Spirit's horse tossed his head, but he hung on to the reins.

"Yes. I'm on my way to the cabin Luke shares with his brother Jake. It's just down the street."

"I see you there safe."

Bethany nodded her thanks and continued walking. When they reached the cabin, Warring Spirit paused.

"Luke will want to say hello. Please don't leave just yet." Bethany knocked on the door. "Luke?"

It opened no more than a minute later. "Beth. What are you

doing here?" Luke's sandy-brown hair was still wet, but his clothes looked dry. "I know you wouldn't venture out here alone at night." He dipped his head.

Hearing the warning in his tone, Bethany felt glad she could reply that she hadn't. "No, Warring Spirit accompanied me." She turned to the side so he'd see the brave. "Luke, I was so scared when I saw you enter that burning building."

"I'm sorry I frightened you, Beth." Luke set his arm around her, giving her shoulders a series of short hugs. In spite of his change of clothes, he still smelled like smoke.

Warring Spirit's horse whinnied as another rumble of thunder reverberated through the air and finally shook the very ground on which they stood.

"Your God is very powerful, Preacher Luke McCabe." Warring Spirit stepped forward.

"He saw you rescue Chicago Joe too," Bethany explained.

"Ah..." Looking at the other man, Luke said, "Yes, my God is all powerful. Won't you come in? I will tell you all about Him."

"Yes." Warring Spirit tossed the reins around the hitching post, leaving his animal standing beneath the cabin's overhang.

Bethany entered the home and immediately felt the cold and damp that the change in weather had brought.

Luke strode to the hearth and hunkered in front of the hearth. "Have a seat, Warring Spirit, while I make a fire."

"Your God is powerful through the fire."

"Yes, He protected me tonight. He is not only powerful, but He is a good God—and a God of peace."

"Tell me more."

Bethany took it upon herself to make a pot of coffee. As it cooked on the stove, she went around the cabin and closed the wooden shutters. At one point, she caught Luke's gaze, and it was if, just by looking into their depths, she could read his very thoughts. *Pray, Beth.* She smiled. She would.

Father God, open Warring Spirit's mind so that he will understand the truth as Luke presents it.

When the coffee finished brewing, she poured it into two tin cups and served the men.

"Mmm...good. Warm to my innards." Warring Spirit nodded his thanks, and Bethany realized then that he'd likely been caught in that first downpour too.

"Thank you, Beth." Luke raised his cup.

She smiled again. "You're welcome." She crossed the cabin and sat at the large table while Luke continued to converse with the Indian brave. A comfortable, easy feeling enveloped her as the warmth from the fire took the chill from the air. She ran her finger along a scar on the tabletop and silently made another petition to God for the salvation of Warring Spirit's soul. She realized then that Chicago Joe's rescue hadn't been so much to save that evil woman's life but to give time to save her soul. And to demonstrate God's love to those who witnessed Luke's daring. Like Warring Spirit—

And perhaps even like herself. For the first time Bethany felt as though she was part of the very fabric of Luke's ministry. Oh, she'd helped him numerous times on the trail. But tonight she felt as though she actually... *belonged.*

"My God came to earth in the form of a man—like you and me." Luke spoke in a slow and steady voice. "He said that no greater love has any man than this, that a man lay down his life for a friend. So that's what my God did, Warring Spirit. He gave His human life and suffered the sins of all mankind so that you and I can live one day in eternity with Him. His name is Jesus Christ, and all you have to do is confess your wrongdoings to Him and believe."

Warring Spirit sat back in the wooden armchair. His deerskin-encased legs were stretched out in front of him. "I believe because I see with my eyes His power through the fire."

With her gaze fixed on Luke, Bethany smiled. She loved him, and now she realized that she belonged with him. Suddenly her plans of returning to Jericho Junction for good disappeared like a puffy white cloud on a windy day. If Luke wanted to live in Silverstone, then Bethany knew she wanted to stay here with him. She simply couldn't imagine a life without Luke McCabe.

Which meant leaving the territory was no longer an option.

"So. You never did say what happened to Old Man Potter, our host this evening." Annetta lay down on her hard bedroll. Jake had packed two, one with each horse, and now she thanked God for his wisdom in doing so.

A small fire crackled at a safe distance between their bedrolls while outside thunder shook the barn's walls and the very ground they lay on.

"He took consumption and died is what I heard when I got back to Silverstone a couple of months ago."

Lightning flashed and lit up the barn.

"Pneumonia?" Annetta brought the blanket up higher, over her chin.

"I 'spect. A friend found him dead in the house. Since Potter was loved by most of the townsfolk, everyone shared responsibilities of taking on his animals, cleaning out the barn and his house."

"He didn't have any family?"

"None. A wife and a couple of sons. But Old Man Potter outlived them all."

"Let me get this straight. He had pneumonia, was loved by all, but had no one to take care of him?"

Jake paused, and she could just make out his expression through the flames of their dwindling campfire. "I reckon that about sums it up."

A spark of determination caused Annetta to sit straight up. "Jake, Mr. Potter is the very reason I think Silverstone needs a hospital."

"Hospital?" Rolling onto his side, he pushed up on one elbow. "There's barely enough folks sick to keep you busy as it is."

"Not true. I just don't have an adequate facility in which to treat patients. My little clinic is too small and very indiscreet for the ladies—some men too. Consequently the only men coming through my doors are those wounded by gunfire or pierced by arrows, and half of them are unconscious."

"Hmm…"

Annetta sensed he was both listening and taking her seriously. She pressed on. "You know the story of Mrs. Jonas, right?"

"Died after childbirth."

"Yes, but it was so unnecessary. According to what Ralph's eldest daughter, Lacey, has told me, the baby was delivered without complications. It was hours later that Mrs. Jonas began to hemorrhage. As a physician, I could have saved her life…in a hospital…where I could have operated, possibly stopped her bleeding, and she could have recovered." Annetta tried to keep the disgust from her voice. "Lacey said her father insisted Mrs. Jonas help with chores shortly after Michael was born. Can you imagine? After delivering a baby the poor woman hadn't been allowed even one day's rest."

"I know, Netta. Some men have as much sense as bullfrogs."

"And just as much sensitivity."

Jake released an audible sigh.

"Anyway, my hope was to see a hospital erected near the church—on the very spot where you're constructing the rectory, in fact."

"My father's benefactor purchased three hundred acres on which I built that church, the cabin, and now Luke and Bethany's new home."

"Oh, I'm not disputing your claim or your right to build." Annetta wished she'd never even broached the subject. "It's just that...well, when I first got to town, I imagined a hospital right there, near the church where visitors could stop in and pray for their sick or injured loved ones. And perhaps you and Luke would visit the patients..."

Jake was silent.

Annetta feared she'd crossed the line with him now. "A silly pipe dream is all it was. Please don't be offended."

"Offended? Are you kidding?" Jake chuckled. "I think it's a great idea."

"You do?" Annetta folded her legs and peered across the way at him.

"I'll build you your hospital. I'll just move my plans for the rectory someplace else. As I said, we've got plenty of land to work with."

"Jake..." Annetta couldn't believe that he'd agreed to her idea. She never thought she'd see a hospital in Silverstone. "I'm so filled with gratitude that I don't know what to say."

"You just said it." He laughed again. "'Course we'll have to get the town board to approve it. But I doubt there'll be a problem. Ed Winters wants to see this town grow. Keeping folks alive is one good way to do it."

Annetta giggled—actually giggled. Then she stood and walked around to Jake's side of the campfire and knelt beside him. "Thank you."

"You're welcome." He sat up, his arms supporting him, and she hugged him around the shoulders. "And thank you for having the foresight and seeing the need."

Sitting back, she stared at him, smiling. The dying embers from the fire cast a soft glow all around them, and Annetta felt her feelings for this man mounting. She guessed from the way he looked back that he had strong feelings for her too.

Reaching out, Jake plucked a piece of straw from her hair, and she realized what a wreck she must look like. Dirt had smudged both her riding skirt and blouse, and she'd lost several hairpins.

Thunder rumbled, long and low, and Jake winced and moved to stretch his leg.

"Is it bothering you?"

"Usually does when it rains. But I'm fine."

The physician in Annetta grew curious. "Did the ball fracture your leg?"

"Yep. It shot clean through the front and exited the back of my calf, although I likely have lead fragments in the bone. At least that's what my family doctor in Jericho Junction said."

"It probably wasn't set correctly." She reached out to touch his shinbone then paused. "May I? As a physician?"

"Annetta, I think we should probably get some shut-eye. My leg is just fine."

"But what if I can fix it and reduce your pain?"

He didn't reply, and Annetta took his silence as permission to examine his lower leg. She didn't even need for him to roll up his trousers. Through the woven fabric she ran her fingers down the length of his tibia and found a lump halfway down about the size of a small plum.

"Mmm-hmm, just as I suspected. It wasn't set properly."

"Well, I can't very well harbor a grudge. The medic on the battlefield did what he could. He had worse injuries than mine to deal with."

"I understand." Annetta thought about several different ways she could go about repairing the disfigured bone, the most obvious being to rebreak it. "Jake, will you consider allowing me to try and fix your leg? I believe I can. And wait!" She moved forward quickly and put her fingertips over his lips. "Before you answer me, please know that you would be doing me another great favor." Slowly she drew her hand away and sat back on her haunches. "If I fixed your leg, I'd earn the respect and gain the confidence of both the men and women in Silverstone. I wouldn't be seen as 'the doctor who should have been a man.' I'd be seen as *their* doctor."

After a heavy, weighted silence, Jake finally replied. "I'll think about it." His grumbled reply rolled like the thunder.

"Thank you." Annetta smiled, sensing he'd eventually agree. "And guess what?"

"What?"

"I won't even charge you for my services, Preacher."

He groaned and stretched out on his bedroll. "Get back on your side of the campfire, will you? I've got to get some sleep."

She laughed and stood. "All right." She softened her tone, wishing she could curl up beside him. "Good night, Jake."

"G'night, Netta." His tone seemed to caress her. "Sleep well."

TWENTY-TWO

ANOTHER DOWNPOUR CAME AND WENT, AND BY THE TIME Warring Spirit took his leave only a few errant raindrops fell from the sky. Bethany thought the cool, clean air felt refreshing after all the months of tireless, thick heat. Luke took her hand and wrapped it around his arm as they headed for the boardinghouse.

"I need to speak with you about an important matter." She regarded him askance. "That's the second reason I came to see you tonight."

"What's on your mind, Beth?"

"It's Angie," she whispered. "I'm hiding her in my room."

Luke paused right there on the boardwalk. "You're... what?"

"I managed to sneak her into the boardinghouse during all the commotion." Bethany searched for his expression in the darkness. "Luke, we have to help her escape to San Francisco. She says she has a sister there who will take her in."

He let out a long, slow whistle. "San Fran, eh? That's a long ways from Silverstone."

"Does that mean it's impossible?"

"No. With God nothing is impossible."

Bethany sighed with relief while giving herself a bit of chastening for doubting.

They began walking again. There were still a few men talking in front of the boardinghouse, although it seemed strangely quiet without the bawdy music from the saloon.

Luke opened the door, and Bethany stepped inside.

"There's something else, Luke."

He held out his hand, indicating the parlor. Bethany took his lead and, once inside, lit one of the small tabletop lamps. A soft glow filled the room.

Luke removed his hat before lowering himself onto the settee, and Bethany sat beside him. Their gazes met, and she realized Luke's eyelashes had been singed in the rescue. Once again she thanked God that He'd spared Luke's life.

He took her hand. "What is it, Beth? Tell me."

She blinked, recalling the pressing issue regarding Angie's impending escape. "Angie said once Chicago Joe notices that she's missing, Chicago Joe will send her hired man, Dirk Crawford, to find and…perhaps even kill her." Bethany wetted her lips. "Angie told me my life may be in danger as well because I'm the one hiding her."

A glint entered Luke's blue eyes. "I can handle Dirk Crawford. Don't worry about him."

A frown furrowed her brown. "You've had run-ins with him in the past?"

"You might say so. Jake told me that Crawford mistreated Annetta yesterday. Even so, Annetta tended to Chicago Joe's medical needs."

"He mistreated Annetta?" Bethany squared her shoulders, feeling some of her original fight course through her veins. "The brute."

"Like I said, I can handle him. And I'll let the Winterses know you're hiding Angie here, with my say-so. They shouldn't object when I explain we're looking to move her." Luke took her chin, and his thumb brushed against her bottom lip. "Don't worry about that man. Don't give him a second thought."

"All right." There was only one man crowding her thoughts at the moment. "Luke, I felt so scared when you ran in to save Chicago Joe."

"Well, you can see that I'm just fine."

"I know, but…" She wanted to say she loved him, wanted to be near him always, even if it meant remaining in Silverstone the rest of her life. But she couldn't think of where to begin.

Then suddenly Luke lowered his head and touched his mouth to hers in a feathery-light kiss. Next he sighed and pushed to his feet. "I reckon it's time I get back home. I'll think on what to do about Angie, but it's too late to do anything now. And I'd like to talk to Jake about it."

"But…" She wished he'd stay, although she realized what just occurred bordered on improper. "Yes, I suppose you should."

Luke grinned as he donned his wide-brimmed hat. "You still want to wait until spring to get married?"

"Actually…" Bethany stood. "I've been thinking about that."

"And?"

"I'll marry you anytime, Luke McCabe."

He tipped his head and stepped forward. "Even if it means living here instead of Jericho Junction?"

"Yes." Oddly she felt no regrets. "My place as your wife is by your side, wherever that may be and…I want to be your wife, Luke."

He held her by the shoulders. "You're sure?"

"I've never been more sure of anything in my life."

A light entered his eyes, and a broad smile curved his lips. He looked like he might erupt into one of those famous McCabe whoops. Bethany touched her finger to her lips in hopes of reminding him of the people sleeping in the boardinghouse. It worked. Luke refrained, much to Bethany's relief. Instead, he pulled her to him and kissed her square on the lips without apology.

"G'night, Beth," he whispered at last.

She knew he was happy that she'd changed her mind. "Good night, Luke." She extinguished the light and then he walked her to the steps. She began ascending with only one backward glance. He watched her. A question swirled in her brain. What about love?

Upstairs, she stood at her bedroom door, listening to Luke's booted footfalls echo on the hardwood floor. She heard the murmur of voices as Luke talked to the Winterses.

Entering her room, she found Angie asleep on the bed and baby Michael still sleeping soundly in his makeshift cradle. She unbuttoned the back of her dress and slipped into her night-clothes. Taking a spare blanket from the wardrobe, she made herself a bed on the floor.

She lay down, stretched, and silence engulfed her. In those moments, Bethany felt her excitement in becoming Mrs. Luke McCabe waning, overshadowed by words unspoken.

I love you.

Would she ever hear those words from Luke?

I love you.

Bethany deduced they were the three most abused and underused words in the English language.

The next morning Luke awoke and washed up. As he buttoned a freshly laundered shirt, he stared out his bedroom window. The early morning sky waxed glorious as the sun stretched its golden fingers over the mountain peaks and onto a sleeping desert below. Luke paused for a few minutes to admire God's handiwork. Then he left his bedroom and peered into Jake's. No one there. Hopefully Jake had found a place to hunker down for the night.

Leaving the cabin, Luke made his way to the boardinghouse. Layers of sand and dust covered most of the wooden walk so he traipsed along close to the buildings. He'd gotten about halfway there when he heard riders approaching. He turned a hopeful gaze on them and wasn't disappointed. Jake and Annetta slowed the horses as they rode through town and halted in front of the clinic.

"Well, well, look what the cat dragged in." Luke gazed up at his brother and smiled. *Thank You, Jesus.* He turned to Annetta and dipped the brim of his hat. "Dr. Cavanaugh."

"Hello, Reverend."

Luke chuckled at their feigned formality.

Jake dismounted and helped Annetta to the ground. Luke thought her appearance was somewhat disheveled, but she looked otherwise unharmed.

"We made it to Old Man Potter's barn just as the storm hit." Jake glanced over his shoulder toward the ruins of the saloon and brothel. "*Whoo-whee!* What's happened over there?"

"I'd say God's judgment." Luke continued to grin.

"Was anyone injured?" Annetta gaped at the empty side of the street, save for the sheriff's office. A cast-iron cookstove stood amidst the cinder and ashes.

"No one hurt or killed," Luke assured her.

"What about Chicago Joe and her hired gun—or whatever he is?" Jake swung both horses' reins around the hitching post. The animals drank from the overfilled trough beneath it.

"She and Crawford left town, but she vowed to come back."

"Hmm…"

Luke turned to Annetta. "How was the circuit?"

"Well…" She flicked a glance at Jake. "I'd say it's been a life-altering experience."

"Is that right?" Luke inched the front of his hat up a little higher.

"Yes. I've seen God do some amazing things in the last twenty-four hours."

Luke didn't miss the smile she sent to Jake. He tucked his chin and grinned.

"But if you'll both excuse me, I'd like to wash up and change."

Luke stepped aside and watched his brother unnecessarily tug at Cannonball's saddle straps. He was sweet on her, all right.

"See you later, Netta."

"Yes, perhaps you will." On that rather audacious note, she strode to the clinic, unlocked the door, and entered without so much as a backward glance. She closed the door behind her.

Jake's face reddened with chagrin. Then he shook his head, and he grinned all the while. "Nothin' like a sassy woman."

Folding his arms, Luke drew in a deep breath. "I trust you were a perfect gentleman where the doctor's concerned."

"Of course." Jake walked over and leaned his forearm on Luke's shoulder. "And it was the fight of my life."

Luke arched a brow. "Yeah?"

Jake nodded.

"You falling in love with her?"

"I think...well, yes, I reckon I am."

"I knew it."

"You think you're so smart." Jake gave him a brotherly shove. "You go get your breakfast. I'm going home to clean up first, maybe get some shut-eye."

Luke eyed his brother's dusty figure and red-rimmed eyes and figured his news about Angie could wait. "You do that."

Bethany saw Luke striding for the boardinghouse and snagged a hold of his shirtsleeve as soon as he crossed the threshold.

"Well, g'mornin', Beth." He smiled and removed his hat.

She noted the light in his blue eyes then saw the back of Jake's dusty coat as he headed home. "They made it back safely."

"They did. Can't you tell? I'm rejoicing."

"You always find something to be happy about." Bethany meant it as a compliment, but it didn't come out as such. She pushed out a smile. Between talking with Angie since sunup and caring for Michael, who fussed and cried for a good hour, not to mention having slept on the hard floor, exhaustion weighed on her limbs.

Luke didn't seem to notice her waspish mood. He glanced around the lobby and sent a look into the parlor. "Where's your guest?"

"Upstairs. She's feeding Michael the pap that Rosalinda was kind enough to prepare."

"Ah." Turning slightly, Luke nodded toward the dining room. "You ready to eat?"

"No…um…" Bethany shifted her stance. "Luke, I need to talk to you about Angie. She's terrified. I relayed what you said last night, that you can handle Dirk Crawford, but she has her doubts."

"You too?"

"No." Bethany shook her head. "I have complete confidence in you." She meant each word.

"Glad to hear it." He narrowed his gaze and worked the side of his mouth between his teeth. "Well, Crawford is a viable concern, I'll grant Miss Angie that much." He thought a moment more. "Tell you what, why don't you go eat some breakfast and maybe take a plate up for Angie. I'll talk to Jake, and we'll figure something out."

"Thank you, Luke."

"You bet."

He smiled into her eyes, and Bethany's heart swelled with love. However, almost as quickly, insecurity gripped her. In another place and at another time, Luke McCabe wouldn't even know she stood in the same room as he did. Sharing her room with Angie Brown last night proved a cruel reminder of just what a plain little field mouse she really was. Angie possessed a natural beauty, evident from her blonde hair and blue eyes to her well-turned ankles.

"Beth? What is it?"

"Oh, nothing." She'd feel foolish, telling him the truth. She ran her hand down the skirt of her light-blue dress. "As I said, I'm tired."

"Well, get some nourishment and then rest. I s'pect Ralph Jonas will come for his boy soon."

"I have my doubts about that too. In order for the older children to come to school, Mr. Jonas needs someone to mind the younger ones."

"Will Angie watch the baby for a while so you can teach?"

"I think so."

"Good. That's one problem solved...for now."

"For now," Bethany repeated. "But Angie can't remain in my room for days on end."

"An obvious point. The Winterses have been gracious thus far, but we can't push them."

"Will you keep me abreast of the situation?"

Luke nodded. "You have my word, Beth."

She expelled a long, slow breath. That's all she needed to keep her courage from crumbling.

"Tell you what." Luke took her by the elbow and led her outside. "Let's go talk to Sheriff Montaño. He's really the one who should know you're hiding Angie and there could be trouble because of it."

She nodded and glanced across the street at the adobe building. "You're right. Let's go."

TWENTY-THREE

LUKE EASED HIMSELF INTO A CHAIR INSIDE THE ADOBE government building. Beth had already been seated beside him. The smell of smoke still permeated the air. Only the thick clay walls had saved this place from burning along with the saloon and brothel.

"What can I do for you?" Montaño's dark eyes bounced between the two of them.

"We need your assistance in getting someone out of town," Luke said. "Quick."

"Oh? And let me guess. This has to do with one of Chicago Joe's girls?"

"How did you know?" Beth scooted to the edge of her seat.

"I guessed." He smiled and met Luke's gaze. "I know our little schoolteacher here has made friends with a certain young woman of questionable reputation." Montaño considered Bethany openly, wearing an expression of obvious fondness that set Luke's jaw on edge. But his jealousy dissipated somewhat when Beth had the good grace to lower her gaze.

Montaño looked back at Luke. "I understand you two are betrothed. Trudy Winters told me."

"That's right." Luke set his arm across the back of Beth's chair. "Setting the date soon."

Beth gave a nod. "But we haven't made a public announcement because we're still waiting for my father to give us his permission."

"I don't expect problems." Luke felt confident about that.

"Nor do I." Beth met Luke's gaze and smiled.

"Ah," Montaño said with a slight grin. "Love is in the air. There will be wedding bells ringing soon."

"That's right. But, Sheriff, we didn't come here today to discuss Beth and me," Luke stated. "We came here to discuss Miss Angie Brown."

Montaño folded his tanned arms across his chest. "What about her?"

"Well," Beth began, "she wants to begin a new life—a decent Christian life. But she can't stay here because she fears Chicago Joe will send that blackheart Crawford back for her. She fears he'll kill her…and possibly others."

"*Sí, chiquita*, he will try." A troubled look wafted across the sheriff's dark features. "However, I expect more soldiers from Fort Yuma today. While they are here, Crawford will not try anything. He is a coward."

Luke figured. "You planning on going after the cattle rustlers with those soldiers?" He knew the subject had been on the minds of many.

Montaño nodded. "A couple of outlaws has been robbing, looting, and murdering in towns and ranches up and down the river and making the scene look like Indian raids. I suspect they are renegade half-breeds who know Indian customs and yet are well versed in the white man's ways."

"So it's pretty much just as you suspected."

"*Sí.*"

"Do you mind?" Exasperation lined Beth's tone. "I came here seeking assistance and protection for Angie—perhaps even the entire town."

Luke raised his brows, but then supposed Beth had the right to be a bit testy.

"Yes, of course." Montaño inclined his head. "As you were saying?"

"Angie said that man named Crawford has friends in Arizona City and they're bad men too."

"Very bad men." The sheriff grinned and fingered his slim mustache.

"You're not taking me or this threat seriously."

"Oh, but I am."

Beth shot to her feet before Luke could stop her. "You're patronizing me." She sent a stone cold look his way. "Maybe you both are."

"Now, Beth, I'm doing no such thing."

"Neither of you is taking this matter to heart. But if you could just stop laughing at me long enough to hear what I have in mind, some lives might be spared."

Luke stood and placed his hand on Beth's shoulder. "No one's laughing." He looked at Montaño, grinning. "Leastwise not me."

Beth shook off his hold and stepped toward the sheriff. "Angie has a relative in San Francisco, a stepsister who will take her in."

"San Francisco, California?" Montaño did laugh at that one, with head tipped back.

Beth glared at him. "Your behavior is despicable."

"I'd have to agree, Sheriff," Luke put in.

The man in black sobered. "My apologies, Miz Stafford." He bowed and his expression showed traces of genuine remorse, although the spark of infuriation in Beth's eyes said she thought he mocked her once more.

"Fine. Have your fun."

"Beth, hold on now..." Luke reached for her elbow.

She sidestepped him and moved to the door. "I'm going to take my intended's advice and find some breakfast. Then I have school to teach. I trust that while I'm teaching you two men will come up with some kind of plan to help Angie escape."

"We will, Beth. I promise."

Luke caught the grateful look in her eyes before she whirled out of the sheriff's office, closing the door behind her with a resounding slam.

Montaño's chortles caused him to turn slowly back around.

"Are you *loco*, man?" Luke gritted his teeth. "I've lived through one war and don't expect to live through another with my usually very sweet-spirited fiancée." He watched her safely cross Main Street.

"Oh, *sí*." The sheriff raised his hands, palms out. "You have your hands full, Reverend. I admire you."

Luke tamped down his frustration and returned his attention to the sheriff.

"I will make you a deal."

"What sort of deal?" Luke gazed back at Montaño.

"I was planning on riding out with the soldiers today to warn the tribes to be on the lookout for a couple outlaws posing as Indians and to assure them of our protection from vengeful white folk. If you take my place, I will take care of getting Angie out of town."

"How do you aim to do that?"

He shrugged. "Dirk Crawford isn't the only one with friends in Arizona City. Meanwhile, I will keep my eyes out for him."

Luke tipped his head. "Think he'll return?"

"Perhaps. It depends how valuable Angie's services have been to Chicago Joe."

Luke bristled and wished the saloon and brothel would have burned a long time ago.

"In either case, Angie will need respectable clothing and some money."

"That's right. She will." Rubbing the back of his neck, Luke decided to entrust the clothing task to Beth. Perhaps it would suffice in letting her know he hadn't taken her burden lightly. He really wanted to help.

"I will be in touch, Reverend."

"Sooner than later, I hope."

"I will do my best."

Luke donned his hat and stepped out of the sheriff's office. He let his eyes adjust to the bright sunshine before making his way to the boardinghouse, where he would tell Beth of the day's plans over breakfast.

The day at the schoolhouse seemed never ending. The children fidgeted all morning, and the older ones wanted to talk about the fire last night and how Reverend Luke saved a "bad lady" from dying in the blaze. Bethany made time for a discussion, and once again she felt a connectedness to the McCabes, as though their ministry had now become her own. She loved the children, all of them. She admired their inquisitiveness. However, after ninety minutes of answering questions and surmising the will of God, Bethany steered her students' minds to arithmetic and ignored the groans accompanying her decision.

Lunchtime came, and while the children ate, Bethany ran to the boardinghouse and had Rosalinda prepare a meal for Angie and pap for Michael. She felt relieved that the Hispanic cook didn't ask questions. Then back at the schoolyard, Bethany called the students to return to the classroom. She'd hoped to see Luke in the course of the noon recess, but it wasn't to be.

As the afternoon dragged on, Bethany tried to get the children to focus on their topics but to no avail. Finally she realized she felt as restless as her pupils.

At last the school day came to a close. Bethany dismissed the children and waited around for Luke. He usually walked her to the boardinghouse—even insisted upon it. But this evening he was nowhere in sight. His ride with the soldiers must have taken longer than he'd planned.

Frustration built inside her like a thundercloud as Bethany

walked home alone. But as she entered the boardinghouse, she realized she wasn't ready to face anyone, especially not Angie. Her gumption and patience were gone. Fear and insecurity had taken their places. She had no news to bring of any plans for escape, and the thought of disappointing her new friend was unbearable.

Making her way through the lobby and around the guests, Bethany headed to the back door and stepped out into the courtyard. Back home in Wisconsin, she'd often walk off her wayward emotions. She checked the timepiece pinned to the bodice of her simple light blue dress. She still had time before supper.

With purpose in each stride, Bethany headed toward the other end of town and made her way along the rocky pathway. She felt completely safe since the day had passed without Crawford or Chicago Joe showing up and looking for Angie. Besides, Luke had brought her out this way last week—when he'd proposed.

But had he meant it? Or had he been coerced by Mr. Winters's threat to bring her before the school board? And all because of a certain swarthy sheriff.

Well, Luke had more in common with Sheriff Montaño than he realized. They both thought she was some hilarious joke. Why, those two behaved like naughty schoolboys this morning, smirking at their teacher. Even though over breakfast Luke had reassured her that Montaño had promised to work on Angie's rescue, she still had her doubts.

Coming to the end of the trail, Bethany found a large rock to sit upon. *Lord Jesus, I'm so confused.*

Only moments passed before a decisive *click* came from somewhere behind her, shaking Bethany from her thoughts. Slowly, she turned and peered in horror at the gun leveled at her. Every muscle tensed while her gaze moved to the scruffy man behind the weapon.

She refused to gasp or to react at all.

He sneered. "Well, well, lookie here what I found." His dark brown, shaggy hair brushed against his shoulders as he turned his head and called out. "Come see what I got, Digger!"

While the man holding the gun watched his comrade approach, Bethany removed her timepiece and slipped it into the sleeve of her dress. She felt certain she had run into two-bit outlaws, and once they discovered she had nothing of value, they'd set her free.

The man called Digger came into view. He was also dark-headed and resembled an Indian brave, although he appeared much less unkempt than his companion.

"Whadda ya think?"

"Boss won't like it, Mal." Digger combed his fingers through thick hair.

"Boss don't gotta know. I aim to have my way with this little thing, and then I'll kill her."

Bethany felt the blood drain from her face.

Digger shrugged. "Well, just be quick about it. I don't want Montaño on our heels."

She slowly shook her head. This couldn't be happening. Why had she felt so complacent...so safe?

Mal leered again and came toward her.

Bethany's heart drummed out a frantic beat.

He inched closer, a diabolical gleam in his eye.

"Montaño? You mentioned him." She didn't know what she was saying, but buying time seemed the only way to stay alive. "Do you mean Sheriff Montaño?"

He paused.

Digger did too. "What about him, missy?"

"I recently left his office." They didn't have to know how much time had actually past. "We were discussing something of great importance."

Both men gaped at her, and Digger's face reddened in anger.

"You got Paden Montaño's woman, you fool! He'll kill us fer sure!"

"She ain't his woman. Look at her. Why, she looks like a...a *schoolteacher!*"

"I am a schoolteacher."

"Well, what do you know?" Mal pointed his gun toward the sky and jutted out one hip. "One plus one equals two." He laughed.

Bethany wasn't amused for a second.

"Turn her loose, Mal. We got enough demons riding our backs. And if she's some kind of acquaintance of Montaño, she's not worth risking Crawford's wrath."

The man named Mal considered Bethany through a narrowed gaze. "Maybe we can strike a deal. A pardon in exchange for the sheriff's sweet schoolteacher here."

Bethany cringed. All she could think about was what Luke would have to say about this. She'd ignored his warnings, and even more, she'd let down Angie now for sure.

"All right. We'll take her with us and then send a right fine message to the good sheriff. I s'pect that Crawford won't mind us coming up with a plan of our own fer once."

"Crawford?" Bethany knew that name. "Is he your boss?"

"The very same," Digger told her.

Bethany's gaze fell on each of the outlaws. Had they been looking for Angie?

"Enough talking." Mal's jaw dropped slightly as an indignant expression crossed his mangy face. "This little lady and I have unfinished business."

Bethany folded her arms tightly and shuddered in disgust at his inference. Glancing around, she wondered how she'd ever manage to get herself out of this situation. Behind her a steep cliff descended sharply. Jumping meant certain death. Then again, she'd prefer it to enduring the profound depravity lurking in the minds of these two outlaws.

"I don't care what you do," Digger said. "But wait till we strike a bargain with Montaño. Then you can deliver up his woman any way you want."

As the two conspired, Bethany stepped backward until she leaned up against three large boulders standing to the side of the embankment. The middle one stood at least five feet high. Mal, with his gun still drawn, strode toward her and grabbed her arm.

"Get your filthy hands off of me." Bethany pushed him away with every ounce of strength she possessed. She no longer cared if he shot her. If he planned to kill her regardless, she'd fight him to the death.

Mal sneered, and she slapped his face with her one free hand.

In retribution, he used his gun to strike a blow to her head, knocking her to the ground. Her vision blurred, and then she was roughly jerked to her feet. Bethany staggered slightly.

"Do that again, missy, and I'll put a bullet right through you."

"Go ahead." She tasted blood. "I'd rather die than let you touch me."

Wearing a furious expression, Mal pressed the cold metal gun barrel hard against her cheek. His breath smelled rancid, but Bethany was unable to turn her face away. She braced herself for the inevitable. The thought that she'd soon be in the arms of her Savior brought a measure of comfort.

A heartbeat later, Mal's gaze moved up over Bethany's head. and the look on his face seemed a blend of surprise and terror. Just then an arrow caught him square in the chest, and he fell backward. Digger shouted and ran. Bethany dove to the ground and lay there, tense and unmoving, until very shortly all became deathly quiet.

Ever so slowly, gingerly, she lifted her pounding head. Her jaw ached terribly where she'd been hit. With blurred vision, she scanned the scene before her. She made out her attacker, Mal. He was obviously dead. Digger, too, an arrow protruding from his neck.

Endeavoring to stand, she caught sight of the coppery brave watching her.

"Warring Spirit," she murmured. Was she safe now?

"Preacher Luke McCabe's woman."

Her knees gave way. The world spun crazily around her until it disappeared within a blanket of murky blackness.

TWENTY-FOUR

Luke sat through supper wondering when Beth would come down. He had spent the day with soldiers from the military outpost near the Yuma Crossing. They had visited several Indian villages, assuring residents of the soldiers' protection and asking them to keep an eye out for the outlaws who were doing the cattle rustling.

Luke checked in at the schoolhouse on his ride into town but found it empty. He assumed that Bethany was with Angie, but when she didn't appear for the meal, he began to wonder.

"'Scuse me." Luke stood and politely left the dining room and took the stairs two by two. Upstairs he knocked on Beth's door.

No answer.

"Miss Brown?" He kept his voice low. "It's Luke McCabe."

The door opened a crack, and a pair of blue eyes stared back at him.

"Is Beth with you?"

"No." Angie opened the door a bit wider, and Luke saw that she held the Jonas baby in her arms. Apparently Ralph never came to pick him up. "I haven't seen Bethany since noontime when she brought me some lunch and pap for Michael."

"All right. Well, I'll see to it you and the baby get some supper now." Luke's gut crimped. It wasn't like Beth to disappear like this.

"I hope Bethany is all right." The concern in Angie's tone echoed the growing unease in Luke's heart.

Still, he prayed for the best. "I'm sure she's fine. When she arrives, please tell her I'm looking for her."

"You mean you can't find her?"

"I'm just startin' to look. She'll turn up."

"Alive, I hope."

Luke refused to reply. "Keep this door closed."

"I will."

Back downstairs, Luke reclaimed his seat at the dining room table with Jake and Annetta, who were the only ones left in the room. When Rosalinda entered the room, he waved her over and quietly asked if she'd fix a plate that he could take to a friend. He would also need pap for an infant. The woman nodded and, thankfully, asked no questions.

"You got something on your mind?" Jake sipped his coffee. "You haven't said a word in a long while, and I noticed Beth ain't here. You two have a quarrel?"

Beside him Annetta chuckled quietly.

"No." Luke sat back and pursed his lips. "Not that I'm aware of anyway. But there is a situation I haven't told you about yet."

Luke leaned forward, glad no one else was within earshot. "Last night Beth helped one of the working girls across the street escape. Chicago Joe left town without her. She's upstairs in Beth's room. But we've got to get her out of town before she's missed." He looked directly at Jake. "Montaño has been informed because there's a concern that Crawford might come gunning for her."

Jake sat back in his chair, a frown creasing his forehead.

Annetta looked alarmed.

Jake set his hand on the forearm of her blouse's lacy sleeve. "I saw Montaño around town today. I'm sure he's keeping a lookout."

"He probably is. But Beth's missing. I can't find her anywhere. I've checked her room, and Angie said she hadn't been in the room since lunchtime."

Jake rubbed his whiskered jaw with his other hand. "Isn't like her to go anywhere without leaving word."

"I know."

"Oh, heaven help her..." Annetta paled.

"What is it?" Jake immediately looked concerned.

"That man, Crawford...do you think he came back? Maybe he discovered Bethany is the one who helped Angie."

She'd spoken aloud Luke's worst fears. He turned to Annetta. "Would you bring the dinner to Angie and make sure she and the baby are cared for while we search for Bethany?"

Her eyes widened, then a determined glint entered her gaze. "I will. Go quickly, Luke."

Bethany moaned and opened her eyes. Her head ached and her body hurt. She tried to focus, suddenly aware of the girl sitting beside her. "Lacey, is that you?"

"Yes, Miss Stafford."

"What are you doing here?"

"I live here."

"What?" Bethany lifted her pounding head and glanced around. The Jonas's barn. "What am I doing here?"

"Warring Spirit brought you. Don't you remember?"

"Warring Spirit..."

"He brought you on his horse, and you looked hurt real bad."

"I don't remember much after seeing Warring Spirit on the ridge."

"Well, he's right here."

Bethany squinted into the dimly lit barn and could just barely make out the figure of the Indian brave standing nearby, arms folded across his chest.

Then her gaze fell on Ralph Jonas, who stood with his hands on his hips.

"I need to get back to the boardinghouse and help...my friend."

"Miss Stafford, you can't go anywhere right now." Lacey put her hands on Bethany's shoulders and pressed her back down into the straw. "Warring Spirit brought you here because he couldn't ride into town for fear someone'd shoot him. Pa said you should stay here, and he's even letting you rest in his barn."

"I'm...grateful." Bethany closed her eyes. She supposed this barn was a far sight better than the pitiful structure the Jonases called a house.

Except Bethany didn't trust Ralph Jonas.

"But, no..." Again, she struggled to sit.

"Please rest, Miss Stafford," Lacey pleaded.

"I have to get back to town. Warring Spirit, please take me back."

The brave's voice sounded nearer, and Bethany looked to see him kneeling at her side. "I no take you. The white men will see and say I hurt you."

"I will say you helped me, not hurt me." Bethany thought her voice sounded far away. Was she losing consciousness again?

"You're staying here with me," Mr. Jonas said. "So hurry up and get well. I got young'uns that need tending to."

"Pa, speaking of..." Lacey's voice sounded pained. "Where's Michael if Miss Stafford is here?"

"He's safe with my friend," Bethany quickly said. "Except...I must get back. Warring Spirit, if you won't take me, will you fetch Luke?"

He paused, but then agreed. "I will find Preacher Luke McCabe."

"Oh, don't bother," Jonas said. "I'd say she's right where she's suppose to be."

Bethany gasped, and her head began to pound.

Warring Spirit moved between Bethany and Jonas. "Touch her, and Preacher Luke McCabe will kill you."

"Aw, I ain't afraid of him."

The brave stood chest to chest with the farmer. "Then be afraid of *me*."

Lacey inhaled sharply.

"I go to find Preacher Luke McCabe."

"Do what you like, but don't expect me to play nursemaid."

A moment of silence elapsed, and then Bethany heard a tussle ensue. A sickening thud hit the dirt floor.

Lacey gripped Bethany's hand. "They're fighting, Miss Stafford, and now Pa is…"

"Dead?"

"No. He's getting up." Lacey whispered in Bethany's ear. "Warring Spirit hit him square in the jaw before he left. I 'spect Pa deserved it too."

Bethany had seen her fill of violence today. Still, she appreciated Warring Spirit's protection, and with Lacey close by, she felt a tad safer from Mr. Jonas.

"Pa's leavin' the barn now." Lacey dipped a rag in a bucket of cold water, wrung it out, and placed it across Bethany's forehead.

"You're a sweet girl, Lacey."

"Thank you, Miss Stafford." Lacey changed sitting positions. "You've got a nasty gash on the side of your head. Your pretty blue dress is bloodstained. But I've got it soaking."

"Thank you." It took a second, and then another, but finally the shock registered. "My *dress*?" She ran a hand down her torso and realized she lay in a pile of hay wearing nothing more than her camisole and petticoat. "Mercy! I'm undressed in front of men!"

"Pa said it ain't nothin' he's never seen before, and Warring Spirit…well, his people don't dress and live like we do."

Bethany wasn't so injured that she couldn't feel embarrassed.

Her cheeks burned with indignation. Then suddenly she wanted to flee, run as fast and far from the Jonas ranch as possible.

Rolling onto her side, she pushed up onto her elbow.

"Now, Miss Stafford, don't go writhing so. Just rest yourself."

At last she gave in. Besides, how far would she get in her state of undress, unprotected from the elements, Indians, outlaws...and rattlesnakes?

Luke summoned the sheriff, and then he, Montaño, and Jake went out looking for Beth. The evening sun was setting rapidly, and Luke prayed God would make it stand still just as He did for Joshua and afford him extra precious time to search.

When they arrived at the eastern ridge, they found two dead men.

"Any idea who they are, Sheriff?" Jake peered at Montaño from on top of his horse.

"*Sí*. They are despicable outlaws. Malachi Espinosa and Juan 'Digger' Cruz. Both half-breed outlaws. I suspect they were our cattle rustlers."

Luke dismounted. "Looks like the Indians made your job easier, Sheriff."

Montaño inspected them. "*Sí*, but it was only one Indian, judging by the arrows." He walked from where he'd been standing near a large boulder to around the brush. "And I see tracks from only two horses in this immediate area. Could be he took the outlaws' horses."

Something glinted in the late afternoon sun and caught Luke's attention. He stooped to pick it up.

"What did you find over there, Luke?"

He glanced at Jake. "I believe this is Beth's timepiece." He turned the gold watch pin in his palm. "She always wears this on her dress."

"You sure?" Jake dismounted Cannonball and walked up beside him.

"I'm sure. In fact…" He met his brother's gaze. "I want to say Beth's mother left this to her."

Behind them Montaño groaned. "Did you look over the cliff? You may find our little schoolteacher there."

Dread filled Luke's being at the suggestion, but he managed to shake his head in answer. "Reckon I need to do that."

"*Sí, amigo.*"

Jake touched his brother's arm. "Want me to look?"

"No. I'd rather be the one to find her." Luke strode to the edge of the ridge. Squeezing his eyes closed, he prayed he wouldn't see her lying in the ravine. Opening them, he scanned the side of the bluff and the rocky arroyo below. Nothing.

He returned to Jake and the sheriff. "Praise God, she's not there."

Jake let out an audible sigh of relief and got back onto his horse.

Montaño nodded. "You two should keep looking. It could be the Indian took Bethany to his village to be cared for. However, I will not be able to accompany you. I need to put into action the plan to smuggle Angie out of town."

Luke gave him a definite nod. "Very well." Pocketing the watch pin, he mounted his horse and wondered where on this sweet earth Beth could have gone.

In Bethany's room at the boardinghouse, Annetta watched Angie snuggling the Jonas baby and tried not to think about the passing time. Nightfall was coming on, and an eerie hush fell over the town as stores closed up and families gathered around the supper table. Usually music and raucous laughter drifted through the opened front windows. But tonight Main Street stood silent.

"This baby's so sweet." Angie smiled at the infant, sleeping in her arms. "I always wished that I'd have children someday."

"You're young. There's still time."

"What decent man would want to make me his wife?"

"You may be surprised." Annetta thought of Jake and turned away from the windows. Smiling at the young woman, she decided Bethany's dress fit Angie nicely. She looked every bit the respectable woman. "You might meet a man who will understand about your past and love you for who you are."

"A prostitute?" Angie snickered, and Michael stirred. She rocked him. "No, I don't believe it's possible."

"I would guess you were forced into the profession. Most women are." Annetta gathered her skirts and sat down on the adjacent bed. "I admire you for seizing this opportunity to escape it."

"I have Bethany to thank for that, but I haven't escaped it yet."

Annetta lowered her gaze, studying her now-folded hands.

"I hope she's all right," Angie said.

"Yes..." Annetta couldn't dwell one more second on the alternative.

Angie looked down at the baby sleeping peacefully in her lap. "Tell me why this baby boy's father hasn't come for him yet."

Annetta shrugged. "I suppose he got busy with his chores. Ralph Jonas has five other children, all of whom have been sorely neglected since the baby's birth." A surge of anger flared up inside of her. "I'm afraid Mr. Jonas values a goat over his own child."

"Typical of men in general, I'd say."

"A week ago I might have agreed with you." Annetta hadn't been able to stop long enough to marvel at the events from the last two days. "But I've had a change of heart."

"Mm-hmm, I know. You're in love with that ambitious preacher—the older one, with the bad leg. A few of the girls liked to say that if God looks like one of those McCabe brothers, then—"

"Yes, yes, I get the idea."

Angie pressed her lips together.

However, Annetta couldn't deny her growing feelings for Jake.

Now if he'd only return unharmed—and Bethany and Luke with him!

Restless, Annetta stood and wandered to the door. "Would you like some tea? I could brew some."

"That would be nice."

Annetta hurried down the stairs. Just as she reached the first floor, the door opened and the sheriff entered.

"Dr. Cavanaugh," he said. "Just who I was looking for." His gaze quickly appraised their surroundings. No one was nearby. Still, he lowered his voice. "I have come for Angie. Where is she?"

"Upstairs."

Annetta led him back up to Bethany's room. Angie still sat in the chair, holding the baby. But she stood as soon as she saw Montaño enter. A light of recognition entered her pale eyes.

"Good evening, Sheriff."

Annetta hated to think the man might have been a customer.

"*Ándale pues.* We do not have much time." He motioned for Annetta to take Michael, and she hurriedly gathered the baby into her arms. "But I must insist you change into these." Montaño shook out first the dark blue shirt with gold banding, a pair of gray trousers, and a coordinating cap. "Pin up your lovely hair. I'm afraid you will be a soldier tonight."

"What do you have in mind?" Annetta wanted to know.

"I have requested military assistance in patrolling the outskirts of town tonight. Angie will be my partner. But instead of an all-night vigil, she and I will ride south to a secluded dock used by the Confederates years ago. A friend of mine will be waiting with his river steamer. When I explained to him that my sister—"

"Sister?" Angie giggled.

Montaño ignored her. "—had entangled herself in a most unfortunate situation, he agreed to waive his ninety-dollar passenger fee. He has also promised to see my darling sister safely onto an ocean vessel at the mouth of the Colorado."

Angie inhaled sharply. "I'm on my way to San Francisco?"

"*Sí.*" Montaño's mustache twitched.

Squealing with delight, Angie flung herself into his arms. "Thank you. Oh, thank you!"

As she watched, Annetta got the feeling Paden Montaño rather liked the attention in spite of his annoyed frown.

"No time for this now. Change your clothes. Roll your dress in a woolen blanket. I will ready the horses."

The sheriff strode to the door. "We ride in an hour's time."

"Sheriff?" Annetta followed him down the stairway. "You left town with Jake and Luke…did you find any sign of Bethany? And where are the McCabes now?"

"They are still searching for her. Now, if you will excuse me. Everything is happening all at once. But I will return for Angie soon."

After he left, Annetta replayed their conversation over in her mind. She had a hunch the sheriff didn't tell her the complete truth. Was Bethany in danger? She closed her eyes and prayed again that Jake and Luke would find Bethany safe and unharmed.

TWENTY-FIVE

DARKNESS SETTLED OVER THE TERRITORY. IT WASN'T easy, but Luke finally agreed to ride back to Silverstone. Earlier they'd followed the tracks at the ridge for about a half-mile, but then they'd lost them.

Reaching their cabin, Luke dismounted. Behind him, Jake slowed his horse.

"Want me to take Cannonball to the stables?"

"Sure." Luke tossed his brother the reins. But when Jake didn't move, Luke followed his line of vision.

A man stepped out of the shadows.

"Warring Spirit."

"Who is this one who rides with you?" The brave took two guarded steps forward.

"This here's my older brother, Jake. He's a preacher too." Luke turned to him. "And this is the Indian I told you about. We met over at Harlan's place."

"Pleased to meet you, Warring Spirit." Jake slowly got off his horse.

Warring Spirit stepped toward them. "You look for your woman, Preacher Luke McCabe?"

Luke's senses heightened. "Beth? You've seen her?"

"She rests at Jonas ranch."

"Rests?" Luke hurled a glance at Jake and then looked back at Warring Spirit. "What's she doing at Ralph Jonas's place?'

With hand motions and broken English, Warring Spirit

explained how he'd happened upon the two miscreants on the ridge. Luke didn't wait for details. He was ready to ride.

Warring Spirit pulled his horse from its hiding place and mounted up. "You bring medicine woman."

"Beth's injured?" Luke's sense of urgency grew. "Is she going to be all right?"

"She will live. But we go now," he said, pointing to himself and then Luke. "And you bring medicine woman tomorrow." He motioned to Jake.

"We'll be there bright and early."

Luke turned his horse around. "Ready, Warring Spirit?"

He mounted up. "I am ready."

The drumming in Bethany's head lessened, and she felt herself becoming more awake and aware of her surroundings. She opened her eyes only to meet more darkness. The sweet scent of hay tickled her nostrils, and she heard an animal's soft munching nearby.

Slowly she pushed herself up into a sitting position and felt the lightweight quilt that covered her. She felt disturbed by the fact she'd been undressed in front of Ralph Jonas. Bethany cringed. Had the man been any kind of gentleman, he wouldn't have looked.

Feeling too weak to rise, she lay back down on the quilt that had been thrown over the hay. Shafts of moonlight filtered through the narrow cracks in the walls. Somewhere beyond the barn, she thought she heard the soft beat of approaching horses' hooves. Minutes later, the door creaked open.

Fear and dread crept over Bethany. She wouldn't be able to fight off Mr. Jonas or anyone else for that matter. But perhaps it was only one of the children.

"Beth?"

She heard the whispered voice and knew at once to whom it belonged. "Luke?" Relief spread through her. "I'm over here."

"Shh…" His boots crunched along the dirt.

Then he came into view, and Bethany pulled the quilt up higher.

Luke hunkered down beside her. She could barely make out his expression as his hand moved over the top of her head and down to her shoulder. "You all right?"

"I think so, except my head hurts. A vile man hit me in the head with his gun." Bethany shuddered. "He's dead now."

"I know." Luke held his canteen to her lips. "Jake, Montaño, and I found the bodies. Then tonight Warring Spirit told me what happened."

Bethany gave in to the urge to gulp down the cool water.

"Easy. Not so fast."

When she had enough, she pulled back and wiped the moisture off her chin with the back of her hand. "Where's Angie?"

"She and baby Michael are safe with Annetta."

"Good." She strained to see his features in the dark. "Forgive me, Luke, for leaving town alone. I thought that since Crawford hadn't come back that I was safe."

"Shh… I don't want that snake Jonas hearing you and creeping in here." Luke sat down a respectable distance away with his back up against the side of a stall. "I'm afraid of what I'll do to him."

"I feel safe now that you're here."

Luke reached for her hand. "Then go on back to sleep. I'm not going anywhere soon."

A sense of relief filled her. She reclined and closed her eyes. But soon her conscience pricked. "Luke?"

"Hmm?"

"Remember last night when I said I'm ready to marry you any time?"

"You change your mind?"

"No." She thought she heard his weighty sigh. "But I need you to know that I wasn't completely honest with you about my father."

"How so?"

"I didn't really have my father's blessing to come here. But when he realized that I was determined to go, he ordered me out of the house and told me never to come back. I stayed with Mr. and Mrs. Navis while I prepared to leave for Jericho Junction."

"Why didn't you tell me this sooner?"

"I was afraid—afraid you would tell me to go back to my father and that I'd be stuck on that miserable farm forever."

"I didn't realize you disliked farming so much."

"Oh, it's not farming. It's my father. He forced me to do twice the work everyone else did, and there was never talk of my future." Bethany felt glad that Luke didn't pull his hand away. "Meanwhile, my friends were moving on with their lives."

"I reckon it didn't help that my baby sister fell in love with the man you always figured on marrying."

Bethany smiled. "No, that didn't help one bit. However, I'm glad it all played out the way it did. I love you, Luke."

"I love you too, Beth."

Her heart pounded out a beat of happiness. "You do?"

"'Course I do. I asked you to marry me, didn't I?"

"Yes, but…only to save my reputation and the McCabe ministry."

"Beth!" He sounded genuinely shocked. "Is that what you thought?"

"Maybe just a little," she admitted.

Luke reached a hand behind her head and pulled her close until his lips touched hers. "Beth, I think I loved you from the day we met. And if you didn't know that deep down, it's probably my fault for not making my love clear to you."

The admission touched that deep down place in her heart, which had been yearning to hear it.

"As for your father, I'm sorry you've carried that burden around with you for so long. But I want you to understand that you can come to me with anything."

"I do...now. And I will."

"Well, if you want me to, I'll help you try to make the situation with your father right. I'll post another letter to him."

"Thank you." Bethany was only too glad for the way Luke took the news.

"And look what I found." Luke dipped his fingers into the inside pocket of his jacket, retrieved something that glimmered in the moonlight, and then placed it into the palm of Bethany's hand.

It felt cool in her palm. "What is it?"

"Your watch pin. You lost it on the ridge."

Bethany breathed her relief. "I forgot about it. I must have dropped it." She suddenly felt foolish. "I didn't want the outlaws to have it. It's the only thing I have left of my mother's."

"I know. That's why I'm glad I found it for you."

"Luke..." Bethany didn't know how to describe all the love and gratitude she felt for this man.

"Honey, you ought to rest now. You've had more than enough excitement for one day."

"All right, but..." Bethany propped herself up on her elbows. "I want to tell you one more thing. Those evil men who accosted me, Mal and Digger, they talked about having a boss named Crawford."

"Is that a fact?" Luke's tone took on a dangerous edge.

Bethany swallowed. "Yes."

"I'll be sure to give Montaño that bit of news."

Bethany knew Angie wouldn't be the only person who would sleep better with Crawford behind bars.

Luke gave her hand a gentle squeeze. "Go to sleep for a while, Beth. We'll talk more in the morning."

Feeling safe with her beloved nearby, she lay back and allowed her eyelids to flutter closed.

Hours later, Bethany awoke. Instead of darkness, shafts of sunlight streamed in through the crevices of the barn's roof and walls. She sensed a presence and looked to see Lorna and Jeb peering at her with curious smiles. Bethany wanted to shake her head in dismay and would have, if it didn't hurt so much. Little Lorna's face needed a good scrubbing, and Jeb's drawers drooped in a telltale way.

Lorna tiptoed in Bethany's direction and cast a shy glance at Luke. He hadn't moved since last night and snored softly only several feet away. But then Jeb tripped over the toe of Luke's boot, and he awoke with a start.

"Well, g'mornin' to you too, little fella." Luke lifted Jeb back onto his feet and swung his gaze to Bethany. His gaze fell over her, and she fumbled to pull the quilt up above her shoulders.

"Blood stained my dress. Lacey rinsed it out for me."

"I—I beg your pardon, Beth." He pushed to his feet, keeping his gaze averted. "But, um...forgive me." He turned back to her, his eyes trained on her face this time. "Beth, I hate to tell you, but you've got some kind of shiner."

She touched her eye. "Oh, my..."

"Makes me sick to think a man would strike a woman like that."

"He's dead now, Luke. Don't let his actions trouble you."

Luke wagged his head. "Well, I hate to think of what our Savior had to say to him."

Bethany could only imagine.

Luke eyed the little ones gaping up at him. "What do you kids say about rustling up some breakfast?"

Lorna skipped toward him and paused only to slip her hand into Luke's. "I fed the chickens."

"Good for you."

Bethany watched Luke's retreating figure. Lorna chattered happily beside him, and Jeb waddled behind.

Once they'd gone, Bethany worked herself into a sitting position. Next she tried to stand. Her legs wobbled, and the room teetered unnaturally to one side. She quickly lowered herself back on to the hay.

A short while later Lacey strolled into the barn, carrying Bethany's dress. She helped her into it.

"The stain didn't lift, Miss Stafford."

"That's all right."

"It sure is pretty, though."

"Well, thank you. It's a bit tight..." Bethany glanced at Lacey, whose threadbare skirt and ragged blouse looked far worse than a stained blue dress. With Christmas rapidly approaching, Bethany thought if she could somehow round up clothes for the children, they'd make wonderful gifts.

The jangling of harnesses signaled the arrival of a wagon and team of horses just outside of the barn. Lacey ran out to greet the visitors and returned with Annetta on her heels.

"Bethany, we've been so worried about you." Annetta set down her black medical bag and removed her bonnet. "I'm encouraged to see you sitting upright."

"It's an improvement over yesterday evening, but I'm still terribly dizzy."

"What happened?"

As Annetta examined and cleaned the gash on her cheek, Bethany explained. Lacey sat silently nearby, listening.

"Luke warned me not to go off by myself. I should have

listened." Bethany hoped that if anything, Lacey would learn from her lapse in good judgment.

"You've got a fine goose egg here," Annetta said.

"How'd an egg get on Miss Stafford's head?" Lacey appeared mildly alarmed.

"It's an expression." Annetta smiled. "Here, come and feel this fine lump on the side of Miss Stafford's head."

Lacey's fingers ran over the sore spot near Bethany's temple. With a wince, Bethany pulled back.

"Sure feels more like a hen's egg than a goose's egg."

Bethany smiled, and Annetta laughed softly.

"Jake and I rode over here in the wagon. I brought Michael with me. One of the other children has him now."

Bethany thought she correctly read Annetta's thoughts. It certainly didn't speak any better of Ralph Jonas's fathering skills.

"Where's Angie?"

"God willing, she's safely on her way to San Francisco."

"Honestly?" In her excitement Bethany sat up too quickly. The world swam before her eyes until she lay back down.

Annetta patted her shoulder. "Just rest."

"Who is Angie?" Lacey queried.

"A friend of ours." Annetta sent the girl a polite grin. Looking at Bethany, she added, "I no longer believe in coincidences." Annetta's smile reached her eyes, and they warmed to an arresting greenish-brown. "I'm convinced of God's grace."

Bethany marveled at the change in her.

"So..." Annetta stood and brushed the straw off her skirt. "Are you ready to go home?"

Before Bethany could reply, a gunshot split the quiet morning.

Twenty-Six

ALERTED BY THE GUNSHOT, LUKE ROSE FROM THE BREAK-fast table and strode to the door. Even squinting into the bright sunshine, Luke recognized Dirk Crawford in the distance. He rode fast toward the ranch with two other men in tow.

"Hey, Jake? Looks like we got trouble."

"I see 'em." He strode quickly from the Jonas's mud-walled home and to their wagon, where he pulled the rifle out from behind the driver's seat.

Meanwhile Luke shooed the kids out back and ordered Jesse to take himself and his siblings out behind the chicken coop. "Stay as low to the ground as you can until I come for you," he called after him. "I'll explain later."

"Yessir." The lanky boy gathered up the baby and collected more of his siblings as he went.

Satisfied the children would be safe enough, Luke turned his attention to the men riding up the lane, which led to the barn.

Jake hurried to the door, cocked the rifle, and leaned it against the inside of the doorway.

Just then, Luke saw Lacey venturing out from the barn. "Get back, Lacey!" he shouted.

She paused in mid-stride as if she'd heard but didn't understand.

"Run, girl!" Jake hollered.

She wheeled around, but only too late. One of Crawford's men swooped down on her like a hawk. He scooped up Lacey and set her in front of him. She kicked and screamed until the mangy brute pulled out his gun and held it to her head in warning.

Jonas came running from around back. "What in tarnation is goin' on?" He carried a rifle in his right hand. "Put down my girl and state your business."

Crawford dismounted and glared in Luke's direction. "Preacher, I understand you have something that don't belong to you." He spit out a wad of tobacco. "Oh, and, by the way, Chicago Joe sends her regards."

"Don't know what you're talking about, Crawford," Luke said.

"Quit playin' dumb and git your hands out to where I can see 'em."

"Now, just hold on." Jonas swaggered forward and lifted his rifle. "Who do you think you are, coming here and—"

Gunfire exploded. Jake ducked out of the doorway while Luke overturned the rough-hewn dining table so they could have some cover.

As the smoke cleared, Luke glimpsed Jonas's lifeless body sprawled out in the dirt.

"He killed Jonas." Dread and remorse poured over Luke. Jonas's children were now orphaned.

"I figured Crawford wouldn't miss at that close proximity." With his back against the table, Jake readied his revolver. "May God rest Jonas's soul."

"Preacher, do you hear me?"

"I hear you," Luke called back. Rage now coursed through his veins.

"If I don't get Angie back, this here girl's gonna take her place, if you know what I mean."

Jake glanced at Luke. "I'm going to need some backup."

Luke shook his head. "You know I vowed I'd never kill another human being."

"In a perfect world, you wouldn't need to, Luke. But the Territory is hardly that perfect place."

"I reckon you're right at that." All Luke had to do was glimpse Jonas's body then watch Lacey struggle in that outlaw's grasp. Meanwhile there were five other children's lives in jeopardy, and Bethany and Annetta in the barn. Heaven help those women if Crawford and his thugs discovered them.

But Luke wasn't about to let that happen.

He hunkered near the doorway and saw the man who'd snatched Lacey toss her off his saddle. He watched him motion to Jonas's body.

"He's sending Lacey for her pa's gun."

"If I shoot him now, either Crawford or his other cohort will most likely kill her."

"Then hold your fire."

A host of emotions gripped Luke, but righteous anger won out. "If she starts swinging that weapon around, they'll kill her for sure." Luke held his breath as Lacey slowly got to her feet. He knew what he had to do. Crawford and his men weren't reasonable fellows. This situation couldn't be won through a gentlemen's conversation.

God, forgive me for making such a vow that maybe I wasn't supposed to keep in the first place.

Luke grabbed his brother's rifle. His gaze met Jake's. "Get ready to do some fancy shooting." He watched as Lacey moved slowly toward her father's body.

"All right, I will." Jake positioned his revolver and himself just an eyeball above the tabletop. "Divert his attention from the girl."

"Crawford," Luke bellowed, "you are one ugly coward to use a child for one of your pawns."

Crawford fired a shot into the house. Both Luke and Jake ducked behind the table.

Then, just as Luke predicted, Lacey reached her father's gun, whirled around, and miraculously shot her captor clean out of his saddle.

Jake squeezed the trigger of his revolver and killed the other outlaw. Next he fired at Crawford, but missed.

Crawford fired his weapon at them, and the charge whizzed over Luke's head. Then, with the precision he learned and used numerous times during the war, Luke aimed and fired. The lead ball met its mark. Crawford clutched his chest, stumbled a few paces, and dropped facedown into the dirt.

Jake stood and clapped Luke's shoulder. "Nice job. It needed doing."

"I know, and I don't regret it either."

"Good man."

Lacey knelt by her father's body and sobbed. Both Luke and Jake kicked the outlaws' weapons out of their reach, just in case. Luke helped Lacey to her feet and held her against his side.

"Things might look grim now," he told her, "but they'll work out."

She wrapped her skinny arms around his midsection, and together they followed Jake into the barn. Never did Luke see two more frightened women. Annetta held Bethany, and tears streaked their faces.

Lacey ran to Bethany.

Annetta ran to Jake and threw her arms around his waist. She buried her head in his shoulder. "Are they dead, Jake?"

He enveloped her in a protective embrace. "Yes, they are. You don't have to worry about them anymore. You're safe now."

Luke felt like an eavesdropper and stepped away to check on Beth. She and Lacey seemed calmer, but he saw in Beth's eyes a sort of pleading, and somehow he knew her thoughts were on the other Jonas kids.

"I'm going around back to fetch the rest of the young'uns." He knelt beside Beth. "Will you be all right for a time?"

"Yes. It's important to me to know all the children are unharmed."

"I'll go check right now."

"Luke?"

He paused, and Beth clutched the collar of his shirt and pulled him close.

"I'm so glad you're all right. When I heard all the gunfire, I–I…"

"It was terrible, Miss Stafford." Lacey began to cry again.

Luke kissed the side of Beth's head. "Take care of her. I'm just fine. You and I can talk later. Meanwhile, I'll fetch the other kids."

Luke set off through the barn and headed for the chicken coop. When he reached the children, Michael was wailing, and four dirty faces peered back at him.

"You're safe now. But I have some hard news." Dropping down on his haunches he did his best to explain what just happened and that their pa had been killed.

"What's gonna happen to us?" Jesse asked. "We can't stay here."

"You'll come home with me." Luke couldn't imagine why he offered such a fool thing. What would he do with six kids?

He mulled on it for a several seconds and determined that for the time being, he'd love them. Love is what everyone wanted in this world anyway.

Reaching for Jeb, he sat the boy on his knee while hugging little Lorna to his heart. Yep, that's what he'd do. He'd just love them.

EPILOGUE

Journal entry: Wednesday, December 25, 1867

It's Christmas Day, and it's hard to believe I've neglected my diary for two months. So much has happened. I'm suddenly a schoolteacher plus a wife and mother of six children.

Luke and I have been married one month and two days. I couldn't be happier. We are adopting the Jonas children as our own. Even so, we will never let them forget their birth parents and remind them of only the good memories.

Our cabin is comfortable but very cramped. We have three rooms. The boys bunk in one, the girls sleep in the other, and Luke and I make our bed near the hearth in the center room. My only complaint is that I don't often get my husband's attention all to myself.

Jake and Annetta became engaged on Thanksgiving. Surprisingly, the very next day, he allowed Annetta to operate and repair the bone in his leg. I'm happy to report that he is recovering nicely, and he can now walk without the use of his cane. He and Annetta hope to be married in the summer when Jake is finished building our new home, which, I'm glad to report, will be close to theirs. How nice to have them living close by. Annetta has become my good friend. For the time being, Jake is residing in the boardinghouse. He hopes to build a hospital next year. Meanwhile, Annetta has employed Trudy's help and says the young lady will make a fine nurse—or even a doctor someday.

We haven't yet heard from Angie, but we all pray that she safely reached San Francisco. I did, however, receive a telegram from my father giving his permission for our marriage. Perhaps someday I will see him and my brothers and sisters again. I can see why God familiarized me with caring for a large family. I have another one now. I also understand the premonition the Lord sent me. He determined I would be the Jonas children's mother. And so I am. I love each child with all my heart.

I hear Michael waking, and soon all the children will be up and eager to open their Christmas gifts. I sewed each child an article of clothing. The boys will have new shirts and the girls a new dress. Jake and Luke made them toys. The children will be so excited to see them. Then we'll attend church this morning, and later Jake and Annetta will come over for Christmas dinner.

As one might expect, my life is exhilarating. But this is only the beginning of a lifelong adventure. With God in my heart, Luke by my side, and children surrounding us, joy will abound. It does already. Things will never be dull, that's for certain!

But then why would I expect anything less than an exciting existence? I am a McCabe, after all.

Coming in 2012
from Andrea Kuhn Boeshaar—

THREADS OF HOPE

Book 1 in the
Fabric of Time series

CHAPTER ONE

August 1848

I*T LOOKS LIKE NORWAY.*

The thought flittered across nineteen-year-old Kristin Eikaas's mind as Uncle Lars's wagon bumped along the dirt road. The docks of Green Bay, Wisconsin, were behind them, and gently rolling hills, rich farm fields, and green grass stretched before them. The sight caused an ache of homesickness to fill Kristin's being.

"Your trip to America was good, *ja*?" Uncle Lars asked in Norwegian, giving Kristin a sideways glance. He resembled her father so much that her heart twisted painfully with renewed grief. "First a ship across the ocean, then a train to Michigan, and another vessel to cross the lake. It is a long way to go."

"*Ja*, but the trip was fine," Kristin managed to reply despite the tumult inside her. It had been a long journey indeed! "The Olstads made good traveling companions."

Kristin turned and peered down from her perch into the back of the wooden wagon bed. Peder Olstad smiled at her. Just a year older, he was the brother of Kristin's very best friend who had remained in Norway with their mother. But it wouldn't be long, and Sylvia and Mrs. Olstad would come to America too.

"You were right," John Olstad called to Uncle Lars in their

Andrea Kuhn Boeshaar

native tongue. "Lots of fertile land in this part of the country. I hope to purchase some acres soon."

"And after you are a landowner for five years, you can be a citizen of America and you can vote."

The Olstad men smiled broadly and replied in unison, "Oh, ja, ja…"

Uncle Lars grinned, causing dozens of wrinkles to appear around his blue eyes. His face was tanned from farming beneath the hot sun, and his tattered leather hat barely concealed the abundance of platinum curls growing out of his large head. "Oh, ja, this is very good land. I am glad I persuaded Esther to leave the Muskego settlement and move northeast. The deer are plentiful, and fishing is good. Fine lumber up here too."

"I cannot wait for the day when Da owns a farm," Peder said. The warm wind blew his auburn hair outward from his narrow face, and his hazel eyes sparked with enthusiasm, giving the young man a somewhat wild appearance, which always troubled Kristin. "Then soon I will own my own farm too. No longer will we be at a landlord's mercy like we were in Norway."

"Amen!" exclaimed Mr. Olstad, whose appearance was an older, worn-out version of his son's.

"And once you own property," Kristin added, "Sylvia will come to America. I cannot wait. I miss her so much."

Kristin grappled with a fresh onset of tears. Not only was Sylvia her best friend, but also she and the entire Olstad clan had been like family ever since a smallpox epidemic ravaged their little village two years ago, claiming the lives of Kristin's parents and two younger brothers. When her Uncle Lars and Aunt Esther learned of the tragic news, they insisted she come to America and live with them. Uncle Lars and Aunt Esther had left Norway seven years ago, making their dreams of owning land come true. Knowing this from their letters, Kristin had agreed to make the voyage, and her plans to leave Norway had encouraged the

Olstads to do the same. But raising the funds to travel took time and much hard work. While the Olstads scrimped and saved their crop earnings, Kristin did weaving and sewing for those with money to spare. By God's grace, they were finally here. And soon Sylvia and Mrs. Olstad would join them, and they would all find hope and happiness in this new land.

Uncle Lars steered the team of draft horses around a sharp bend in the rutty road. He drove down one incline and up another. On top of the hill Kristin could see Lake Michigan sprawling eastward beyond a lovely white, wood-framed house that suddenly came into view. She then noticed the homestead's large, well-maintained barn and several out buildings, including a tiny cottage, and she marveled at the sight of an American farm. No wonder Mr. Olstad couldn't wait to own one!

Next, she spied a lone figure of a man up ahead. Kristin could just barely make out his faded blue cambric shirt, tan trousers, and the hoe in his hands as he worked the edge of the field. Closer still, she saw his light brown hair sprigging out from beneath his hat. As the wagon rolled past him, the man ceased his labor and turned their way. Although she couldn't see his eyes as he squinted into the sunshine, Kristin did catch sight of his tanned face. She guessed him to be somewhere in his midtwenties and decided he was really quite handsome.

"Do not even acknowledge the likes of him," Uncle Lars spat derisively. "That is Sam Sundberg, and good Christians do not associate with any of the Sundbergs."

Oh, dear, too late! Kristin had already given him a little smile out of sheer politeness. She had assumed he was a friend or neighbor. But at her uncle's warning, she quickly lowered her gaze.

"What is so bad about that family?" Kristin's ever-inquiring nature getting the best of her, and she had to ask.

"They are evil. Karl Sundberg is married to a heathen Indian woman who casts spells on the good people of this community."

"Spells?" Peder's eyes widened.

"*Ja*, spells. Why else would some folks' crops fail while Karl's flourish? He gets richer and richer with his farming in the summer, his logging camps in the winter, and his fur trading with heathen, while good folks like me fall on hard times. Same seed. Same fertile ground. Same golden opportunity." Lars snorted with disgust. "I will tell you why that happens. The Sundbergs have hexed good Christians. Then to add insult to injury, Karl involves himself with the United States government and its Indian affairs. He sees that the Indians are well paid for their land, while those savages murder our women and children, accusing us of stealing the land out from under them. Oh, they are an evil lot, those Sundbergs. Same as the Indians."

Talk of Indians didn't frighten Kristin; rather, it piqued her curiosity. As for the spells…well, those frightened her. She'd grown up around superstitions and had learned to fear them. After all, what if they were true? Even so, she wondered what it would be like to meet an Indian face-to-face—especially if he resembled the fine-looking man they had passed only moments ago.

Unable to help herself, she swung around in the wagon to get one last glimpse of Sam Sundberg. She could hardly believe he was as awful as her uncle described. Why, he even removed his hat and gave her a cordial nod just now.

"Turn around, girl, and mind your manners!" Uncle Lars scolded. His large hand gripped her upper arm, and he gave her a mild shake.

"I–I'm sorry, *Onkel*," Kristin stammered. "But I have never seen an Indian."

"Sam Sundberg is not an Indian. The squaw I referred to is his father's second wife, who is called Mariah. It's the two younger

Sundbergs, Jackson and Mary, who are half-breeds. Not Sam. Still, Sam is just as bad. He calls the Indian woman 'Ma.'"

"Indians. How very interesting," Kristin murmured. "Are there many living in the Wisconsin Territory?"

"As of three months ago we are the State of Wisconsin—no longer a territory," Uncle Lars stated with as much enthusiasm as a stern schoolmaster. "And to answer your question...*ja*, there are too many Indians in this state, if you ask me. You, my *liten niese*, will do well to stay away from them. All of them. You hear?"

"Yes, sir," Kristin replied. She chanced a look at Peder and Mr. Olstad. Both pairs of eyes and stoic expressions seemed to warn her to heed Uncle Lars's instructions, and she had no doubt that they would do the same.

Sam Sundberg wiped the beads of perspiration off his brow then placed his hat back on his head. Who was the little blonde riding next to Lars Eikaas? Sam hadn't seen her before. And the men in the wagon bed...he'd never seen them either.

After a moment's deliberation, he concluded they were the expected arrivals from the "Old Country," as his father liked to refer to Norway. Months ago Sam recalled hearing talk in town about Lars's orphaned niece sailing to America with friends of the family, so he assumed the two red-haired men and the young lady were the topics of that particular conversation. But wouldn't it just serve Lars right if that blonde angel turned the Eikaas's regimented household upside down?

Sam smirked at the very idea. He didn't have to meet that young lady to guess Lars would likely have his hands full. Her second backward glance said all Sam needed to know. The word *plucky* sprang into his mind. He chuckled. Plucky she seemed, indeed. No other female in Brown County would have the tenacity to boldly appraise a man the way she did, even if it had been done in all innocence. No doubt Lars had been acquainting his guests with the Sundberg family, calling them such things as "savages," "heathens," and "half-breeds." What newcomer wouldn't be curious?

A bolt of indignation shot through him, and his mirth was quickly replaced by anger. Although Sam was a full-blooded Norwegian, he took the revilements against his stepmother and half-brother and half-sister as personal affronts. He shook his head in frustration. If only people in this community would take the time to get to know his family. If they'd only try to understand that his mother and siblings were no different from anyone else.

He swallowed a lump of bitterness as, off in the distance, the Eikaas wagon rolled out of sight, leaving brown clouds of dust in its wake. Sam knew his father wouldn't approve of his animosity. Pa would say, "Turn the other cheek." But Sam was tired of turning the other cheek. At twenty-five years old, he'd lived through enough prejudice to last a lifetime. He no longer had the patience for the so-called Christians like Lars Eikaas and his clan…and now add to it his plucky little niece.

Of course, not everyone around here was as intolerant of Indians as the Eikaas family. There were those who actually befriended the native Wisconsinites and stood up to government officials in their stead…like Sam's father, for instance. Like Sam himself.

He returned to his work beneath the hot sunshine and pondered the latest government proposal to remove the Indians from their land. First the Oneida tribe had been forced out, and soon the Menominee band would be "removed" and "civilized." As bad as that was, it irked Sam more to think about how the government figured it knew best for the Indians. Government plans hadn't succeeded in the past, so why would they now? Something else had to be done. Relocating the Menominee would cause those people nothing but misery—they stated as much themselves. Furthermore, they were determined not to give up their last tract of land. Sam predicted this current government proposal would only serve to stir up more violence between Indians and whites.

But not if he could help it.

"Sam!"

Hearing his sister's voice, he looked toward the house. "What is it, Mary?" he called back.

"Ma says to come in for noon dinner."

"Be right there."

Hoe in hand, he trudged across the dark fertile soil. The corn grew high, and Sam expected a good crop this year.

He reached the white clapboard home and quickly washed up, using water from the rain barrel. Entering the mudroom, which was for all intents and purposes a simple lean-to at the back of the house, he hung his hat on a wooden peg and donned a fresh shirt. Ma insisted upon cleanliness at the supper table. Finally presentable, he made his way through the house and into the dining room where a white, frosted cake occupied the middle of the table.

"That looks good enough to eat," Sam teased, although his appetite was getting the better of him by the minute.

Ma gave him a smile and her nut-brown eyes darkened as she set the wooden tureen of turkey and wild rice onto the table. "Since it's Rachel's last day with us, I thought I would prepare an extra-special dessert."

Sam glanced across the table at the glowing bride-to-be. In less than twenty-four hours, Rachel Brecker would become Mrs. Luke Smith. But for the remainder of today, she'd fulfill her duties as Ma's hired girl who helped with the cooking, cleaning, sewing, washing, and ironing...and whatever else women were wont to do around the house.

They all sat down, Mary taking her seat beside Rachel. Sam helped his mother into her place at the head of the table then lowered himself into his chair next to his younger brother, Jackson, who'd been named after Major General Andrew Jackson, the seventh president of this great country.

"Sam?"

Ma's silky voice pulled him from his musing.

"Since your father is away, will you please ask God's blessing on our food?"

He gave his mother a respectful nod, and all heads bowed. "Dearest Lord, we thank Thee for Thy provisions. Strengthen and nourish us with this meal so we may glorify Thee with our labors. In Jesus's name, amen."

The women served themselves, and then between Sam and eighteen-year-old Jackson, they scraped the bowl clean.

"Good thing Pa's not home from his meetings in town," Jackson muttered with a smirk.

"If your father were home," Ma retorted, "I would have made more food."

"Should have made more anyhow." Jackson gave her a teasing grin. "No seconds." He clanged the bowl and spoon together as if to prove his point.

"You have seconds on your plate already," Ma said. "Why, I have never seen anyone consume as much food as you do, Jackson."

A guilty grin curved the corners of his mouth.

Sam had to chuckle at the good-natured bantering. But in the next moment, he wondered if his family behaved oddly. Didn't all families enjoy meals together? Tease and laugh together? Tell stories once the sun went down? According to Rachel, they didn't. The ebony-haired, dark-eyed young woman had grown up without a mother and had a drunkard for a father...until Ma got wind of the situation and took her in. She allowed Rachel to live in the guesthouse, which had originally been built years ago to accommodate Ma's ailing mother. And now, as a result of the Sundberg's generosity, Rachel would soon marry a fine man.

Sam took a bite of his meal, chewed, and looked across the table at his fifteen-year-old half-sister. Both she and Jackson resembled their mother, dark brown hair, dark brown eyes, and graceful, willowy frames, while Sam took after his father, blue eyes and stocky build, measuring just under six feet. Yet, in spite of the outward dissimilarities, the five Sundbergs were a closely knit family, and Sam felt grateful that he'd known nothing but happiness throughout his childhood. He had no recollection whatsoever of his biological mother who had taken ill and died during the voyage from Norway to America.

Sam had been but a toddler when she went home to be with the Lord, and soon after disembarking in Philadelphia, his father met another Norwegian couple. They helped care for Sam and eventually persuaded Pa to take his young son and move with them to Wisconsin, known back then as the "Michigan Territory." Pa seized the opportunity, believing the promises westward expansion touted, and he was not disappointed. He learned to trap and trade and became a successful businessman. In time, he saved enough funds to make his dreams of owning land and farming a reality.

Then, when Sam was three years old, his father met and married Mariah, an Oneida squaw. Like her, many Oneida were Christians and fairly well educated due to the missionaries who had lived among them. Sam took to his new mother immediately, and she to him. Through the years, Ma cherished and admonished him as though he were her own son. As far as Sam was concerned, he was her own son—and Mariah, his own mother.

They were a family.

"Was that the Eikaas wagon driving by not long ago?" Mary asked.

Sam snapped from his reverie. "Yes, it was. It appears Lars has relatives in town."

"He didn't stop and visit, did he?" Mary's eyes were as round as gingersnaps.

Sam chuckled. "No, of course not. I can't recall the last time Lars Eikaas spoke to me…or any of the Sundbergs, for that matter. It's just a hunch on my part. A while back I'd heard that Lars's niece was coming to America, accompanied by family members, and since I didn't recognize the three passengers in the wagon this morning, I drew my own conclusions."

"Is she pretty?" Jackson's cheeks bulged with food.

"Is who pretty?"

"Eikaas's niece…is she pretty?"

Sam recalled the plucky blonde whose large, cornflower-blue eyes looked back at him with interest from beneath her bonnet. She'd worn a dark skirt and a lavender blouse. And pretty? As much as Sam hated to admit it, she was about the prettiest young lady he'd ever set eyes on.

Jackson elbowed him. "Hey, I asked you a question."

Sam gave his younger brother an annoyed look. "Yeah, I s'pose she's pretty. But don't go getting any big ideas about courting her. She's an Eikaas."

Sam forked another bite of food into his mouth, wondering who he was trying to warn…Jackson or himself!

Kristin looked around the one-room log hut with its unhewn walls and narrow loft above. Disappointment riddled her being like buckshot. Although she knew she should feel grateful for journeying safely this far, and now to have a roof over her head, she couldn't seem to shake her displeasure at seeing her relatives'

living quarters. Having glimpsed the Sundberg farm, Kristin had mistakenly assumed that all American farms looked as picturesque.

"Here is your trunk of belongings," Uncle Lars said, carrying the wooden chest in on one of his broad shoulders. With a grunt, he set it down in the far corner of the cabin.

"Tonight you will sleep in the loft with your cousins." Aunt Esther's tone left no room for questions or argument. Her dark-brown hair was tightly pinned into a bun, and wearing a plain brown dress with a tan apron pinned to its front, the older woman looked as drab as her surroundings. "Your uncle and I sleep on a pallet by the hearth."

"Yes, *Tante. Takk*—thank you. I am sure I will be very comfortable."

"Come, let us eat." Aunt Esther walked toward the doorway. "I cook outside during the summer months."

Kristin nodded. She'd glimpsed the large pot dangling over the open circle of flames in the nearby yard. "I've prepared venison stew," Aunt Esther continued.

"It sounds delicious." Kristin's stomach growled in anticipation. She'd eaten very little on the ship this morning. Excitement plus the waves on Lake Michigan made eating impossible. But after disembarking in Green Bay, her stomach began to settle, and now she was famished.

Aunt Esther called everyone to the table, which occupied an entire corner of the cabin. Her three children, two girls and one boy who ranged in age from seven to sixteen, came in from outside, as did the Olstads. After a wooden bowl filled with stew was set before each person, the family clasped hands and recited a standard Norwegian prayer...

I Jesu navn gar vi til bords—We sit down in the name of Jesus,

Spise drikke pa ditt ord—To eat and drink according to Your word,

Deg Gud til are, oss til gavn—To Your honor, Oh Lord, and for our benefit,

Sa far vi mat i Jesu navn—We receive food in the name of Jesus.

"Amen."

Having said grace, hands were released, and everyone picked up a wooden spoon and began to eat. Kristin noticed her cousins, Inga and Anna, eyeing her with interest. They resembled their father, with blonde curls and blue eyes.

"What do you like to do on sunny afternoons such as this one?" she asked cheerfully, hoping to start conversation. After all, Inga's age was close to hers. Perhaps her cousin would help her meet friends.

"We do not talk at the table," Aunt Esther informed her. "We eat, not talk."

"Yes, *Tante*." Kristin glanced at Peder and Mr. Olstad, who replied with noncommittal shrugs and kept eating.

Silently, Kristin did the same.

When the meal ended, the girls cleared the table and the men took young Erik and ambled outside.

"May I help with cleaning up?" Kristin asked her aunt.

"No. You rest today and regain your strength. Tomorrow we are invited to a wedding, the day after is the Sabbath. Then beginning on Monday, you will have chores like everyone else."

Kristin nodded. She'd expected that she would have to earn her keep somehow, and she certainly wasn't afraid of hard work. However, her aunt's brusque manner caused her to feel more homesick than ever. She missed her deceased parents and little brothers. Why did God take them, leaving her to live life without them? And Sylvia…how she missed her best friend!

Walking to the other side of the cabin, Kristin opened her trunk and began sorting through her belongings. Had she made a mistake coming to America?

Lord, I know You led me here...didn't You? Weren't those inner promptings from You?

Tired from her travels and feeling more than a little discouraged, Kristin knelt by the trunk. Her fingers reverently glided over a soft knitted shawl that had once belonged to her mother. Lydia Eikaas had been an excellent seamstress, spinning the wool into yarn and thread, weaving and sewing garments, and she'd taught Kristin everything she knew about the craft. Surely Kristin could now put her skills to good use in this new country, this land of opportunity.

She sighed and glanced over to where her aunt and two cousins were still busy straightening up after the meal. Inga and Anna barely smiled, and her aunt's expression seemed permanently frozen into a frown. Is that what this country really afforded...misery?

Allowing her gaze to wander around the dismal cabin once more, Kristin began to wish she had not come to America.

Experience the *inspirational* sagas
of the McCabe family in the

SEASONS OF REDEMPTION
SERIES

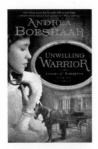

The War Between the States has Valerie Fontaine frightened about her future. When her father is arrested, she is forced to flee the city or be taken into custody. Will the war keep her from her newfound love?

978-1-59979-985-8 / $10.99

Sarah McCabe's new job in the city is giving her a firsthand taste of the life she has always desired—a life of luxury, culture, and social privilege. Sarah knows exactly what she wants...but what does God want for her?

978-1-61638-023-6 / $12.99

Nurse Fields is drawn to a blind patient searching for his past. But will his recovery reveal the secret she is trying to keep?

978-1-61638-192-9 / $12.99